N. J. Crisp started his writing career in the fifties when he published a number of short stories. He quickly moved on to television drama and has become well known for his contributions to series including *Dixon of Dock Green, Doctor Finlay's Casebook, Spytrap* and *Colditz*. With Gerard Glaister he co-devised *The Expert, The Brothers* and *Oil Strike North*. This is his first novel.

D1380770

N. J. Crisp

The Gotland Deal

Futura Publications Limited
A Futura Book

A Futura Book

First published in Great Britain in 1976
by Weidenfeld & Nicolson Ltd

First Futura Publications edition 1976

Copyright © N. J. Crisp 1976

ISBN 0 8600 7113 8
Printed in Great Britain by
Hazell Watson & Viney Ltd
Aylesbury, Bucks

Futura Publications Limited
110 Warner Road,
Camberwell, London SE5

Author's Note

Over a number of years I have written for several television series, concerning the police, forensic scientists, espionage, and so on. This has meant talking to many experts and advisers in these and related fields.

Some of the material which I have not used for television is in this book. I cannot acknowledge those advisers as I would wish. They are men who prefer to remain unknown by name. But I hope that all of them, and especially the one who has been so kind as to read the manuscript of this novel, make suggestions, and correct certain inaccuracies will accept my sincere, if too generalized, thanks.

The above should not be taken to imply any claim to documentary truth in this book. The events are purely imaginary, and it is a work of fiction.

My apologies to Paddington and Notting Hill Police Stations (and the officers who man them) who in real life cover most of the areas north of Hyde Park which, in the following pages, I have assigned to Bayswater.

Bayswater Police Station does not exist, nor, to the best of my knowledge and belief, do any of the people mentioned in this book, with the exception of Mr Ben Maile, the artist. I hope he will forgive the reference to him and to his beautiful painting, *Trawlers at Sunset*.

N. J. CRISP
London 1976

1

The West Indian girl lay on her back, her eyes staring up at the sky. A thin rain was falling, and her fine-boned face glistened. Her blouse was ripped open, and stained. Blood trailed thickly down her body. The source of the blood was her left breast. The oozing had stopped.

It was getting crowded in the basement area. Detective Inspector Sidney Kenyon picked his way across her angled, spread-eagled legs, and climbed the steep metal stairs to the pavement. It was five o'clock in the afternoon, but under the low hanging clouds which had blanketed London all day, it was dark. It was a cold November day and the persistent, nagging rain made it worse. Kenyon shivered, crossed the road, got into his car, and sat behind the steering wheel.

Since Detective Inspector Kenyon had been stationed at Bayswater Police Station, parts of Notting Hill had gone up in the world. Bassett Place, W11 was not among them. The houses crumbled, paint blistered and peeled and the dark, mildewed rooms were crammed with human beings, mostly coloured and poor. Now and then, as in the fashionable and expensive Hyde Park area, which was also in Kenyon's patch, one of them met a violent death.

Kenyon's lunch had consisted of a cheese roll and three large whiskies in the Bristol Arms, near Paddington Station. The resultant lift, which he had needed after being up most of the night, had long since gone and had been replaced by a residual sourness at the back of his throat.

The early morning raids had been a waste of time. There were no explosives in those houses off the Harrow Road, only antagonistic and resentful families. One young construction worker had thrown a bottle at Kenyon, which missed, shattered against a door, and cut the forehead of the Superintendent in charge of the operation. The young construction worker had been hauled off to Bayswater Police Station and charged, and that was the total bag for half a night's work.

Kenyon opened his mouth wide and yawned. He either needed to go to bed, or else renew that whisky-given lift in the very near future, and he did not expect to get much sleep tonight either. He lit a cigarette, and stared through the rain-dimpled windscreen, waiting. The cigarette tasted foul. He needed something to drink, tea would do, and then the cigarette would be enjoyable, or at least not actively unpleasant as it was now. A small cafe was open along the road, the window proclaiming 'Fresh Sandwiches Cut While You Wait' and Kenyon half thought of going in and ordering egg and bacon, and toast and tea, in the hope of deceiving his body with a substitute breakfast into acting as though it were rested and refreshed after a night's sleep. But he could not be bothered.

He glanced across the road at the two police cars, their blue roof lights revolving silently. The rigged-up spot lights glared down into the basement area, huge shadows postured and paused on the front of the house, as people went up and down the metal stairs and moved about in the congested basement area – police surgeon, photographer, detectives, uniformed coppers, fingerprints, forensic, representatives of the trades who congregate round violent death: Kenyon could be over there talking to them, and getting wet with them in the now thickening rain, but there was no point. He would take over later when such information as there was had been assembled. Until then, he was drier, if not much warmer, sitting in his car.

Black faces paused now and then, and peered at him with no great friendliness, through the windows of his car, associating him with the leisurely, spotlighted activity across the road. Kenyon took no notice of them, was hardly aware of them. His world was not theirs, and in his world of theft and fraud and violence, of blackmail and rape and death, spontaneous affection rarely came his way. He mostly settled for nervous respect, founded on apprehension.

Three cigarettes later, his Detective Sergeant, Len Mallory, crossed the road, opened the door and got into the passenger seat. 'I'm soaking bloody wet' Mallory said, unnecessarily.

Lionel Mallory had contracted his christian name to Len during his first week at Police Training School. His mother's admiration for the great Lionel Barrymore had led to a plethora of nicknames, all of which he disliked. As a nineteen-year-old constable, he had capitulated to the rough, male ribbing he got, preferring the anonymity of being one of the lads.

Late one night, in Kenyon's flat, half drunk on Kenyon's whisky, he had related this, his good-looking face creased with laughter as he told the story. Kenyon thought it showed weakness, and privately slightly despised him for it. You sailed under your own colours as far as Kenyon was concerned, and if you compromised or trimmed, as any sensible man must from time to time, then it was in the face of some overwhelming threat to position or personal safety, not stupid jokes.

Kenyon had said none of these things, preferring to listen in silence and top up Mallory's glass. Mallory was a good Detective Sergeant, painstaking and efficient. They got on well together, and made a good team. Kenyon had no intention of risking an effective working relationship over something so peripheral as slight moral cowardice and inverted snobbery. But he mentally pencilled in a small query about Mallory's character in the long run. Like any other policeman, he did not use the word 'character' about his colleagues in the strictly conventional sense, confining it to such attributes as guts, loyalty, toughness and reliability in an emergency.

In any case, Mallory was still in his twenties, and the next few years' pressures could make him. Or break him. Kenyon was only five years older, but in the CID, five years was a long time. His morning face in the shaving mirror still looked young, but the outward appearance deceived only a few of his clients, and not them for very long. No working detective in Central London remained young inside himself for more than a few years, not even Mallory, Kenyon supposed, as he looked at the cheerful, fresh face beside him. Mallory was scrubbing his wet hair with a handkerchief.

'She was stabbed once,' Mallory said. 'Probably held down, at the time. There were bruises on her throat.'

'I saw them,' Kenyon said, waiting to be told something he did not already know. He had wandered round, before he decided that it was too wet and uncomfortable over there, studied the dead girl, walked in and out of the basement room, which contained a double bed, some rudimentary, grimy furniture, including a wardrobe with both men's and women's clothes in it, and a tattered carpet, on which there were blood stains. It had all registered in his mind, not consciously, but without effort, as everything registered, every moment of his waking life, because looking at things and people in that way was his trade, and he could not help it any more.

He had inspected the lavatory, which was along a stone-floored passage, lacked lavatory paper and, by the look of it, was shared by a number of tenants, and which had told him nothing apart from that. On the second floor he had found the bathroom, equipped with a gas heater and a meter, but no plug for the bath. It was painfully obvious that it served every human being crammed in that house. He had looked at the pay telephone in the communal hall, noted the copy of today's *Times* tucked behind the box, and wondered if anyone in that house read it, or if it was destined for the lavatory.

Kenyon knew that the West Indian girl had not died at once. He knew that she had been stabbed in the basement room, and had crawled across the floor while her pounding heart had pumped her life's blood out of her body, on to the carpet, on to the wood floor near the door, on to the stone step outside the door, until she had grasped for the metal stairs, rolled over on to her back, and stared up at the sky for the last time.

Kenyon knew all that as though he had been there at the time and seen it happen. If this case ran true to form, he knew the rest already too, but he waited for Mallory to tell him. Mallory had been left over there to ask questions, and get wet, which was what

Kenyon had done when he was a Detective Sergeant. In two hours' time there would be a post mortem on the girl, which Kenyon had already arranged. An electric saw would slice into her head, and the skull would be lifted like the lid of a box. Her organs would be removed and examined and a detailed report would be at Kenyon's disposal. The forensic report would form part of the evidence in court, but Kenyon did not need it yet. He knew enough already.

'Her name's Jenny Abel,' Mallory said. He twisted Kenyon's driving mirror round until he could see his reflection, and combed his hair carefully into place. 'She's lived there for three months with another spade called Winston Peters. Apparently she used to screw around on the side as well. No sign of any weapon.'

Kenyon could have written this down beforehand with ninety per cent accuracy, apart from the names. But you could never tell. It might have been different this time.

Mallory put his comb away, satisfied. His hair hung naturally, in the casual style he affected, and which he maintained by fortnightly visits to a hairdresser in the Kings Road.

Kenyon adjusted his mirror until he could see out of the rear window again. 'Where's Winston likely to be?'

'One of three places,' Mallory said. 'Unless he's heading for somewhere a long way away.'

'Let's go and find him,' Kenyon said. Men like Winston Peters rarely ran away. They might be able to get it wrapped up in time. With any luck Kenyon might not have to make the phone call he would have had to make, had this case turned out to be different in some way.

They found Winston Peters at eight o'clock. He was gyrating and shaking to Reggae music, an intent, broad smile fixed on his face.

Kenyon and Mallory were the only two whites in the dimly lit, crowded, smoke-filled, underground club. Otherwise, it was full of spooks. The customers who were not dancing were clustered round tiny tables. They looked at Kenyon and Mallory, and knew who they were, but they continued to pass their joints from hand to hand while they stared at the two white policemen.

' I need a drink,' Kenyon said. ' There's no hurry.' Mallory did not hear. The music was deafening. Kenyon took his arm, guided him to the bar, and ordered two large whiskies.

No trained police dog was needed to sniff out the marijuana in here, Kenyon thought. The whole bloody place stank of it. He found the characteristic smell quite pleasant, although, when he had tried smoking the stuff, it had done nothing for him. He supposed he had too much self control to allow the drug to take effect. Or else he was too used to his own drugs, he reflected, as he sipped whisky, and inhaled on his cigarette. He decided to have another drink and get back that lift he would need. He had a fair idea what was going to happen next.

The Reggae music was coming from a vast, elaborate juke-box, flashing with multi-coloured lights. In the blessed moment of comparative silence while the records changed, Kenyon got hold of the barman.

' Tell Winston Peters we'd like a quiet word with him outside,' Kenyon said.

' Who?' the barman enquired, his face growing puzzled.

' Don't get clever,' Kenyon said, wearily. ' Just tell that one. Him. Whatever you call him.'

He nodded at the young man on the dance floor, whose description matched that which Mallory had obtained from reluctant neighbours : twenty-five years old, six feet tall, well built, black face, small beard, wearing a blue light-weight suit and heavy rings on his left hand.

' Oh,' the barman said. ' Speedy.'

' Speedy,' Kenyon agreed.

The music started again. The barman crossed to Winston Peters, spoke to him, and returned to the bar. Winston Peters began dancing again.

' What did he say?' Mallory asked loudly.

The barman shrugged. ' Nothing.'

They watched Peters as he twisted and turned and shook to the music, perspiration dripping from his face.

' He's doped to the eyeballs,' Mallory said into Kenyon's ear. ' If he flies any higher, he'll go into orbit.'

Kenyon did not answer. He tried not to allow Mallory's habit of stating the obvious to irritate him unduly. After the third whisky, Kenyon became bored with waiting. As the music died for a few seconds, he crossed to Winston Peters. Mallory followed.

'Police,' Kenyon said. 'We're enquiring into the death of Miss Jenny Abel. We think you may be able to help us.'

Peters stared back, his chest heaving, apparently not comprehending.

'Let's go somewhere quiet,' Kenyon said, and took Peters' arm, just as the music started again.

Winston Peters went berserk. Kenyon and Mallory were expecting this, which was just as well since Winston Peters was holding a knife, screaming savagely, and doing his utmost to plunge the knife into Kenyon or Mallory or both. It took a little while, as they stumbled round with the Reggae music throbbing and pounding, to overpower Peters. Kenyon's jaw was aching, and Mallory was bleeding from the forearm by the time they had Winston Peters pinned down on the dance floor.

It could have been achieved more quickly. Both Kenyon and Mallory were skilful exponents of painful and damaging blows which would have left Peters writhing in helpless agony on the floor. Both men were careful not to use them. Both were well aware of the angry, hostile faces which surrounded them as they scuffled and grappled and avoided that knife. Neither had the slightest ambition to become involved in any extension of the affray, which would certainly put them both in hospital.

Eventually, they had the man on his back, Kenyon kneeling on his chest, Mallory holding his legs. Kenyon looked into Peters' eyes and saw a change there. The muscular body was limp underneath him. Kenyon stood up, and helped Winston Peters to his feet. Mallory picked up the knife. Kenyon looked for the exit. There was a group of people blocking their path, but Kenyon led the now listless Peters forward, just the same. The group did not give way.

Kenyon stopped. 'Excuse me,' he said, politely.

The leader of the group, a huge, grimly scowling man, took no notice. 'Speedy?' he said, enquiring.

Peters did not answer. He appeared to be studying his shoes.

'Speedy?' the leader of the group repeated.

Kenyon knew that it was not over yet. They did not want to let him go. They wanted to do something, they wanted the excuse to do something now, at the last minute.

Peters continued to look at his shoes. 'It's OK,' he said.

'You sure?'

'Yes. It's OK.'

The group slowly parted.

'Thank you,' Kenyon said.

They sat in the detention room. Kenyon wondered how many months, if you added it all up, he had spent doing this, sitting in the bare, forbidding room. The steel door, which had a barred aperture, could not be opened from the inside.

All those hours talking, asking questions, sometimes cajoling patiently, sometimes raising his voice and shouting, pretending an anger he did not feel, sometimes outlining in a flat, deadly voice, for the benefit of some surly, unco-operative villain, the unpleasant fate which he, Detective Inspector Sidney Kenyon, could personally guarantee, unless the villain would reveal whatever piece of information it was he needed at the time. If you totted up all those hours and projected them into Kenyon's future career, it would amount to years – as many years in this prison-like atmosphere, probably, as many of his clients would ever spend inside. Except that Kenyon could stand up and bang on the door, and the constable standing outside would let him out. He could do that. His clients could not.

Not that there was any need for cajolery or mock bullying with Winston Peters. Peters was talking, his deep voice a flat monotone, the sentences interspersed with long silences which neither Kenyon nor Mallory broke. Mallory would stop writing on the statement form, Kenyon would light another cigarette. They knew they only had to wait. Winston Peters wanted to talk. He needed to talk.

'Three months we've been together,' Winston Peters said. 'And it was fine. It was great. Until she got this job. She told me she was a dancer. I wanted to go and see the act, but she said no, it was a very high-class club, and they wouldn't let me in. I believed her. I believed everything she ever said. But last night I was in the West End and I thought, hell, they can only say piss off, we don't have niggers in here. So I went along.'

Winston Peters stopped talking. Mallory went on writing for a few seconds, his Parker pen flowing across the page. Then he stopped writing, and waited patiently. The statement would be a paraphrased précis of Winston Peters' words, using such direct quotations as would be helpful in establishing that he had murdered Jenny Abel.

Kenyon lit a cigarette, and offered the packet to Peters. Peters took one. Kenyon lit it for him.

'They let me in,' Peters said. 'There was no trouble. There were plenty of coloured people there. So was Jenny, but she wasn't any dancer. She was sitting with a white man, a middle-aged creep with a beard. She didn't see me. She was too busy working on the white man. When they left, I followed. They went to a block of flats in Battersea. I waited outside for two hours, but she didn't come out, so I went home. I didn't know what to do. I thought Jenny was different. But she was only just another dirty little whore after all.'

Kenyon already knew, from enquiries carried out while he and Mallory were tracing Peters, that Winston Peters made a living as a small time ponce. He ran two girls from bed-sitters off Queensway, whose clients found them through cards in newsagents' display cases, which would read something like 'Beautiful young coloured lady seeks exciting new position.'

But Kenyon found nothing contradictory in Winston Peters' account of his emotional reaction. In his experience, ponces and prostitutes were more violently jealous and possessive than anyone else. The fact that Winston Peters would almost certainly have persuaded Jenny Abel to go on the game in the end in any event, had nothing to do with it.

'She came home at ten o'clock this morning,' Winston Peters said, in his deep, flat monotone. 'She said one of the other dancers in the show had been taken ill, and she'd stayed the night with her. Only I knew differently, of course.' He sighed, and rubbed his face tiredly. 'I looked in her handbag. There was thirty pounds there. She'd never stayed out all night before. I suppose she saw the chance to make a bit extra, and she thought she could get away with it. She didn't admit it at first. She went on lying. We rowed all day, off and on. One time I went to the lavatory. She must have thought I'd gone out. I found her dialling a number in the hall. This creep with the beard maybe. I dragged her back downstairs and told her she had to quit the club, and she said it was none of my business, and she'd screw who she liked, and the next thing I knew, she was lying on the floor, and there was blood spurting out of her. But I didn't mean to kill her.'

'Just a minute,' Kenyon said. He wanted Winston Peters' admission to be clear, plain and unqualified. He did not want to present some lawyer with a handle in advance which could be used to argue that the knifing had taken place by accident in the course of a struggle. Somebody would probably dream that one up anyway. Kenyon saw no point in helping them.

'Do you always carry a knife?' Kenyon asked.

'Not always,' Peters said.

'Most of the time though.'

'Only to frighten people.'

'How do you carry it? In a sheath?'

'Yes.'

'When Jenny Abel came home at ten o'clock this morning,' Kenyon said, 'were you carrying the knife in the sheath then?'

'Yes.' Peters said.

'So at some point during the quarrel,' Kenyon said, 'you drew the knife from its sheath, and you stabbed Jenny Abel.'

'Yes,' Peters said. 'Though I didn't mean to kill her.'

'There were bruises on Jenny's throat,' Kenyon said, 'suggesting that she'd been held down and then stabbed.'

'I didn't know what I was doing,' Winston Peters said.

Kenyon had long ago noted that Peters was right handed. 'You quarrelled,' Kenyon said. 'You held Jenny down with your left hand, and you stabbed her in the left breast with a knife which you had previously taken out, and which you held in your right hand. Is that what happened?'

'Yes,' Winston Peters agreed, seeming relieved to have the incident so lucidly recalled and clarified. 'That's what happened.'

Mallory was writing busily, and Kenyon was satisfied that the statement would be shaped in such a way as to emphasize the crucial point. Winston Peters' words, 'I did not mean to kill her,' would be recorded. But placed alongside the admission that he had held the woman down by the throat, and stabbed her in the left breast, it would sound pretty weak. Winston Peters might insist on the statement being altered when he read it through before signing it, of course, but Kenyon did not think he would. In any case, that was a chance you had to take.

Kenyon was not under the illusion that a confession at this stage would mean an automatic conviction. Solicitors and barristers did not make a living out of 'Guilty' pleas. Well, what they would cook up at a later stage was their business, but it was no part of Kenyon's job to help them. *He* might decide to help Winston Peters, by putting his evidence, when it came to trial, in a certain way, but if he did, that would be a personal and private decision on Kenyon's part. Kenyon well knew how, with a well judged sentence in his evidence, to put a defendant in a good light, and provoke sympathy for him. He had done it many times, when he felt sorry for a man he had arrested and charged. But Winston Peters had committed murder, no question. If his sentence were to be alleviated, it would be through him, Detective Inspector Kenyon, not some well paid barrister who had never even spoken to Peters. That was the way Sidney Kenyon saw it.

Winston Peters' face was working strangely. 'I wanted to hurt her,' he said, 'but I didn't want her to be dead.' He began to cry. 'God in heaven, believe me. Please believe me.'

Winston Peters sat there, choking on his sobs, his shoulders heaving, tears running down his black face.

Kenyon put his hand on the man's shoulder, and squeezed it. 'Come on Winston,' he said. 'The bad part's over. You'll be all right. Would you like something to eat?'

Peters shook his head.

'Tea then,' Kenyon said. 'There's no hurry. We'll have a cup of tea and a bit of a chat before we go on. Eh? How about that?'

Peters managed something approaching a grateful smile, thankful, Kenyon knew, to be treated like a human being. Well, why the hell not? He was a human being. Kenyon banged on the door, and ordered some tea. Mallory coaxed Peters into accepting another cigarette.

They took Peters through the statement slowly and carefully. Winston Peters signed it. Kenyon witnessed it. They took him to the Charge Room where he was charged, and saw him locked into a cell.

Kenyon glanced at his watch as he and Mallory climbed the stairs to the first floor. 'Not bad,' he said, pleased. 'A murder case wrapped up in five and a half hours.'

Bayswater Police Station was an old building, which had seen better days. It was due to be refurbished in a year's time, and demolished and rebuilt in five. Meantime, the stone stairways, echoing corridors, and inadequate facilities reminded Kenyon of a workhouse.

'He didn't want to change his statement, either,' Mallory said, smiling good-naturedly. 'Not a word. Nothing.'

'Since he was crying half the time,' Kenyon said, 'he probably couldn't even read it, poor sod.'

They turned into the CID office, from where the Detective Sergeants and Detective Constables worked. Kenyon had a small, glass-walled office in one corner, which was cramped and paper-strewn. Just now, all the desks except one were unoccupied, most of their owners at home, one or two out on cases.

'Any messages for me?' Kenyon enquired of the only man there.

The young man in shirt sleeves, Detective Constable Michael Meacher, groped for pieces of paper. 'Two, sir.'

'Feel like a quick one to celebrate?' Mallory asked, putting on his raincoat.

'Not tonight,' Kenyon said. 'I've got something on.'

'OK. See you in court.'

'Yes. Good night, Len.' Kenyon turned to Meacher. 'What are they?'

'A Miss Sarah Brooks phoned,' Meacher said. 'She lives at

Flat 31, Cleeve Court, Rockstone Gardens, W2. She wants you to go round and see her.'

Kenyon nodded. He knew the whereabouts of Cleeve Court, as he knew every club, pub, hotel, shop, garage, restaurant, school, and block of flats in every street in the area north of Hyde Park which made up the Bayswater Division. 'What about?'

'She wouldn't say, sir. She said it was very urgent, but it was a private matter and she wanted to see the Detective Inspector personally.'

'She can get screwed,' Kenyon said.

'From the sound of her voice,' Meacher said, grinning, 'there might be some good screwing there too. She had a nice voice.'

Meacher was fresh faced, eager and twenty-four years old. 'The only trouble with that young man,' Detective Superintendent Pinder had said to Kenyon one night in the Police Club, 'is that he's cunt mad.' Mostly from a temporary lack of it, Kenyon thought.

Meacher's very first case in CID had been to investigate a break in. The occupant of the flat, a bright eyed lady of thirty-six, whose age temporarily matched her bust measurement, had shown him how the bedroom window had been forced. She had then shown him a number of rather more interesting things in bed. At the end of six weeks, Meacher was tired but happy, and the affair was over. The lady's husband, an engineer officer on an oil tanker, had returned home. Meacher had chafed impatiently, but the husband had given up the sea, and was home for good. Besotted by recollections of former delights, Meacher had called one day when he knew the husband was out, but a coldly indignantly virtuous lady bust size thirty-six had slammed the door in his face.

Ever since then, Meacher had eagerly anticipated a similar turn of good fortune, but so far it had not happened. Kenyon devoutly wished that he would get himself fixed up again, and then he might stop thinking about it all the time.

'Go and see her in the morning,' Kenyon said.

'Right, sir,' Meacher said, calculating his chances.

'Not on your own doorstep again, for Christ's sake,' Kenyon

said. 'Never screw around on your own patch. It's asking for trouble. Screw around on someone else's.'

'I don't know what you mean, sir,' Meacher said. He was convinced that his visits to the accommodating and educational lady were a secret, known only to himself.

Kenyon gave up. 'What was the other message?'

'Another lady, sir. She didn't leave her name. She said it wasn't important.'

'All right,' Kenyon said. He went into his office, thought about taking his electric razor to the washroom and having a shave, but decided he could not be bothered.

He eyed the telephone, hesitating.

Meacher was leaving. 'Good night, sir.'

'Good night, Mike.' Kenyon decided not to phone. He was ready to leave now, and he could be there in fifteen minutes anyway.

Kenyon drove along Bayswater Road to Marble Arch, turned into Edgware Road, followed it until it became Maida Vale, and kept going. It was still raining steadily and for a while the windscreen misted up, and it was cold, but soon the blower fan cleared the windscreen, and the car became pleasantly warm.

Kenyon could feel himself relaxing, discarding the pressures of the last few hours. It had not been a bad day after all. Whether or not a murder case was easy to solve did not show up on the statistics. Kenyon had a one hundred per cent success rate when it came to murder. Admittedly, it was usually a relatively simple crime, since you rarely had to look outside family or lovers, but it still looked good on his personal files.

He drove to a street in Kilburn, and parked. He then walked two hundred yards to another street, hunching into his collar against the rain. There appeared to be no lights on, but the living room faced the back garden. He tried the back door. It was locked. Irritated, the rain dripping from his hair, he put his finger on the door bell, and kept it there. A light went on in the kitchen. The door was unlocked. Kenyon went in.

'You took your time,' he said. 'A man could drown out there.'

Molly closed the door. Her feet were bare. Her short nightdress was nearly transparent, and Kenyon could see her breasts and a hint of pubic hair.

'I phoned,' Molly said.

'I know.' Kenyon took off his raincoat, pitched it on a chair, dried his face with a towel. 'I've been on a murder case. I only got the message twenty minutes ago. It didn't seem worth phoning back. Were you in bed?'

'Yes,' Molly said.

Kenyon put his hands on her cream-fleshed shoulders, ran them slowly down to her breasts. He felt her nipples rise at once. That was one thing he liked about Molly. No one had to turn her on. She was a self starter.

'A good place to be,' Kenyon said. 'Let's go.'

'Don't you want a drink?' Molly asked.

'No,' Kenyon said.

He kissed her. Her lips parted at once. He slid his right hand down her short nightdress, lifted it, and massaged her gently, feeling the other lips grow warmly moist.

'You bastard,' Molly said. 'That's not fair.' Her voice was unsteady.

Molly liked to start quickly, as though she were being raped, and then slow down until neither could keep it up any longer. She turned her head to one side, her eyes closed, her lips parted, she groaned, and her arms clamped him tight.

Kenyon lay on his back. His heart was still beating hard, but soon it would slow down. They would talk idly for a while, and then she would fall silent, look at him fixedly, and begin to kiss his body, throwing the covers back as her exploring lips moved down his stomach. Then they would begin again. That was how it always was.

Except tonight.

'I think my husband knows,' Molly said.

Kenyon looked at her. She was staring up at the ceiling. Her breasts which looked large in a brassiere, seemed less large now.

'How?' Kenyon asked.

'Something he said.'

'When?'

'This morning. When he was packing his suitcase.'

'You stupid, bloody cow,' Kenyon said.

He got out of bed, and pulled his trousers on.

'I did phone you,' Molly said, 'but you didn't call back.'

She got out of bed, and stood up. Her breasts became large again.

'Why the hell didn't you tell me as soon as I got here?' Kenyon demanded.

'I would have done,' Molly said, 'but you started touching me up. You made me want it. Anyway, he might not come back. I was only saying.'

Kenyon was sitting in the kitchen drinking coffee when there was the sound of the key in the back door, and Gerald Pearson walked in. He was a man of medium height, with butter-coloured hair, and pinched lips. He looked at Kenyon with what might have been disappointment.

'Gerald, darling,' Molly said, surprised, 'I wasn't expecting you home tonight.' She was fully, indeed primly, dressed.

'The new area manager rearranged my calls,' Pearson said. 'So I shan't have to be away so much in future.'

'My husband's a salesman,' Molly told Kenyon.

'I see,' Kenyon said.

'This is Detective Inspector Kenyon, Gerald,' Molly said. 'This is my husband, Mr Kenyon.'

'How do you do,' Kenyon said.

Pearson shook his umbrella, which deposited a considerable amount of water on the floor.

'Is there something wrong with the car?' Molly asked. 'Did you have to walk?'

'I couldn't park anywhere near the house,' Pearson said.

You bloody liar, Kenyon thought. You had it all worked out. Creep in, creep up the stairs, catch me screwing your wife. You think yourself bloody lucky it didn't work out, mate. I'd have rammed your teeth down your throat.

Kenyon knew that his anger was unreasonable, but while it was one thing to screw a married woman, it was quite another when you met the husband of the woman you were screwing. A very convenient arrangement had come to an end. Which was hard luck on Molly as well, he thought. Judging from the look of this prick. Once a month, in and out like a rabbit, and the rest of the time going to strip clubs and looking at it. No wonder she was always ready.

'Mr Kenyon called about the burglary,' Molly said.

'What burglary?' Pearson asked, sulkily.

'There have been a number of break-ins near here, Mr Pearson,' Kenyon said. Which was a safe statement to make about anywhere in London. 'I'm making enquiries about anything suspicious you may have noticed.'

'I haven't seen anything, Gerald,' Molly said. 'Have you?'

'It's rather late for that sort of call, isn't it?' Pearson asked. He was not quite looking into Kenyon's eyes. His gaze was directed at Kenyon's neatly knotted tie.

'I would have been earlier,' Kenyon said, 'but I was delayed by a murder investigation which took priority.'

Pearson's eyes blinked two or three times. 'How interesting,' he said. Murder belonged on the television screen as far as he was concerned, a prelude to the News, which pictured equally unreal deaths. He could not quite adjust to the idea that there really were men who dealt with murder in the way he called on his prospects, as part of their day to day work.

Kenyon could see the man's brain failing to cope with this different kind of reality. He had seen it before, and knew that that was why he was a policeman. It pleased him to be different from, outside, the great majority of people. It gave him a kick.

He stood up. 'Thank you for the coffee, Mrs Pearson. I'll say good night.'

'Where are you stationed?' asked Pearson. 'In case we need to get in touch with you.'

'If you think you have any information about the break-ins,' Kenyon said, 'get in touch with your local police station.'

'Then I don't suppose we shall see you again,' Pearson said, not quite bold enough to insist on an answer to his question.

Kenyon gave it to him anyway. 'I'm at Bayswater, Mr Pearson,' he said. 'If you'd like to talk to me personally, I'll be only too glad to come and see you any time.'

'I don't suppose that will be necessary,' Pearson said, staring straight at Kenyon's tie.

No, it won't, Kenyon thought, as he let himself out, and walked back to his car. You haven't got enough guts to come straight out with it, and say, listen you, stay away from my bloody wife, he thought, disgusted.

Kenyon drove back to Paddington. His mood grew blacker as he spent ten minutes trying to find somewhere to park near his flat. All the residents' parking strips were occupied, and in the end he manoeuvred into a space in Queen's Gardens, and walked through the rain, which seemed determined to break some sort of record.

Kenyon lived in a basement flat in Gloucester Terrace. The air inside struck him with that peculiar below-ground-level chill, but he preferred the interior warmth of a whisky to switching on the electric fire. He liked his flat, on the whole. It was convenient for the police station and, at night, with the curtains drawn and the standard lamps on, it was comfortable and pleasant. But in the day time, despite the tiny patio, it was dark and gloomy and if he spent much time there, he found it claustrophobic and lonely. Still, it served well enough. It was really only somewhere to sleep.

For all his weariness, Kenyon was restless that night. Normally, the pressures of a job which could extend through sixteen hours a day, seven days a week, unless he made a conscious effort to take time off, kept introspection at bay. But tonight, he looked at himself without much pleasure.

He had quite liked Molly, without feeling any great attachment to her. She matched him in bed, and her aimless chatter was agreeable enough, when they were not contemplating the carnal, which was not very often. He had used her, he knew, to deal with a strong, natural instinct, which otherwise got in the way. She had used him in exactly the same fashion. It had been a very satisfactory, almost routine arrangement, about which he had felt no shame, regret or remorse.

So why now? Not because of any fear that Pearson might

report him. That would take a degree of determination which Pearson lacked. Just because Gerald Pearson, formerly merely a name hardly mentioned, had turned into a human being, a man with butter-coloured hair and pinched lips, who fixed his eyes on people's ties? But Kenyon had thought him an odious, little creep, and disliked him on sight. It did not make sense.

Kenyon turned over on to his other side, and sought for sleep. Perhaps he should have got married, in which case presumably complicated incidents like tonight's would not occur. Although, judging from some of his married colleagues, Kenyon thought, he would not take any bets on that.

2

The hearing in the Magistrate's Court the following morning, a Saturday, was brief and formal. Winston Peters was remanded in custody for eight days.

Kenyon recognized the solicitor who was representing Winston Peters. Barker was thirty years old, brisk, energetic and ingenious. He had a nice, open smile, which he directed at Kenyon in the corridor outside the court.

'Could I have a word, Inspector Kenyon?' he said.

'Guilty,' Kenyon said.

'Oh, I don't know,' Barker said. 'I think he's got chances.'

'You're kidding,' Kenyon said. 'Try reading the statement.'

They were talking quietly in a corner where a bay window looked out on to a yard. Mallory was waiting a few yards off.

Kenyon knew what this little chat was meant to help establish, but it was up to Barker to make the running.

'You'll never get away with more than manslaughter,' Barker said.

'I'll bet a fiver on murder,' Kenyon offered.

'According to my client,' Barker said, 'there was a quarrel. The girl picked up the knife. Peters tried to take it away from her. There was a struggle, in the course of which she was accidentally stabbed.'

'His memory's improved since last night,' Kenyon remarked affably. 'He didn't say that when he coughed.'

'Possibly,' Barker suggested tentatively, 'the questions put to him were framed in such a way that the truth didn't come out.'

'You'd have forensic to deal with. The bruises on Jenny's throat.'

'Evidence of the struggle?' Barker suggested.

'You can try it,' Kenyon said, 'but I don't fancy his chances.'

'Oh, I don't know. My client was shocked and grief-stricken when he made that statement. Probably overcome with remorse.'

'That's true,' Kenyon agreed.

'Under arrest. Being interrogated by the police for the first time in his life. Hardly knowing what he was saying. Possibly being led – quite unintentionally of course – in the wrong direction. Not realizing what he was admitting. Imagine,' Barker said softly, rehearsing the rough draft of a brief he might later construct for the learned counsel who would never meet Winston Peters, 'imagine the man's feelings. Deeply in love with a girl, whom he was shocked to discover was a common prostitute. Horrified by the fact that he has accidentally brought about her death. Confronted by trained and experienced detectives, a man with no criminal record, an ordinary citizen, a man of previous good character –'

'He's a ponce,' Kenyon said.

Barker's eyes flickered. 'I understood he drove a mini cab.'

'So he does,' Kenyon said. 'Now and then, when he feels like it. He's also a ponce.'

'He's never been charged with any such offence,' Barker said.

'Just the same,' Kenyon said, 'I expect the prosecution will manage to bring it out.'

Barker discarded his rough draft, and tried something else. 'We might go for diminished responsibility on the grounds of severe provocation,' he said.

'Last night,' Kenyon said, 'he stuck a knife in Jenny Abel, and killed her. A knife which he makes a practice of carrying. Those are the facts.'

Barker had lost his smile, and was looking worried. 'When I was talking to him,' he said, 'I couldn't help feeling sorry for him.'

Kenyon felt some sympathy for Barker, who played it straight, unlike some solicitors Kenyon knew.

'So did I,' he said. 'He broke down and cried like a baby when he was making his statement.'

'This severe emotional stress which you noticed,' Barker said, 'was it present when you arrested him in the first place?'

'He didn't seem to know what he was doing,' Kenyon admitted.

Barker was looking more cheerful when Kenyon left him. Kenyon knew that he need not have given the solicitor the peg on which he might hang severe provocation and diminished responsibility. But he did not regret it. Kenyon had looked at the haggard, drawn, hopeless face of Winston Peters in the dock, and felt compassion for him. Presumably he really had felt love, whatever that meant, for Jenny Abel. What did it matter if he got five years instead of ten? Let the poor bastard come out while he still had some life left in him.

As it happened, Winston Peters had very little life left before him. That night, in his cell, he carefully ripped his shirt and trousers into long strips, tied them together, knotted them to the barred window and hanged himself.

Kenyon and Mallory went back to Bayswater Police Station, and climbed the stairs to CID. Kenyon's head was beginning to ache, and the few hours of restless sleep he had finally achieved had done little to make him feel less tired. He considered taking Sunday off, and spending the day in bed. He occasionally did this when his body showed signs of failing to meet the demands which he made upon it.

Detective Constable Meacher was there. 'I went round to see Miss Brooks, sir,' he said.

'Who?' Kenyon had forgotten about Miss Brooks.

'Any luck, Mike?' Mallory enquired salaciously.

'No. Oh, she's not bad looking, but she's an iceberg. There's nothing doing there,' Meacher said, with all the authority of his vast experience.

'Never mind your bloody sexual fantasies,' Kenyon said. His tiredness was making him irritable.

'Find yourself a nice policewoman,' Mallory advised.

'The nice ones are all attached, and the rest are butch,' Meacher said, wistfully.

'You're beginning to bore me, Meacher,' Kenyon said. 'How would you like to go back on the beat?'

'Sorry, sir,' Meacher said, not liking the idea at all.

'Well. What's her problem?'

'I don't know, sir. She wouldn't tell me.'

'But I told you,' Kenyon said, dangerously. 'I told you to go and deal with it.'

'Yes, I know, sir, and I tried,' Meacher said, beginning to look genuinely apprehensive. 'But she just wouldn't talk to me. She was perfectly polite and she said it was something to do with a break-in.'

'She's lucky to get a detective at all for that,' Kenyon said. 'Even you,' he added. 'Uniform Branch deal with minor crime these days.'

'Well, that's the point, sir.'

'What is?'

'She said it was such a serious matter, that she must see you personally.'

Kenyon lit a cigarette. Miss Brooks was beginning to annoy him.

'She said she'd be in all day,' Meacher said. 'So, whenever it was convenient for you.'

'If there's one thing I can't stand,' Kenyon said, 'it's stupid women who imagine I'm going to come running, tugging my forelock. I think I'll go and tell her so. Do you want to come?' he asked Mallory.

'I can't wait,' Mallory said.

'She's probably lost her bloody budgie,' Kenyon said.

Rockstone Gardens had been built when the grace of the Regency age still influenced Victorian builders. Originally massive family houses, they had all now been converted into expensive flats, and the residents were beginning to refer to the area as Lancaster Gate rather than Paddington. Cleeve Court, at one time five houses which had been largely gutted, except for the facade, and rebuilt as a single unit of luxury flats of varying sizes, was the largest conversion in Rockstone Gardens. The work had been completed six years before.

Flat 31 was on the top floor. There were two small passenger lifts in Cleeve Court, but Kenyon chose to climb an elegant flight of stairs, a part of the original building which had survived. This was habit. Kenyon thought you got a better impression, a better feel of a place, from walking up stairs. You got nothing out of a lift.

He noted that Cleeve Court boasted a hall porter, that the carpet on the stairs was thick and expensive, that the sound-proofing was good, and that the lighting came from chandeliers. This meant that the service charges were high, which he could have guessed anyway, and was not much to get from a long and exhausting climb.

Kenyon rang the doorbell of Flat 31. Sarah Brooks opened the door.

'Miss Brooks?' Kenyon said. 'I'm Detective Inspector Kenyon. This is my colleague, Detective Sergeant Mallory.'

'Come in,' Sarah Brooks said.

The flat was no surprise. Kenyon had anticipated it. Ingeniously carved out of the former servants' quarters to form a small pent-house, the living room was separated from a terrace by sliding glass doors, through which could be seen the topmost branches of the trees in the gardens, bare now, but no doubt a pleasant sight in the summer. Elegant and well placed furniture made the living room seem larger than it really was. Pictures hung on the walls, one of them an original.

But Miss Brooks was a surprise.

'Can I offer you a drink?' she asked.

'Please,' Mallory said, promptly. 'Whisky.'

'The same for me,' Kenyon said.

'Do sit down,' Sarah Brooks said.

Kenyon sat, vaguely uncomfortable in his raincoat, and looked at Sarah Brooks as she fixed the drinks. Meacher had dismissed her as not bad looking, which only showed, Kenyon thought, his youthful, massive lack of taste. He guessed that she was about thirty. Her voice was softly modulated. She wore her fair hair short. Her mouth was well shaped, and she evidently well knew that her wide blue eyes were her best feature, and made them up accordingly. She seemed completely composed, and not at all like the neurotic frump Kenyon had half anticipated.

'It's extremely good of you to come like this,' Sarah Brooks said. 'I am grateful.'

She wore a white dress, and as she bent over the drinks table, Kenyon found himself watching the line of her thigh, the curves of her small, but firm, breasts.

For Christ's sake, stop it, he told himself. You're getting as bad as Meacher.

'Thank you,' he said, taking the whisky from Sarah Brooks. 'Thank you,' he said again, as she offered him a jug of water. He added some to his whisky, for the sake of appearances.

'Do please smoke,' Sarah Brooks said, offering a box of cigarettes. 'I'm sorry, I should have asked you to take your coats off. Just put them down anywhere.'

Kenyon caught Mallory's eye. Mallory winked. Sitting with a generous glass of whisky, served by a fanciable lady, in an expensively comfortable flat, while smoking her cigarettes, made a pleasant change from some of the grubbier and more unpleasant things they were obliged to do from time to time.

'Perks,' Mallory said softly.

'Pardon?' Sarah Brooks asked.

'Good health,' Mallory said.

'Oh. Yes.' Sarah Brooks had not poured a drink for herself, but she lit a cigarette. 'I told the young Detective Constable a little,' she said.

'You've had a break-in,' Kenyon said.

'Yes, but not in the ordinary way.'

Her expression was serious. Kenyon had not seen her smile yet. Her face was troubled, but then it often affected people that way, the thought of some stranger prowling round, prying into personal possessions.

Mallory voiced Kenyon's thoughts.

'It's not that,' Sarah Brooks said.

'When was this?' Kenyon asked.

'Yesterday,' Sarah Brooks said. 'I came home just after six. The front door was closed, but it wasn't locked. I knew then.'

Kenyon registered his first mental query. People often swore that they had locked their doors, when they had not.

'What was missing?' he asked.

'Nothing,' Sarah Brooks said.

'You're quite sure?'

'Yes.'

'Isn't that an original picture?' Kenyon asked.

'Yes. It's by Ben Maile. *Trawlers at Sunset.*'

'Worth a bit, I should imagine.'

'They weren't after things like that,' Sarah Brooks said with a trace of impatience, as though speaking to a somewhat backward child. Kenyon found this irritating. 'I have some jewellery as well. That wasn't touched.'

'Then you can't be sure anyone was in here at all,' Kenyon said.

'If you'll come with me,' Sarah Brooks said. 'I'll show you.'

Kenyon and Mallory finished their drinks, put down empty glasses and stood up.

'First of all, that was open,' Sarah Brooks said, indicating the sliding door. 'I think I disturbed them, and they went out that way. All the sun terraces are adjoining. There's a way on to the fire escape at the end.'

'You keep saying "they", Miss Brooks,' Mallory remarked.

'That's how I think of them,' she said. 'But of course, there might have been only one.'

'I see,' Mallory said, in the tone policemen use when they do not wish to be rude. Kenyon knew how he felt.

'We'll start in the bedroom,' Sarah Brooks said.

There was another sun terrace off the bedroom, which faced the rear of the block. White, louvred, fitted wardrobes, covered one wall. A large, double divan was covered by a pink satin bedspread. Feminine things stood on the dressing table. No male things.

'There,' Sarah Brooks said, pointing.

'Where?'

'My pots of cream. They've been probed. See for yourself.'

Kenyon took the tops off jars of cold cream, moisturizing cream, and vanishing cream. Inside each of them, the cream formed a tiny vortex, as though a thin probe had been inserted.

'I see.' This time it was Kenyon who said it, neutrally.

'And then, in the bathroom . . .' Sarah Brooks led the way to the bathroom.

There was a pink bathroom suite, with matching towels. Bars of soap sat in a tray above the washbasin, and in a recess above the bath.

'Look at the soap,' Sarah Brooks said.

Kenyon looked at her blankly.

'Pick them up,' she said impatiently.

Kenyon did so. Each cake of soap came apart. Each had been cut down the middle.

'Oh, and the bath was running,' Sarah Brooks said.

'The bath?'

'Yes. The cold water tap had been turned full on.'

'Are you implying that your intruders intended to take a cold bath, Miss Brooks?' Mallory asked.

'I'm simply telling you what I found, Sergeant,' Sarah Brooks said. 'But I doubt if anyone intended to take a bath. The plug wasn't in.'

She led the way to the kitchen. Kenyon had grasped roughly what Miss Brooks was showing them, by now. He wondered if she was going to try and account for it.

In the kitchen, Sarah Brooks pointed to an empty packet of soap powder. 'That was nearly full. It's been emptied. The soap, again, it's been cut in half. And there's this.'

She showed them a plastic bottle of washing up liquid. The bottle had been slit neatly down one side, apparently with a razor.

'Anything else?' Kenyon asked.

'No, that's all. Let me give you another drink.'

'Thank you,' Kenyon said, and followed her into the living room. 'Do you have any idea how your intruders might have got in?' he asked.

'No. Whisky again?'

'Please.'

Mallory went off to the front door. Kenyon accepted his drink. 'Thank you.'

They could hear Mallory opening and closing the front door. Sarah Brooks lit a cigarette. He was watching her closely this time, and he saw that for all her apparent self-possession she was nervous. Perhaps more than nervous. Perhaps afraid. Perhaps something else.

Mallory came back. 'That's not a very good front-door lock you've got, Miss Brooks,' he said. 'It looks fine, but anyone can open it from the outside by just sliding a table knife behind the beading.'

Kenyon looked at him sharply. 'Has it been forced?'

Mallory shrugged. 'There are a few scratches. Hard to tell. Could be wear and tear. Could be not.'

'There's something else,' Sarah Brooks said. 'The last few days I think I've been followed.'

'Who by?'

'I don't know.'

'Who do you imagine?' Kenyon insisted.

'The same people presumably who broke into my flat, and searched it,' Sarah Brooks said.

Kenyon looked at Mallory who was sitting in an armchair, legs crossed. Mallory did not look up. He was studying his whisky with all the intensity of a man gazing into a crystal ball, and waiting for the cloudiness to clear.

'What do you think they hoped to find?' Kenyon asked.

'I don't know,' Sarah Brooks said. She tapped her cigarette on the edge of an ashtray two or three times, although there was no ash on the end of it. 'I don't understand why the cold water tap was left running.'

'Possibly to drain the cold water tank,' Mallory said, finding his thought, it seemed, in the depths of his whisky glass.

'Why?'

'People sometimes use a cold water tank as a hiding place,' Kenyon said.

'For things like diamonds,' Mallory said. 'That's where we found the Steiner stones, remember?' he reminded Kenyon, whose memory did not need jogging, since on that occasion they had both been shot at.

Sarah Brooks laughed shortly, without much humour, but the low sound was musical and pleasant, just the same. 'They weren't looking for diamonds,' she said.

'Something small though,' Kenyon said, helpfully. 'Something which could be hidden in a pot of cream, or a cake of soap.'

Sarah Brooks shrugged.

'What's your occupation, Miss Brooks?' Kenyon asked.

'Civil servant.'

'With?'

'The Foreign Office. I'm a translator.'

'Which languages?'

'Russian and German.'

'I see,' Kenyon said. He was beginning to enjoy the complexity of the picture he was building up, which he could later accept, or reject. 'What sort of translating? Conferences? That sort of thing?'

'Yes. I used to travel a good deal,' Sarah Brooks said, 'doing simultaneous translation. Lately, I've been engaged on other kinds of translation.'

'What other kinds?'

'Documents of various sorts,' Sarah Brooks said.

Which was good and vague, Kenyon thought. She was being evasive, or at least less than forthcoming. Normally, Kenyon might have adopted a hard line, snapped, become impatient, decided to bear down on her. But it was comfortable, sitting here in this warm flat, drinking whisky. And the scenery, in the form of Sarah Brooks, was agreeable. Kenyon had no urgent desire to be anywhere else.

'Are these various documents ever microfilmed?' Kenyon enquired.

'Not by me,' Sarah Brooks said, sharply. 'There are procedures laid down.'

'You appear to hold a fairly responsible position,' Kenyon said. 'Suppose you needed to refer back to some previous translation, for example? I presume, you have access to microfilmed records?'

'Only through the proper channels,' Sarah Brooks said. 'And there are strict checks.'

Kenyon finished his whisky, leaned forward, and put his glass down on to a coffee table. His eyes rested briefly on the curve of her crossed legs.

'Are the documents themselves of any great significance?' he asked.

'Diplomatically, yes. For policy purposes.'

Kenyon smiled at her kindly. 'You asked to see me, Miss Brooks,' he said, 'and here I am. You've had a break in, but nothing was stolen. Do you know how many break-ins we get in this area? Thousands are reported in the course of a year. You've been lucky. Nothing was missing. But your flat was searched for something – or so you believe – a small object, which might have been concealed in a jar of face cream, or a hollowed out cake of soap. Precious stones are one possibility. You say that's not so. All right, then what? A roll of microfilm seems another possibility. I could be wrong about that, of course.'

He gave Sarah Brooks the opportunity to tell him that he was. She was looking at him hard, as though trying to make up her mind about something. Then she glanced at Mallory uncertainly, and stubbed out her cigarette, screwing the butt into the ashtray.

'I've worked with Detective Sergeant Mallory for two years,' Kenyon said. 'Anything you may wish to say to me can be said in front of him.'

He thought that she was trying to make up her mind whether to trust him.

'A certain part of my work,' Sarah Brooks said, 'involves decoding.'

'Decoding what?'

'I have a security classification,' Sarah Brooks said. 'I've worked for the Foreign Office ever since I left college. There's no reason why I should not be trusted.'

'Is that what you believe?' Kenyon asked. 'That you're under surveillance?'

'My flat being searched was the last straw,' Sarah Brooks said. She reached for another cigarette, tapped the end on the coffee

36

table nervously, and dropped it. Her fingers were shaking slightly. 'For some time now, I've begun to suspect what was happening.' In an attempt to control her voice, it had gone up a pitch. 'I've had the feeling I was being watched. My mail is always late . . .'

'So's most of mine,' Kenyon said.

'I think it's been intercepted,' Sarah Brooks said. She waved at the telephone. 'I hear noises on the phone. I think it's been tapped.'

Kenyon remained unimpressed. Paddington Telephone Exchange was old and out of date. You were lucky if your call did not fail entirely, or result in a crossed line. A few weird clicks was the normal. It was the clear, trouble-free line which was being tapped.

'My car has been searched,' Sarah Brooks said. 'Things inside it haven't been in the same place. My handbag's been searched too, and my desk.'

'Did you complain about this?' Kenyon asked.

'Yes, but it didn't do the slightest good. I was told I was imagining things. Well, those cakes of soap aren't imagination, Inspector Kenyon. Someone did that.'

'Yes,' Kenyon said. 'Someone did.'

He remembered being called out once to see a beautiful, if neurotic, woman, whose lovely breasts were pouring with blood from a dozen cuts. Her lover, who happened to be a Cabinet Minister, had done it, she said. Kenyon had thought this one was a nasty, in view of the possible political implications, and trod slowly, and with caution. It was just as well, since it had transpired that the lady had smashed a toothglass and done it herself when the Cabinet Minister was not even in the house. A horrified maid had seen her do it.

'I'm being investigated by some branch of the security services,' Sarah Brooks said. 'I resent that because I haven't done anything, but apart from that I find their methods hateful and very disturbing.'

She was certainly disturbed all right, Kenyon thought. 'I'm not certain what you expect me to do about it, Miss Brooks,' he said.

'I don't know who they are,' Sarah Brooks said. 'I've never seen a face. They're just doing these things and to be honest, I'm getting very frightened. It so happens that I'm alone. I wonder how far they're prepared to go.' She shuddered slightly. Her tongue ran over her lips. 'All this is happening to me, Inspector, for no reason. None at all. I'm the victim of someone's paranoia. That seems to me to be persecution, pure and simple. There are supposed to be laws in this country. Are the security services above the law?'

Kenyon preferred to treat the question as a rhetorical one. Any answer would have been decidedly ambivalent, and less than reassuring. He waited for Sarah Brooks to go on.

'I don't know if I can expect anything, Inspector Kenyon,' Sarah Brooks said, 'but what I'd like is your help. When they broke into this flat, they went too far. They broke the law, and I'm entitled to call in the police.' She was breathing deeply, and had difficulty in going on. She bit her lip, and fingered the pyramid-shaped ring she wore on her right hand. 'I want it stopped,' she said, despairingly. 'I want protection.'

3

Kenyon and Mallory bought pork pies in a pub round the corner. They had talked to Sarah Brooks for another half an hour, and Kenyon had promised her he would look into it. Kenyon cut into his pork pie, and lost a piece of crust, which fell into a puddle of beer on the table.

'Oh, shit,' he said.

'Temper,' Mallory said.

Kenyon forked another piece more successfully, put it in his mouth, and chewed. The pub had been 'done up' a year ago by the brewers, whose ambition it seemed to be to deprive all their pubs of any soul and character they might have possessed. The pork pie had never had either, and bore a strong resemblance to plastic.

'What do you think, Len?' Kenyon asked.

'I don't know.'

'Nor me.'

'None of the things she told us can be proved,' Mallory said. 'She could have done them all herself.'

'Yes, but why should she?' Kenyon argued.

'Come on, Sid,' Mallory said. 'You'd have to ask a head shrinker "why". Why do people turn up at the nick, and confess to murders they haven't committed? The fact is, they do.'

'I know,' Kenyon said. He was feeling unaccountably depressed. He was reluctant to write off as a nut that slim, good-looking woman in the white dress.

They finished their pork pies in silence. Mallory lit a cigarette. 'She's very convincing though,' he said, thoughtfully.

Kenyon woke up on Sunday morning, and decided to compromise. He would read the papers in bed until lunchtime, have a bath, and then possibly do a little work in the afternoon. He ran his bath very hot, and then lay there soaking, staring fixedly at the shower attachment without seeing it. After half an hour, he sighed, stood up in the bath, soaped himself all over, and turned on the shower.

Kenyon thought that he was lucky. Nature had given him a tall, muscular build, and although years of hurried meals and snatched sandwiches at odd times had made him about half a stone over weight, despite the fact that he smoked too much, and used whisky the way some people used pills, so far his body had taken it without complaint or apparent deterioration. His stomach was still flat, and his thighs and shoulders still strong.

He turned the shower on to cold, turned his face to the icy spray, and stood there until he shivered. As good as a week's holiday, he told himself. He dried himself, wrapped himself in a towelling dressing gown, stood in front of the mirror, and shaved. It was a pleasure to shave in a leisurely way, to take his time, instead of hurriedly mowing the stubble with an electric razor in a few borrowed moments.

Kenyon had a deceptively gentle face. The high, broad forehead topped blue eyes which often looked amused when he was not. He had inherited his father's long, straight nose, which was a little too long, and his mother's prominent cheekbones. His mouth tilted at the corners, up or down, depending on his mood, and revealed strong, slightly uneven teeth when he smiled. As a package, Kenyon did not think much of it. He had been slightly surprised when he found that some women found him attractive. Now, he accepted that good fortune might occasionally overtake him. He wondered how Molly's Sunday was going. He suspected that she could handle Gerald Pearson without too much difficulty. He speculated what his successor in Molly's bed would be like, without too much interest. He was sure there would be one, wished Molly well, and forgot about her.

Kenyon left his car where it was, and walked. The weather had relented slightly, and a chilly sun brightened the streets and squares of Paddington. There was no hall porter on duty at

Cleeve Court, but Kenyon found him dozing in his flat, and stirred him into consciousness. The hall porter had not seen anyone he did not know enter the building on Friday. Yes, he did hold duplicate keys for all the flats, but none were missing, and none had been borrowed. Kenyon thanked him, and left him, bleary eyed, contemplating the undressed beauties in the *Sunday People*.

Kenyon spent the rest of the afternoon interviewing the residents on the top floor of Cleeve Court. They all agreed that anyone could walk along the length of the sun terraces. Some of them did not like it, and had complained to the managing agents, but it was part of the fire escape arrangements. None of them had seen anyone moving along the sun terraces late Friday afternoon. But since it had been dark, and most of them had their curtains drawn, that did not prove very much, one way or another.

Kenyon prowled all over the building, apparently aimlessly, but in reality following his nose, and waiting for some indication of the unusual, which had served him well many times in the past. But nothing could have been more normal.

Cleeve Court had a small garden at the rear, for the use of residents, a patch of well-kept grass, two wooden bench seats, a child's swing, and some flower beds. Kenyon stood in the garden, looked up, located Sarah Brooks' flat, with its rear sun terrace opening off her bedroom. Anyone could get on to that sun terrace from the roof, and the fire escape arrangements for the adjoining buildings called for people to cross the roof of Cleeve Court.

No cat burglar was necessary. Anyone who was not crippled could manage it easily, which he supposed was the idea. He thought gloomily that it might be a good idea for the Fire Department to liaise more closely with the police. Fire escape routes were only too often an open door for men looking for an easy entry, with other ideas in mind. But had someone gone into Sarah's flat, and searched it? A part of Kenyon believed her, but it was not the professional part, he knew that.

He was aware of a vague hope that he might see her during the afternoon, but her sliding windows were closed, and there was no sign of life. Perhaps she was out. The simple way to establish that would be to ring her doorbell, but he did not. He could have done. He had a good enough excuse, God knows. But although he found the idea of looking into those splendid blue eyes aesthetically pleasing, that was a compartmented personal feeling. The copper in Kenyon, which was most of him, had other people to talk to before he sought Sarah Brooks out again.

That evening he heard that he would never speak to Winston Peters again. Kenyon experienced genuine regret. The man's death seemed such a waste. He was glad that he was not responsible for the safety of prisoners in those cells. Whoever was, would be for it.

Kenyon drove to the Foreign and Commonwealth Office in Downing Street on Monday morning. He flashed his police identification, which got him a parking place in the yard at the rear. He went inside, filled in a form, received a pass, and was shown up to see Mr Everitt, who was Sarah Brooks' Establishment Officer.

'Good morning, Inspector,' Everitt said, shaking hands warmly. 'Do sit down. What can I do for you?'

Kenyon told him. Everitt listened attentively. Everitt was polished, polite, and sounded as though he had been educated at Eton and Oxford, which he probably had. The office in which they talked struck Kenyon as incredibly luxurious and spacious, compared with his own little hutch at Bayswater Police Station.

'I am aware of most of this, of course, Inspector,' Everitt said. 'Sarah came to see me about it. She's under a complete misapprehension, as I'm sure you know.'

'No, I don't know,' Kenyon said, with an abruptness calculatedly just this side of rudeness.

'Pure fantasy, old chap,' Everitt said, smiling pleasantly. 'All of it.'

Kenyon was not an especially class-conscious man. Crime was not confined to any one income bracket. The biggest swindler Kenyon had ever nailed was listed in *Debrett's Peerage*. The most vicious killer had been an effete, soft-spoken man, an habitué of the trendy, expensive night clubs for the leisured, and who briefly, at one time, fluttered on the fringe of Princess Margaret's circle.

The old school tie meant nothing in the Police Force, and coppers had no respect for it, nor for rank and position. But the bland Everitt annoyed Kenyon. His cordiality was patronizing.

'Miss Brooks has supplied chapter and verse,' Kenyon said. I'll need rather more than vague generalizations from you before I dismiss the matter.'

Everitt sighed, clasped his hands, and made sure that it was clear he was consulting his watch. 'Sarah made certain allegations,' he said patiently. 'I found her manner slightly hysterical, but it is my duty to protect her welfare. I consulted Security, who assured me that she was not under surveillance of any kind.'

'Not even a classification check?'

'No routine check would go to such lengths, Inspector,' Everitt said. 'I strongly advised her to consult her doctor, and suggested that it would be a good idea to take some leave, and have a complete rest. She's very conscientious. I suspect she's been overworking.'

'Would Security inform you if they were investigating one of your staff?' Kenyon asked.

'Of course,' Everitt said, looking Kenyon straight in the eye, in the manner of a man well accustomed to telling blatant lies.

Kenyon stood up. If only Everitt would commit some offence which would bring him into the Interview Room in Bayswater Police Station. What a pleasure it would be to deal with Everitt in those circumstances.

'I'm wasting your time, Mr Everitt,' Kenyon said. 'And you're wasting mine. I think I'd better talk to the Security Officer concerned.'

'I thought I'd made it quite plain,' Everitt said, 'that no one is concerned.'

'You said you'd consulted Security,' Kenyon said. 'Which I assume is staffed by individuals. I presume you talked to one of them.'

'I sent an urgent confidential memo,' Everitt said, stiffly.

'Did you get a reply?'

'Are you being facetious, Inspector? Of course, I got a reply.

How else could I have given you the facts?' Everitt said, stressing the word 'facts' heavily.

'The man who signed the reply,' Kenyon said. 'If he revealed his identity. He'll do.'

Tight lipped, Everitt made a phone call. When he hung up, he said, ' In half an hour. You'll have to go somewhere else.'

' I know where to go,' Kenyon said.

Kenyon drove to Queen Anne's Gate, parked his car, and entered a building. Here too, he received a pass, and was directed to the first floor. There, he waited, while a telephone call was made, after which he received another pass.

A man in a porter's uniform led him into a lift. They rode to the top floor, and walked along several corridors. Kenyon strongly doubted if they were in the original building, by the time they arrived at a door. He also thought that the man in porter's uniform was remarkably young and well educated to be a porter, and that the gun he was carrying was not totally concealed.

' Tom Bradley,' Tom Bradley said, shaking Kenyon's hand, with a firm, muscular grip. ' Glad to meet you. Take a pew. Make yourself comfortable. Feel like some coffee? Or would you rather have a snort?' He dug a bottle of whisky out of a desk drawer.

' Coffee,' Kenyon said. ' I have occasional illusions about cutting down.'

' So do I,' Bradley said. ' I feel it shows strength of character if I don't have one till lunchtime. Get back you,' he said, stuffing the whisky bottle back into the overcrowded drawer. 'Right,' he said, picking up a file. ' I know what this is about. I've been going through the lady's security file again, while you were on your way over. Let's get that out of the way, and then we can have a quiet natter.'

Bradley was a big man of forty-five, with greying hair, and Kenyon had warmed to him at once. He was obviously a professional, thank God. Impossible to guess his background, or whether he was really with the Security Department of the Foreign Office, or some less clearly defined organization. But Kenyon felt that they might at least speak the same language.

'Is Sarah Brooks under surveillance?' Kenyon asked, without preamble.

'No.'

'Everitt told me that he'd be informed, but I wanted to hear it from you.'

'Lance Everitt is a prize cunt,' Bradley said. 'Whoever selected him for that job had his brains in his arse. Forget Everitt. I'm telling you.'

'All right,' Kenyon said. 'You've told me. Now convince me.'

'OK. First, civil servants who go bent, or get careless, are my pigeon, so I'd know if anything was on. Second, she's not under suspicion. There's not a word in here,' Bradley said, riffling the pages of the file like a gambler shuffling a pack of cards, 'which might indicate she's not a loyal, dedicated lady which I'm sure she is. Third, I wouldn't bother much if she weren't. She's not important enough.'

'She has access to microfilmed documents,' Kenyon said.

'Christ almighty,' Bradley said, 'if you only knew the kind of time-wasting crap our diplomats think the Foreign Office ought to have on record. I wouldn't give a shit if she delivered the whole bloody lot to the Russian Embassy.'

'Since part of her work is decoding,' Kenyon said, 'some of it must be secret stuff.'

Bradley roared with laughter. 'I'm sorry,' he said, choking into his handkerchief. 'You ought to be right, of course. But these people use code to tell you it's snowing in Moscow in January. It makes them feel important.'

Kenyon's neck prickled at the back, under his collar. Someone was leading him up the garden, and if Sarah Brooks was convincing, Tom Bradley was even more so.

'What security classification is she?' he asked.

'Relatively low,' Bradley said. 'She has no access whatever to information which is at all sensitive. It wouldn't worry me if she turned out to be Mata Hari in disguise. She doesn't know anything worth knowing. No,' he said, closing his file, 'I'm afraid Sarah Brooks isn't quite as important as she apparently thinks she is.'

'On the other hand,' Kenyon said, 'if you did have her under surveillance, you probably wouldn't tell me anyway.'

'Damn right, I wouldn't,' Bradley agreed.

'You could be giving me a load of cobblers.'

'True. I'm not. But I could be.'

'I expect you're a high class liar when it suits you,' Kenyon said.

'I expect you are too,' Bradley said. 'It kind of goes with the job, in my experience.' He looked at his watch. 'I don't know where that bloody coffee's got to. If you'll excuse me for a few minutes, I'll go and chase it up.'

Bradley went out, closing the door behind him. Sarah Brooks' security file lay on his desk. Kenyon picked it up, and read through it. There was not much to read. Her security classification, twice upgraded in the course of her career, was still short of access to top secret material. Her screening, which was ordinary to the point of dullness, with not a question mark in her life, let alone a suspicion. A series of annual reviews and comments, repeatedly confirming that no queries had arisen about Sarah Brooks.

Ten minutes later, Bradley came back with two cups of coffee. 'Sorry to have been so long,' he said. 'I hope you weren't bored.'

Kenyon took his coffee. 'Thank you.' He spooned in sugar, and stirred it. 'I've been thinking,' he said. 'Suppose it wasn't information. Suppose Miss Brooks had struck up some sort of acquaintance with someone whom you might disapprove of.'

'Don't remember anything like that,' Bradley said, 'but let's check.' He skimmed through the file, enjoying the game he was playing. 'No, nothing here, no Czech journalists, no East German agricultural experts, not so much as a Russian piccolo player. I'm sorry I can't show you this file,' he said apologetically, 'but it's for my eyes only. You understand.'

'If you were giving her the works,' Kenyon said, 'it might not be her real file anyway. You might prefer to use a dummy, in case I can read upside down. Or in case you left it lying around for someone to look at.'

'Jesus Christ,' Bradley said, grinning, 'the villains in Bayswater must love a suspicious bastard like you. You'll have to believe somebody or other sooner or later. I don't know what more I can say, except hurry up and finish this horse piss they call coffee, and let's give ourselves a snort to take the taste away.'

Crime in Bayswater rolled on as relentlessly and unendingly as the waters of the River Thames. Any changes of level served only to increase or temporarily diminish the size of the backlog. The overworked handful of men who dealt with it just kept on going.

For the next few days, Kenyon had little time to spare for Sarah Brooks. Other cases which flowed in took priority, including a grievous bodily harm, in which the victim had lost an eye; a rape, which Kenyon did not believe was anything of the kind; criminal assault upon a girl aged four; and a tip-off from an informant about a Long Firm Fraud.

It had seemed to Kenyon that Sarah Brooks lived at a somewhat expensive address for a civil servant. He snatched a few minutes with the managing agents of Cleeve Court who told him that Sarah Brooks had bought her flat four years before on a ninety-nine year lease. A deposit of twenty-five per cent of the purchase price had been paid, and the remainder was on a twenty year mortgage.

Kenyon looked up her salary in the civil service list. She was quite well paid. The flat was well within her means. But four years before, her salary had been considerably lower. He wondered how she had managed to find the twenty-five per cent deposit.

His Long Firm Fraud informant was a hollow-chested, forty-year-old, small-time villain called Jackie, who had been a guest of Her Majesty on several occasions. Jackie was married, with five children, and played both sides against the middle in a pretty successful effort to keep them well clothed, well fed, and well housed. Kenyon met him in a dingy cafe off Praed Street, where they drank stewed tea, and bargained. Kenyon thought that Jackie was a high class snout, and was prepared to take him seriously.

'It's good, Mr Kenyon,' Jackie said, 'but I don't want to say too much until I know what the score is.'

'You know the score,' Kenyon said. 'I'm supposed to report

it to the Long Firm Fraud Squad at Scotland Yard, and let them handle it.'

'I've got problems with them,' Jackie said, gazing at Kenyon, with melancholy eyes. 'What you might call a personality clash.'

'Nobody loves you, Jackie,' Kenyon said. 'It's time you faced up to that.'

'If it's handled right,' Jackie said, 'there's a nice reward comes my way from the insurance company. Otherwise, there's no point.'

'If it's as good as you say it is,' Kenyon said, 'I might be able to keep it to myself, and just tell the Yard I'd made a raid on the strength of your information, and struck lucky.'

'That's what I had in mind, Mr Kenyon,' Jackie said. 'I thought we might be able to come to some arrangement.'

The firm in question had an impressive name. The premises from which they operated were considerably less impressive and consisted of a tumbledown warehouse, with inadequate loading and unloading facilities in a gloomy area of North Kensington. The company was properly constituted, but anyone could set up or buy a company. The Directors' names did not appear in Criminal Records, but front men were easily hired to become directors. Consignments of perfume and cosmetics had been ordered, and promptly paid for. Long Firm Fraud men were patient people. The first thing they had to do was to establish a good credit record.

It was conceivable that the company in question was legitimate, that it was operated by straight businessmen who had overlooked the fact that a wholesaler's warehouse needed good loading bays and a clear approach road, and who would eventually enlarge their presently negligible sales force. Kenyon thought it more likely that, having established a reputation for quick payment, a series of much larger orders would be placed in the near future. That as soon as the goods were delivered, the warehouse would be left empty, and the invoices unpaid. That the perfumes and cosmetics thus acquired, which could easily be worth £200,000 or more, would then be fed through various outlets, and sold to those who liked to buy cheaply.

Six months work, profit say £100,000 and upwards. Tax free,

of course. Not bad. Kenyon hoped to turn this particular operation into a loss-making one for those concerned, plus a period of enforced idleness in one of Her Majesty's Prisons.

Kenyon was briefing Detective Constable Meacher about the Long Firm Fraud, when Sarah Brooks telephoned him.

'Kenyon,' he said, into the phone.

'It's Sarah Brooks,' she said. 'I wondered if you'd managed to find out anything yet.'

'I'm afraid not,' Kenyon said.

'Oh. It's several days since we talked. I thought perhaps . . .'

'I'm still making enquiries,' Kenyon said.

There was silence. No sound came from the earpiece.

'Hullo,' Kenyon said. 'Hullo.'

'Yes, I heard you.'

'Sorry. I thought we'd been cut off.'

'No, I . . . it's just that I had hoped . . . there's really no one else I can turn to . . . I don't know if you thought I was being silly . . .'

'Not at all,' Kenyon said, politely.

'I can't help being frightened. I try, but I can't help it.'

'I'd like to talk to you again fairly soon,' Kenyon said. 'When would it be convenient to call?'

'Any evening,' Sarah Brooks said. 'Or the weekend, of course.'

Kenyon hung up, pondered briefly the implications of that 'any evening', and resumed briefing Meacher.

'Put your scruffiest clothes on,' he said, 'and stop shaving for a couple of days. You're out of work. There's a café, a betting shop, and a pub, all within a hundred yards of the warehouse. Drift around between the three. Try and find out what's going on, without making yourself conspicuous. I want to know the state of play. If you're absolutely certain you're not known to any of the people you see coming and going at the warehouse, you can try asking for a job. Ring in twice a day, but otherwise stay away from the nick, until you're pulled off.'

'OK, sir.' Meacher was delighted. He had visions of making a name for himself. If it all came off, Kenyon, for his part, would receive three hundred pounds in cash out of Jackie's reward, which no one but he and Jackie would know about. Kenyon thought he would put it towards a new car.

Kenyon rang a friend of his, and was lucky enough to find him in. 'Fancy a quick one some time soon?' he enquired.

'It's a bit dodgy at the moment. My social life's come to a halt.'

'This isn't entirely social,' Kenyon told him. 'Any time. I don't care how late it is.'

'Eleven o'clock tonight. Unless you've started going to bed early.'

'I haven't,' Kenyon said. 'And let's make it my place. This is private.'

Kenyon got home at ten o'clock. He switched the television set on, and made himself a sandwich. At eleven o'clock, a horror movie started. Kenyon watched it through to the end. The blood and gore left him unmoved. Real blood did nothing to him, let alone the make believe variety. But he enjoyed the picture's Gothic bravado. He turned it off at the end, poured a whisky, and sat waiting. There were some documents in his brief case, which he ought to look at before the morning, but he would set his alarm, and study those over breakfast. Kenyon enjoyed cooking and eating his solitary breakfast.

At one o'clock, he gave up, and put the whisky bottle away. The telephone rang. Kenyon picked it up.

'Sorry. Got delayed. Too late now?'

'No,' Kenyon said.

'Ten minutes.'

Kenyon fetched the whisky bottle out again, filled a jug with water, put some ice cubes in an ice bucket, and placed the collection on a table, together with a clean glass for his visitor.

The door bell rang. 'Hullo,' Kenyon said, into his entryphone.

'Steve.'

'Come in.'

Kenyon pushed the button to release the house door, and opened the front door to his flat.

Steve Rimmer came down the stairs. 'Hullo, Sid,' he said. 'What a time to arrive.'

'Doesn't matter,' Kenyon said. 'It's good to see you again.'

They shook hands. Kenyon ushered him in, and pointed to the table. 'All set up, ready and waiting. Help yourself.'

'God, I need one too,' Rimmer said. He put four ice cubes in the tall glass, poured whisky carefully over the ice, and added a dash of water, which was the way he always took his whisky. 'I'm frozen stiff. I've been out with the special squad.'

'Sit down,' Kenyon said. 'Anything happen?'

'No,' Rimmer said, sprawling in an armchair. 'False alarm. Cheers.'

'Cheers,' Kenyon said, and poured a drink for himself.

Steve Rimmer was almost exactly the same age as Kenyon. They had struck up a firm friendship when they were at Police Training School together. Their paths had diverged when Rimmer went into Special Branch, and for some years now, their meetings had been infrequent.

Rimmer was a comfortably ordinary-looking man, whose face it would be hard to recall and describe. This was a useful asset in some of the more bizarre activities which Special Branch got up to.

'Still leading a monk-like existence?' Rimmer asked. 'Or is there a little lady tucked up out of sight in the bedroom?'

'I'm what you might call in between,' Kenyon said.

'Troilism yet,' Rimmer said.

'No such luck,' Kenyon said. 'One down, and nowhere to go.'

'Time we got you married,' Rimmer said. 'I don't see why the general misery shouldn't be spread about a bit.'

'Don't be such a bloody hypocrite,' Kenyon said. Rimmer was married to a raven-haired beauty called Ann. They lived in a pleasant, semi-detached house in Hendon.

Rimmer grinned. 'Ann always sticks up for you too,' he said. 'I try and tell her that you're nothing but a bloody ram, and you're not afraid of becoming a dirty old man so much as afraid you won't. She claims you haven't met the right girl yet. Still a romantic, my wife.'

'How is she?'

'She gets a bit pissed off,' Rimmer said. 'I can't say I blame her. Wandering in at all hours, away for days at a time, it's not most people's idea of marriage. Not mine, really, to tell the truth,' he added, after a pause.

Kenyon topped up Rimmer's glass. 'The baby all right?' he enquired. Steve Rimmer was a good friend, but just the same Kenyon wanted him to be relaxed and chatty before they got to the point. What Kenyon wanted to know would need some digging, and it would have to be very unofficial.

'Baby? You're out of date, mate. He's now a butch youth of eighteen months,' Rimmer said, with feeling. 'Don't fall for that patter of tiny feet stuff. Mine sounds as though he's got wooden clogs on. He thunders about like a bloody elephant. Especially at six o'clock in the morning. He climbs out of his cot sublimely convinced that I ought to be up at dawn, and it's his job in life to see to it.'

Rimmer went into a lengthy anecdote concerning one of his son's more spectacular misdemeanours, although his smiling gestures betokened acute pride in his offspring. Kenyon wondered how it was possible to shut off sections of one's mind as completely as Rimmer appeared to do. He also wondered if Ann knew exactly what her husband was involved in.

It was doubtful if the general public quite realized how often the police were armed. Tomorrow at twelve noon Kenyon would issue thirty-eights to himself, Mallory and a Detective Constable. They would pose as customers in a bank near Queensway from twelve-thirty onwards. If the tip-off Kenyon had received was good, the bank would be raided at one-thirty. It was unlikely, though not absolutely certain, that the robbers would choose to shoot it out with three armed policemen. Any copper with a gun was an authorized shot, who was not going to miss, and the villains knew it. Apart from the unpredictable psychotics, most of them would drop their guns, become peaceful and co-operative and swear that they had been forced to take part by threats. The lawyers would later introduce evidence about childhood deprivation and social maltreatment.

That was one thing. But the special squad, armed with machine guns, which Steve Rimmer was attached to, was another. Kenyon wondered where Rimmer had been tonight, and why he had been delayed, but he did not ask. Rimmer was cryptically vague about his recent assignment.

Kenyon supposed that he would probably have the doubtful privilege of being one of the first generation of policemen present when gun battles with terrorists were fought out with machine guns in the streets of London. Special Branch seemed to think it was going to happen one day. And Special Branch had a reputation for good intelligence.

Rimmer finished his anecdote. Kenyon topped up his glass. Rimmer issued an invitation to Sunday lunch some time. Kenyon promised to ring Ann, and confirm in the near future. The flat was soothingly warm. The two men were sprawled opposite each other, drinking, smoking, talking idly, as they had done many times before their careers diverged. Kenyon judged that there would not be a better moment.

'I ran into someone you might know, the other day,' he said, casually.

'Is this the private matter?' Rimmer asked. He seemed no less relaxed and friendly, but Kenyon knew that the brain behind those smiling eyes was suddenly observant and careful. Rimmer's life often depended on not being taken unawares. He was not likely to lose the habit, even in the company of a close friend, Kenyon reflected.

'Yes,' Kenyon said. 'A fellow called Tom Bradley.' He was stubbing out a cigarette, but he was also watching Rimmer closely. He saw the momentary flicker in his eyes as Rimmer sipped his drink.

'Oh, yes,' Rimmer said.

'Come on,' Kenyon said. 'The Old Pals Act takes precedence over the Official Secrets Act.'

Rimmer grinned. 'A bit surprised to find you mixing at his level, that's all,' he said.

'What do you know about him?'

'Why?'

'I've never met a big wheel like Bradley before,' Kenyon said, dealing back the card he had just been played. 'I'm curious about his background, that's all.'

'I don't know much about him myself,' Rimmer said, gesturing vaguely. 'Formerly Naval Intelligence, I think.'

Kenyon ignored the qualifying 'I think', and pressed on, treating it as a fact. 'What was he before he went into Intelligence? Regular Navy?'

'A Dartmouth cadet,' Rimmer said. 'Served on destroyers for a few years, and then transferred. He was a brilliant Russian scholar. Spent some time in Washington, too.'

'What sort of rank, before he left the Navy?'

'Commander. In so far as rank meant anything, in his line of work.'

'But a mister, now.'

'That's right. Plain Mr Bradley.'

Kenyon thought of the bluff, hearty, 'I'm-just-one-of-the-boys-like-you,' Bradley that he had met. The Regular Navy still turned men into officers and gentlemen, with clipped, laconic accents. Somewhere, Bradley had lost all that. Or adopted a different façade for his interview with Kenyon. That might mean nothing. But there was a conceivable explanation. Kenyon's job took him from the dregs to the cream. You adapted yourself according to what you wanted. Kenyon could talk like a villain when speaking to villains, especially if he wanted to convey a certain impression, usually of the misleading variety.

'What department does he work for?' Kenyon asked.

'You must know that, if you were talking to him,' Rimmer said.

'I got shunted,' Kenyon explained.

'I think he runs his own outfit,' Rimmer said, which was probably accurate, but less than explicit. 'Now let's turn this into two-way traffic, shall we? What were you doing with Tom Bradley?'

Kenyon told him about Sarah Brooks, outlining it as a routine police enquiry, on behalf of a spinster lady. He did not say so, but anyone listening would infer that the lady in question was probably in late middle age, and grey and bespectacled into the bargain.

Rimmer sat quietly, his eyes fixed on Kenyon. 'No, thanks,' he said, when Kenyon finished and moved to refill his glass. Rimmer seemed somewhat amused.

'This Sarah Brooks,' he said. 'This spinster. Somewhere around thirty or so? Good figure? In fact, decidedly bedworthy? Good to look at? The tired DI's dream, by any chance?'

'Not bad,' Kenyon said, annoyed with himself. 'Have you met her?'

'I don't have to,' Rimmer said. 'You fancy this bird like mad, otherwise you wouldn't be giving her the time of day.'

'She's very convincing,' Kenyon said, quoting Mallory.

'Come off it,' Rimmer said, grinning at him. 'All the trouble you've been to, the Foreign Office, Bradley, me. Bloody hell, the workload you've got, and you spend all this time on Sarah Brooks. If you didn't have visions of laying her, you'd have made one phone call and dropped it.'

'All right,' Kenyon said. 'She's a nice, attractive girl. Woman,' he corrected himself. 'But not the kind to get neurotic over nothing. At least, I don't think she is. But someone's conning me. Either Miss Brooks, or the people I've talked to.'

'The delicious Sarah,' Rimmer said.

'Could be,' Kenyon said. 'But I need some bugger I can trust who's not going to feed me a load of crap. I'm electing you.'

'Thanks very much,' Rimmer said.

'I want to know if she's under surveillance, or being investigated, by her own people, Special Branch, DI this, MI that, or Uncle Tom Cobley. Or perhaps it's some foreign mob.'

'Jesus Christ,' Rimmer said, 'you're really clutching at straws, aren't you. If the KGB had the slightest interest in her, someone else'd be taking it seriously, besides you.'

'Will you have an ask around for me?'

Rimmer looked at his watch, and stood up. 'All right,' he said. Kenyon saw him to the door.

'I think it'll be a waste of time,' Rimmer said. 'Why don't you just slide into her bed, and take her mind off it?'

'I should think Tom Bradley's a busy man,' Kenyon said. 'I

wonder why he'd take two hours of his time to assure me there was nothing in it.'

'Because you were making a bloody nuisance of yourself over nothing,' Rimmer suggested.

But despite Rimmer's friendly smile, Kenyon knew that he was wondering about that too.

4

At one-thirty the following afternoon, Kenyon was filling in a bank pay-in slip. Mallory was queuing for foreign exchange. The Detective Constable was near the door, studying literature on personal loans.

The minute hand of the clock flicked forward, each half minute. Kenyon's jacket was unbuttoned. His gun could be in his hand, aimed, in a second. He was conscious that his heart beat had speeded up. There seemed to be something in his throat, and he kept swallowing. If the bank was going to be hit, the villains would probably not open fire, but they might. Kenyon hoped they would not be carrying shot-guns. He had a fear of being blinded.

One-thirty became one-thirty-one, one-thirty-five, one-forty-five. The raid was late. Or perhaps their information was bad. At three-thirty, when the bank closed, nothing had happened. Kenyon's feet ached, and he felt drained by his continuous concentration and expectation. This let-down was almost worse than if he had been forced to open fire.

The three policemen climbed into Kenyon's car, and drove back to the station to hand in their guns.

'And the bloody pubs aren't even open,' Mallory said.

'I've got a bottle in my office,' Kenyon said.

'Thank Christ for that.'

As Kenyon reversed into his space in the car yard, he said, 'Oh, go and see Sarah Brooks again, some time, will you?'

'All right,' Mallory said. 'Any special line?'

'Spend some time with her. Get her to talk again. See what your second thoughts are.'

57

'OK,' Mallory said. 'Do you want to come along as well?'

'No,' Kenyon said.

It was several days before Mallory found time to spend half an evening with Sarah Brooks. The man who had assaulted the four-year-old girl had been identified, and there was an All Stations Message out for him. The grievous bodily harm victim who had lost an eye was still in hospital, and his assailant had been charged after being arrested, fighting drunk, by two PC's in a patrol car. The rape accusation had been withdrawn, much to the relief of the married man named as the assailant, who swore to Kenyon that he would never pick up a housewife in a Paddington pub again as long as he lived.

Meacher looked like fulfilling his ambition and making a name for himself. If Meacher had got it right, a swoop at a particular time on a certain day would net a very good Long Firm Fraud gang and also result, probably, in a commendation for Meacher. Kenyon remembered his own first commendation and he knew how important it was to a young detective. He wondered if that three hundred pounds that would come his way would enable him to run to a Volvo he coveted.

And as the crimes were investigated, more crime rolled into Kenyon's office daily.

Steve Rimmer telephoned, and Kenyon met him for a hurried Chinese meal, which Rimmer ate enthusiastically. Kenyon did not much like Chinese food, and drank a good deal of Chablis to hide the taste of it. Too much wine, he thought, later. It had given him a headache. Or perhaps the headache had other causes.

The restaurant had been empty except for the waiters, and themselves. Kenyon was not surprised. Why anyone should pay good money for chop suey was beyond him. Rimmer helped himself to another portion.

'I've put out a few feelers,' Rimmer said. 'I'm ashamed of the lies I told, but if there was a dodgy file anywhere on Sarah Brooks, I should have got a sniff of it.'

'No sniff?'

'Not a whiff, not a trace. Good, pure, clean, fresh air surrounding that lady. Special Branch don't know about her. Nor do any of the security services, as far as I know.'

Kenyon had expected this, but he was disappointed. 'What about the high-powered Tom Bradley? Why did he come into the picture?'

'Maybe it just happened to land on his desk.'

'A routine, small-time enquiry?' Kenyon objected.

'Look,' Rimmer said. He lowered his voice, even though the two Chinese waiters were at the far end of the restaurant, gossiping. 'Security may do some pretty bizarre things, but their day to day admin is still Civil Service. If the Foreign Office memo of enquiry found its way to him he'd deal with it.'

'Why not pass the buck to a junior?'

'Or that,' Rimmer said. 'Or there may be some aspect I don't know. I'll admit,' he said, speaking very softly, 'that Bradley runs a very private show. I'd never have got any details. But I'd have got a reaction, Sid. I wasn't taking much of a chance, because I think your Miss Brooks is a phoney. But if she'd been on Bradley's books, he'd have wanted to know who was putting out those feelers. Instead, nothing. They don't give a damn.'

Rimmer finished his meal, smothered a burp, and looked at his watch. 'Must go,' he said. 'Sorry.' He produced his wallet.

'On me,' Kenyon said. 'With apologies for wasting your time.'

Kenyon was walking the three hundred yards back to Bayswater Police Station, when Mallory's car drew up alongside. Kenyon got in.

'I've just spent two and a half hours with Miss Brooks,' Mallory said.

'Yes?'

'A bloody attractive woman,' Mallory said.

'You didn't need two and a half hours to find that out.'

'No.'

Mallory drove into the Car Yard. 'Going home now?' he asked.

'Yes.'

Mallory parked beside Kenyon's car, and switched off. A van drew in, and a dog handler got out, and led his animal towards the station.

Kenyon noted that two Flying Squad cars were parked in the car yard. He spared a moment to wonder what that bloody lot were doing on his patch. They came and went these bastards, and you never knew what they were up to until they had done it.

'I think I've made up my mind,' Mallory said. His dark silhouette was leaning against the driver's door. He fumbled for a cigarette, and lit it, the flame briefly illuminating his face. 'I've listened to her, and she's still convincing. I've looked at her, and she's nice to look at. There's fear in those eyes of hers perhaps. But fear of what? Could be herself. Could be that part of her knows it's all a game.'

'That's what you think?'

'Second thoughts, you asked for. All right. On the whole, I don't believe her.'

'Thanks, Len,' Kenyon said. 'Goodnight.'

He got out, climbed into his own car, and drove home. That was when he noticed his headache coming on.

The door of Flat 31 opened. 'Come in, Inspector,' Sarah Brooks said.

'Thank you.' Kenyon went inside.

He had telephoned her at the Foreign Office, and suggested he should call. Her cool voice had agreed.

He thought that she had bathed and changed after she got home from work. Her perfume was freshly applied. He liked all of it.

'Whisky again?' Sarah Brooks glanced at him enquiringly.

'Not yet,' Kenyon said. She sat opposite him. She was wearing a white blouse, and a black skirt. Kenyon was not at all sure that she was wearing a brassiere. He did his best to dismiss that as an unimportant question.

'Miss Brooks,' he said, 'since you first made your complaint . . .'

He gave it to her in officialese. He could hear his own voice, as he explained in neutral tones, but he had no need to think about what he was saying. He could use these stilted phrases all night, and concentrate on watching someone, as he was watching Sarah Brooks now. He did not tell her all of it, but he told her enough. He saw the hint of hope die in her eyes. He saw her look away from him, and begin to fidget. He saw her fingers rotate the pyramid-shaped ring she wore.

'. . . and so, from the enquiries I've made,' Kenyon concluded, 'it would appear that no grounds for your apprehension exist.'

'In that case, there's nothing more to be said.' Sarah Brooks stood up. Kenyon did not move. 'I expect you'd like to go, Inspector,' she said.

'Do you still think you're under surveillance?'

'What does it matter? You've assured me that no grounds exist. Thank you very much Inspector, and I won't take up any more of your time.'

'Sit down, Miss Brooks,' Kenyon said.

She stared at him, her face closed.

'Please,' Kenyon said. 'Sit down.'

She sat on the couch, and tucked her legs up beside her body. It made her look curiously vulnerable.

'The position is this,' Kenyon said. 'I meet all kinds of liars and nuts. In the course of one year, I can get told that London is going to be blown up by a nuclear bomb planted in Victoria Station; that the Queen is going to be kidnapped and held to ransom; and that the Army intend to take over the government at gunpoint. None of these things are actually impossible, just as it's not impossible that something unpleasant is happening to you. First, I try and assess the person telling me. If I think it's worth it, I'll do some checking. The checks on your statements are negative. Strictly speaking I should leave it there. But I'd rather not think you're a liar or a nut. For reasons that don't matter, I'd like to believe you.'

Sarah Brooks had listened to him intently. 'But you don't,' she said.

'I'd find it hard, unless you can tell me a great deal more.'

'I've told you everything already,' she said despairingly.

'If you're free for dinner,' Kenyon said, 'it might be easier to talk over a meal.'

That surprised her. When she looked at him now, it was different. Perhaps for the first time she was seeing him as a man, rather than as a policeman, who, like a plumber, a carpenter or a post office engineer, was just someone who'd do a job she needed done.

'All right,' she said, at last.

They walked to the Royal Lancaster. Kenyon thought that Sarah Brooks would be about five feet seven in her stockinged feet, or around five feet nine in the shoes she was wearing. She walked beside him keeping easily in step. Those slim legs were long as well.

'Two dry martinis,' Kenyon said, in the cocktail bar, forgoing his usual whisky for the sake of simplicity. Besides, he wanted to judge roughly, from his own reaction, the probable effect on Sarah Brooks of whatever alcohol she drank.

The cocktail bar was comfortable, and not too crowded. They studied menus, and gave their orders to the head waiter.

'Good evening, madame,' the head waiter had said, smiling pleasantly. 'Good evening, sir,' with a slightly more formal smile.

Kenyon thought it possible that the head waiter had recognized Sarah Brooks, but had tactfully refrained from saying anything in deference to her unknown companion.

'Why did you choose this place?' Sarah Brooks asked.

'It's quiet,' Kenyon said. He gestured to the bar waiter, indicating 'the same again'. 'We can talk. And if you want to get up and walk out on me, you won't have far to go. Do you come here much?'

'Now and then,' Sarah Brooks said. 'Not recently. Why should I want to walk out on you?'

'You might not feel like telling me the things I want to know.'

'Such as?'

'Later,' Kenyon said. He paid for the second round.

There were other quiet restaurants nearby which were not nearly as expensive. But Kenyon felt that he was having a night out, and anyway, this slim, elegant woman belonged in a place like this. He ordered a bottle of Chambertin with the meal, and was careful to drink no more than Sarah Brooks. When the coffee arrived, and the bottle was nearly empty, he suggested a liqueur. She refused.

Kenyon felt pleasantly warmed and at ease by the food and wine. He hoped that Sarah Brooks would feel a little off guard. Assuming she had anything to guard. Until then, they had talked casually, and Sarah Brooks had seemed to grow more relaxed. He had learned that she enjoyed the theatre, and was an occasional opera goer. She knew most of the European capitals, and told an anecdote about Stockholm. She was much more widely read than Kenyon, but shared his enthusiasm for Hemingway and Chandler.

The West End plays she mentioned were not running any more, and she seemed to watch a lot of television. Kenyon drew his own conclusions. Unless she was far more removed from the normal patterns of behaviour than he thought she was, she had told him a great deal more about herself than she knew.

'All right,' he said, 'shall we get down to the purpose of the meeting?'

She smiled. 'Why is it that people only start talking business with the coffee?'

'Perhaps because they've been enjoying themselves, and don't want to spoil it.'

Again, he caught that quick glance from her blue eyes which told him that she was aware of him as a male.

'Is that what's going to happen?' she asked.

'I don't know. That's up to you. I'm going to get somewhat personal. Can I call you Sarah? It might help a bit. My name's Sidney, or Sid. Please yourself.'

'You mean you want me to look on you as a friend?'

She had not been much affected by the wine after all She was mocking him. Kenyon decided not to have that.

'Sarah,' he said, 'the way you make yourself up indicates that you know perfectly well what an attractive woman you are. If you care to invite me into your bed, I expect I'd enjoy it, but I can find out my chances in that direction with a simple question. I don't have to mess about with the wining and dining and suggestive talk bit. All right?'

Kenyon was aware that he was being less than completely honest, but Sarah Brooks seemed to take his words at face value.

She held his eyes for long enough, to indicate that she would stand up to anything he said, and then nodded. 'All right.'

'You think you're under suspicion. Everyone else denies it. Someone's lying. That someone could be you.'

'It isn't.'

'Convince me.'

'How?'

'If there's any truth in what you say, and I do mean if,' Kenyon said, 'there must be something you haven't told me.'

'I've told you everything that happened.'

'Not about what happened. About yourself.'

'I've told you that, too.'

Kenyon lit a cigarette. He smoked the plain variety. She smoked tipped, so he did not offer her one. 'Tell me how you got your painting. The one by Ben Maile.'

'Why?'

'Look, darling,' Kenyon said, unpleasantly, 'I've got a very good reason for asking. If you don't want to answer, let's just say we've had a nice evening, and forget the whole fucking thing.'

The pinkness in her cheeks came from controlled anger.

'I don't much like being spoken to like that, Inspector,' she said.

'And don't give that "I'm a lady and you're just a common policeman" shit,' Kenyon said. 'I'm leaning over backwards to help you, but if you don't want to help yourself, that's your look-out.' Kenyon gestured to the waiter, and ordered a large brandy for himself. He did not ask Sarah again if she would like anything.

The brandy arrived. Kenyon cupped the glass in his hands.

'You don't always drink whisky, I gather,' Sarah said, her tone brittle.

'I have catholic tastes in drink and women,' Kenyon said. 'Some for one time, some for another. It depends how I feel. Some you just have. Some you take your time over. Sometimes it's a need. Sometimes it's a pleasure. Some have unpleasant after effects. Some don't.'

Sarah seemed averse to pursuing this thread. 'How does my painting come into it?' she asked.

'Perhaps it doesn't,' Kenyon said. 'Let me judge.'

'A few years ago,' Sarah said, 'Ben Maile held a cocktail party at the Dorchester Hotel to launch a signed print. A friend of mine was invited, and took me along. There were a number of originals on sale as well. The one I have was one of the cheapest.'

'How cheap?'

'About five hundred pounds.'

'All right,' Kenyon said, 'I'll use your language, and regard that as cheap. Who paid for it? You?'

'My friend.'

'It's in your flat.'

'It's in my care,' Sarah said.

'I see,' Kenyon said. 'Four years ago, you bought your flat. To obtain a mortgage, you had to find twenty-five percent deposit. Where did the money come from?'

'I don't think that's any of your business,' Sarah said, tightly.

'A good-looking woman civil servant,' Kenyon said. 'I know what your salary was four years ago. You must have saved like bloody mad to find that amount. You didn't even use it all that much at the time. You were abroad a lot, with your conferences, and simultaneous translation.'

'It doesn't cross your mind that my parents might have given it to me?'

'It crosses my mind,' Kenyon said, 'that you don't seem very anxious to answer my questions.'

'I'm not a criminal,' Sarah said, angrily. 'I don't have to account for my private affairs to you.'

'You do if you expect me to help you.'

'Would you get the bill, please?'

Kenyon gestured for the bill, which arrived in an elaborate folder, and was more than Kenyon had expected. He paid by credit card, which postponed the evil day for a month.

'I don't see how it can possibly matter,' Sarah said, 'but a friend of mine lent me part of the money.'

'The same friend who bought the painting?'

'That's of no importance.'

'It sounds like a long-standing relationship,' Kenyon said.

'I've told you what you want to know,' Sarah said, with finality.

'Not quite,' Kenyon said. 'There's one small detail you haven't mentioned. This friend. Was it a man or a woman?'

That was when Sarah Brooks walked out of the dining room of the Royal Lancaster Hotel.

Kenyon did not go after her. He took the head waiter into a quiet corner. The head waiter had never seen Sarah Brooks before in his life. Kenyon produced his warrant card, and repeated his questions. The head waiter's memory took a turn for the better.

He had run out of cigarettes. He bought some on the way out, strolled slowly back to Cleeve Court, and leaned on the doorbell of Flat 31, until Sarah Brooks opened the door.

Kenyon walked in, took off his raincoat, and threw it on the couch.

'If I ask you to leave, and you refuse,' Sarah said, 'am I entitled to send for the police?'

'You can try,' Kenyon said. 'But since I'm a police officer making enquiries, I don't fancy your chances.'

'If you're thinking of asking your simple question,' Sarah said, 'I can give you a simple answer in advance. No. You don't interest me.'

'You're thirty years old,' Kenyon said. 'You're not married. I doubt if you're sexless. You've stopped going to the theatre. The last opera you mentioned was on at Covent Garden a year ago. The odds are you've had something going for a long time, which is now over.'

'I'm not a lesbian,' Sarah Brooks said.

'He was an American, wasn't he?' Kenyon asked.

'How did you know that?'

'The head waiter remembered his generosity.'

Sarah nodded. 'We used to go there sometimes.'

Kenyon picked up a decanter. 'Is this brandy? I'll have one while you talk, if that's all right with you.'

'It's in the past,' Sarah said. 'It's over.'

'Do you really believe you have something to be afraid of, or not?'

'I don't believe it,' Sarah said. 'I know it. I don't know what it is or who it is. But I'm frightened, yes, believe me.'

'As yet,' Kenyon said, 'I don't believe you.'

He gave himself a large brandy, and lit a cigarette.

'It's the usual cliché, a stupid, sordid situation,' Sarah said. 'He's married, with a family. End of story.'

'Details,' Kenyon said.

'So that you can sit there and enjoy it, like some voyeur?' Sarah asked, bitterly.

'Jesus wept,' Kenyon said, tiredly. 'I have to talk to little girls who've been raped. I've seen the body of a dead seventy-year-old grandmother, with a milk bottle stuffed up her vagina. If you think hearing about who you've been screwing is going to give me a kick, you just don't know what goes on in this lousy world of ours.'

'I'm sorry.' She sounded as if she meant it.

'Forget it.'

'But it wasn't just screwing.'

'The word does not spring easily to your lips,' Kenyon said. 'Let's call it making love.'

'Yes, let's.'

'Or as we say in the statements we take,' Kenyon said, 'intercourse took place on a number of occasions. Take that as read, and get on with it.'

He was needling Sarah Brooks, as though he did not like her. He had never felt this intermittent antagonism to a woman before.

'On the biological level,' Sarah said, 'we were attracted to each other the first time we met.'

'When?'

'In Rome, seven years ago. Nothing happened then. Not for over a year in fact. We kept on seeing each other, in various places. As far as you're concerned, intercourse first took place here in London. As far as I was concerned, I'd fallen in love.'

'And him?'

'Yes. It was real,' Sarah said. 'Even to the point that after a few years we'd become comfortably used to each other.'

'Is that why it ended?'

'I think I changed, to some extent,' Sarah said. 'For one thing, my thirtieth birthday arrived. I was twenty-four when it started. The future was tomorrow, perhaps the day after, at most the next time I'd see him again. I suppose it could have gone on for another ten years, by which time I'd have been forty, and probably head of my department. A permanent civil servant in all senses of the word.'

'If there was all this love flying around between you,' Kenyon said, 'why didn't he get a divorce and marry you?'

'He's a Catholic,' Sarah said. 'So is his wife. We talked about it once. Divorce, I mean, and getting married. The religious thing didn't bother me. I'm not anything really. But when we talked, I could see . . . no, I could *feel* . . . the guilt inside him, the guilt he'd always have about his wife and marriage if he ever ended it. Perhaps he'd have done it, if I'd pressed him. I think he would. But I'd have destroyed him. And myself too. We didn't talk about it much after that.'

'Yes,' Kenyon said. 'Screwing around on the side is one thing. "Father I have sinned" in the confessional, and a few quick Hail Marys, and that's OK. Off you go for a bit more sin. But woe betide you if you want to give one woman a civil marriage licence, and screw her for the rest of your life. It's a great religion for a bit of agonized poking after work, so long as you get home at night in time to tuck the kids in.'

'That is the point, isn't it? The children?'

'I don't know,' Kenyon said. 'Where were his children?'

'At home, in his big house in Connecticut, with his wife. He's quite well-to-do.'

'Hence the picture,' Kenyon said, looking at it. 'Hence giving you the deposit to buy this flat.'

'That was a loan, which I've repaid,' Sarah said. 'The picture was a gift.'

'Save those details for the Inland Revenue,' Kenyon said. 'Did he have a name?'

'Harry. Harry Coleman.'

'And Harry ended it, or you ended it, or you both ended it – when?'

'Not long ago. He was being posted away from London. It brought everything to a head. Whether we should go on . . . or not. We decided not.'

'Why did you say "posted away from London"?' Kenyon enquired. 'Was he in the armed forces?'

Sarah shook her head. 'The American Embassy. He's a diplomat.'

Kenyon experienced that strange feeling, which sometimes came to him, when, after countless dead ends, a small gleam of daylight appeared. It was a professional sensation, closely akin to joy.

'You told me he was well-to-do,' he said.

'He's not a career diplomat,' Sarah said. 'He's a high level adviser. That was how we met in Rome, we were both at the same conference. We met again at the Strategic Arms Limitation Talks, and various other meetings. He used to be a Professor of Public Affairs at a New England University. Before that, he was a White House correspondent for a defence magazine.'

'He's done a lot,' Kenyon said. He was taking in what Sarah was saying, but his brain was busy with the pieces which were clicking into place. Except that one piece would not fit, no matter how it was manipulated.

'He's older than I am,' Sarah said. 'He's forty-seven. He's one of those types of Americans I rather admire. They don't work for money, because they don't need it. They've got plenty, and it doesn't mean much to them. Some go into politics, some become academics, others some kind of public service. Harry's interested in politics in the international sense, rather than any particular party . . .'

Kenyon interrupted her. 'Do you have a photograph?'

'Why?' For a few minutes Sarah's face had softened as she talked about Harry Coleman. Now the wariness had returned.

Kenyon smiled at her. 'I'd like to know what he looks like. And you can join me in a brandy, if you'd like to celebrate.'

'Celebrate what?'

'Now you've talked to me I know that someone else lied about something. I'm inclined to think you may be right. That you're under surveillance for some reason.'

'Who lied? What did I say?' She was thoroughly puzzled.

'Could you have kept your affair with Harry Coleman a secret for several years?'

'Well, we didn't go out of our way to broadcast it . . .'

'Did he stay here?'

'Sometimes.'

'And you at his place?'

'Yes.'

'Did you ever go on holiday together?'

'Twice. Why?'

'Where?'

'Italy the first time, and Gotland last summer.'

'Fetch his photograph,' Kenyon said.

Sarah went into her bedroom. Kenyon thought about Tom Bradley, and Sarah Brooks' security file which contained no reference to any relationships she might have formed.

'Not so much as a Russian piccolo player,' Tom Bradley had said.

Kenyon thought that a long-standing affair with a married American diplomat would have justified a note in that file. If the British did not think it was important enough for a passing reference, the CIA would. England was a foreign country to them, with a security record which the Americans did not much admire.

The events surrounding Pontecorvo and Fuchs, Burgess, Maclean and Philby, still rankled with the Americans. They would, at the very least, satisfy themselves that an affair between a high-level diplomatic adviser who knew enough to take part in the SALT negotiations, and a Russian-speaking girl in the British Foreign Office, was harmless. Kenyon thought that something about Harry Coleman should appear in Sarah Brooks' file.

So why didn't it?

5

The studio photograph showed approximately the sort of American Kenyon had expected. A strong, smiling, open face, looking much younger than the forty-five years he had acquired when the photograph was taken. No grey in the dark hair, no lines on the clear forehead.

'I don't suppose this is the only one you've got?' Kenyon said. 'Can I keep this?' She hesitated. 'I may need it,' Kenyon said. 'I don't know.'

Sarah smiled slightly. 'You may as well have it,' she said. 'It only sits in the bottom drawer, with the rest.'

'But you don't throw them away.'

'I don't want to throw them away,' Sarah said.

'He looks like quite a nice sort of chap,' Kenyon said.

'There's a sense in which I came to life with him,' Sarah said. 'He's part owner of a large chunk of my life.'

'Are your parents alive?'

'They live near Winchester. My father's retired. He was a bank manager.' She seemed to have become accustomed to answering his questions.

'Did they ever meet Harry Coleman?'

'I don't think they'd have understood a married Catholic with two children,' Sarah said. 'I never mentioned his name. My mother used to talk wistfully about having grandchildren, but she doesn't any more. I think she's written me off as a confirmed old maid.'

'There are a few things I want to check on,' Kenyon said. 'I won't embarrass you, or reveal what it's about, but I'd like Harry

Coleman's address in America, his phone number if you've got it, where he used to live in London, his department at the Embassy, the extension number, any places you used to visit a lot, where you might be known, and anything else about him which might help me.'

'Help you to do what?' Sarah asked, frowning. 'Harry can't be involved in any way.'

'Police detectives don't much resemble Sherlock Holmes,' Kenyon said. 'Most major crimes are solved because someone grasses—passes information to the police. Gives us a tip-off. Otherwise, it's a process of elimination. I'd like the information, so that I can eliminate Harry Coleman from my enquiries, if you want me to use the formal language. Write it all down, please. You don't mind if I get some fresh air, do you?'

He did not wait to find out if she minded or not. Her curtains were not closed. He slid the glass doors aside, and stepped out on to her balcony. The air outside was cold. There were no clouds in the sky. Kenyon leaned on the balustrade, feeling the moist chill under his fingers. There would be a frost later.

Rockstone Gardens was really a square. In the summer, when the trees were clothed with leaves, two sides of the square would be virtually obscured from the balcony, but now he could see the windows of the surrounding flats – some lit, some dark – and be seen from some of them. Kenyon looked round carefully. Sarah's penthouse flat was on the top floor of Cleeve Court, and all the buildings in the square were the same height. He calculated that there were ten, possibly twelve flats in the square, where a man with field glasses might be able to observe the inside of Sarah's living room, if her curtains were not drawn.

Kenyon shivered and went back inside into the warm.

'Don't you usually draw your curtains at night?' he asked.

'Not always. Why?'

'It helps to keep the heat in,' Kenyon said. 'Cuts your central heating bills.'

He took the sheet of paper she offered him, glanced at it, and put his raincoat on. 'Where did you say he was now? Washington?'

'I didn't say but he isn't. New York. The United Nations. I'd rather you didn't talk to him,' Sarah Brooks said urgently. 'He's gone back to his family. That's the whole point. I don't want that spoiled for him.'

'Don't worry,' Kenyon said. 'Your name won't come up.'

Sarah accompanied him to the door. 'Thanks for dinner,' she said, with a wry smile.

'If anything happens,' Kenyon said, 'phone me. Otherwise, I'll be in touch again in a day or two.'

She nodded. 'Goodnight,' she said.

'Goodnight.'

For a moment Kenyon felt, absurdly, that he should kiss her. Not in the way of a man making a pass, the first move on the road to bed. But as though he knew her well, a comforting *aurevoir* before their next meeting. But the moment passed, and he did not touch her. He rode downstairs in the lift, the photograph of Harry Coleman in his briefcase.

Kenyon wondered whether to go back home and make his phone calls from there. But there was no reason why he should pay instead of the taxpayer. He was a police officer pursuing a legitimate enquiry. He went back to his office at Bayswater police station.

He calculated that it would be early evening in Connecticut, and dialled the fourteen figure number – 0101 for the USA, followed by a three-figure code, and a seven-figure number.

He heard the phone ring five times at the other end, and then a low, reserved woman's voice answered.

'Who's speaking?' Kenyon asked.

'This is Suzanne Coleman,' the distant voice said. 'Who's that?'

The connection was clear and faultless, better than most calls from one London district to another. The distance in the woman's voice came from within herself, not from the thousands of miles which separated them.

'This is Detective Inspector Kenyon, of the Metropolitan Police in London,' Kenyon said. 'We believe Mr Coleman may have witnessed a fatal road accident which took place some time ago, and we'd like to speak to him about it. If he's not at home, could you tell me where I could reach him, please?'

'He's back in London,' Mrs Coleman said. 'You could reach him through the Embassy.'

Kenyon experienced a jolt of disorientation. He had not been prepared for her reply. He stared at the statements and report forms which littered his desk.

'Hullo? Hullo?' the distant woman's voice said.

'Sorry,' Kenyon said, pulling his thoughts back to the present moment. 'I understood that Mr Coleman had returned to America for good.'

'No,' the distant voice said. 'He came home for a vacation in the fall, but he flew back to London three weeks ago.'

'I must have misunderstood,' Kenyon said. 'I thought he was taking up a post at the United Nations, in New York. Perhaps he was merely considering it.'

'Not to my knowledge,' the distant voice said. 'He didn't mention it to me.'

'I have his London address in Mount Street,' Kenyon said, staring at Sarah Brooks' neat handwriting. 'Can you tell me if he's still living there? Has he written to you since his return? Or phoned you perhaps?'

'I received a letter yesterday, mailed from the same apartment,' the distant voice said, puzzlement and caution tinging its low tones. 'Wouldn't it be better to contact my husband direct? Or is there something wrong? Why didn't you telephone his London apartment in the first place?'

Kenyon was annoyed with himself. He had not intended to make Mrs Coleman anxious. 'This is an outstanding enquiry,' Kenyon said, 'and I was relying on an old note in the file. Obviously the officer who telephoned the Embassy when your husband was on leave in America, got some of the details wrong, for which I must apologize. I'll speak to your husband direct, and I'm extremely sorry to have troubled you.'

'That's quite all right,' the distant voice said, apparently re-assured. 'Although I don't know if he'll be able to help you.

He didn't tell me anything about seeing a fatal accident in London anytime, and I'm sure he would have done.'

'We're not at all sure about that,' Kenyon said. 'We're only checking. Thank you again.'

Kenyon hung up. Once more, someone was lying. Once more, the leading candidate was Sarah Brooks. He dialled Coleman's apartment in Mount Street. There were three burr-burrs, and then a click. 'Harry Coleman is out,' a deep, resonant, male tape-recorded American voice said. 'Please leave your name and telephone number, and any message. You may start recording now.'

Silence followed. Kenyon hung up. He glanced at Sarah's notes, and dialled another number, which he knew anyway.

Two FBI men were permanently attached to the American Embassy. Kenyon had met the one who was on duty, but did not know him well enough to try going off the record. The FBI man was vague in the extreme. He was not personally acquainted with all the people who worked at the Embassy, having recently arrived from the States himself, as Inspector Kenyon would know. The necessary records were under lock and key in another part of the building, and in any case he would prefer not to speak on the telephone. It would be better if Kenyon were to call at the Embassy the following day.

Kenyon thanked him politely. He had not given any reason for his enquiry this time, but he was pretty certain the conversation would be recorded. There would be some reaction if anyone was interested in it. Like Harry Coleman himself, perhaps.

Kenyon studied Coleman's photograph, and wondered why he should tell Sarah Brooks that he was leaving England for good, go home for a holiday with his wife and children, and then fly back to London. Or if he had told Sarah anything of the kind.

For an hour, tonight, Kenyon had believed her. His personal wish to believe her had coincided with his professional assessment of such evidence as there was. But now, again, he was far from certain. Either several people were concealing the truth, or just one. Sarah Brooks. The balance of probability indicated

Sarah. Why she should was another matter, and the only conceivable explanation was a medical one.

Kenyon went back over their evening together in his mind. Was that elegant, attractive, educated woman a nutter? He thought not. He had encountered many degrees and varieties of dottiness in the course of his career, and she fitted none of them. But that was only a lay opinion. A psychiatrist might think differently.

And if Sarah had told the truth from the start, then several other people had not. Lance Everitt at the Foreign Office, Tom Bradley, presiding over his mysterious private empire, Harry Coleman, possibly the FBI man at the American Embassy, conceivably Mrs Coleman. Even perhaps, his old mate, Steve Rimmer.

Kenyon could only imagine far fetched explanations for what would amount to a widespread conspiracy of untruth. In his experience, far fetched reasons collapsed in the face of the simple and obvious. In this case to distrust Sarah Brooks, ignore his attraction to her, and face the fact that it all depended on her word. But there was that security file of hers. Why was there no mention of her long-standing affair with Harry Coleman, a high ranking diplomatic adviser? It then occurred to Kenyon, very late in the day, that he only had Sarah's word that Coleman was a man of importance. Or, come to that, that she had ever had an affair with him at all.

Kenyon got in his car. It was now one o'clock in the morning, and the traffic in Park Lane had thinned. He turned into Mayfair, found somewhere to park on a single yellow line, and walked to Coleman's address in Mount Street, which turned out to be a block of extremely expensive flats.

A night porter was dozing behind his desk. Kenyon went straight past without waking him, ascended some lushly carpeted stairs, found Coleman's apartment, and kept his finger on the doorbell for a minute and a half. He could hear the bell ringing inside. It was unlikely that anyone would sleep through that. He went downstairs, and shook the night porter into semi-wakefulness.

Kenyon was treading on very thin ice now, and he knew it. Theoretically he needed a search warrant. In the case of a British subject, he would have had no compunction in ignoring the theory. If coppers always went by the book, and abided faithfully by the Judge's Rules, very few villains would ever appear in court. But this was different. Coleman was a foreign subject, with diplomatic status. An angry complaint to Scotland Yard would blow Kenyon's career sky high. Kenyon was fond of his career. He had every intention of becoming a Detective Chief Superintendent at the very least, and preferably a Commander (Crime).

Kenyon waved his warrant card under the sleepy night porter's nose, and put it away before the man had time to note his name. He talked very fast about lights being seen in an unoccupied flat, and described its location. The night porter dug out duplicate keys, and led Kenyon to Coleman's flat which was large, lavish, and luxurious.

The night porter waited, while Kenyon went through the motions of checking for any signs of forced entry.

'You'd better get back on duty,' Kenyon said. 'I'll make sure nothing's been tampered with. I'll tell you when I've finished.'

The night porter withdrew. He had been watching Kenyon's actions with sleepy curiosity, rather than Kenyon himself. If there was any trouble later, the man did not have Kenyon's name, and his description would fit a lot of police officers. If they put two and two together, Kenyon would swear he had been nowhere near Mount Street that night. Scotland Yard would probably not believe him, but they would pretend to, provided his actions could not be unassailably proven. They would not be anxious to have a good DI sacrificed if it could be avoided. An unpleasant half an hour being told his fortune by the Assistant Commissioner would be the worst that would happen to him.

Kenyon reset the telephone answering device, and played back the tape. There were messages from a wine-merchant, about a delivery of claret, a Savile Row tailor about a suit which was ready for fitting and finally, from Mrs Coleman.

'A policeman called Detective Inspector Kenyon telephoned,' the distant woman's voice said. 'He said you might have witnessed a fatal road accident. I told him I thought not, and he's going to call you at home, or at the Embassy.' There was a long pause and

Kenyon thought the message was over, but then the distant woman's voice resumed, uncertainly, this time. 'I thought I ought to let you know.' Another pause. 'Thank you for your letter. It was good to see you, and the children send their love.' Another pause, longer this time. 'I know we've been through a bad spell, Harry, and I prayed that those lonely years were behind me now. It would have been nice if we could have come to London and set up home there. I wish you could have told me why that wasn't possible just yet, now that we're together again, really together I mean. But if your assignment is so important all I can do is wait as patiently as I can. Call me some time if you can, any time of the day or night, it doesn't matter. If you can't I'll be thinking of you. Goodnight, my dear. And God bless you.'

There were no further messages. Nothing from Sarah Brooks. Kenyon reset the tape. Listening to that distant, woman's voice, in this empty flat had affected him curiously. It made him feel like a voyeur, trespassing in private, deep emotions, which were none of his concern. He shrugged off the feeling, and searched Coleman's flat with skilful, practised speed. It did not take very long. For all the apartment's size and comfort it resembled an overgrown hotel suite, with precious little trace of the absent occupant.

Wardrobes contained suits, shoes, casual clothes, and ties, hung tidily on rails. Drawers revealed neatly laid out shirts, underwear, sweaters and socks. There were expensive suitcases in a store cupboard. The bathroom contained the usual things, together with an electric razor, an electric toothbrush and a water-pik. In the kitchen everything was put away in drawers and fitted cupboards. There was milk in the refrigerator, but very little food. On the other hand, the deep freeze had enough frozen food in it for three months.

The desk in the large living room contained none of the personal items one might expect. No passport, no letters, no bank statements, no cheque book, no bills awaiting payment. Either Coleman had not been here very much for some time, or he kept all his personal belongings in his office at the American Embassy. And Kenyon could hardly bluff his way in there.

He returned the keys of the flat to the night porter and enquired casually where the owner of the flat was and if he was likely to be back soon. The night porter knew the answer to neither question. He spent alternate weeks on day and night duty, could not recall seeing Mr Coleman recently, and assumed he had simply missed him. There was in any case, he pointed out, a residents' car park at the rear of the building, reached through a mews, and Mr Coleman used the rear entrance most of the time, which could not be seen from the desk.

Kenyon thought it was time that he had a word with Detective Superintendent Pinder.

Kenyon was in Pinder's office the following morning, when the call from the American Embassy came through. Kenyon had given his heavily built, florid-faced chief, an outline, omitting certain details, such as his unauthorized search of Coleman's flat. He took the phone from Pinder's outstretched hand and listened to the pleasant, American voice which belonged, it said, to Coleman's assistant.

'Why do you wish to interview Mr Coleman?' it asked.

Kenyon used phrases such as 'may be able to assist us with our enquiries', emphasized that Coleman was in no way involved himself, and asked when it would be convenient to speak to him.

'Harry's out of town for a while,' the assistant said. 'But I'm expecting him to contact me. Why don't you tell me what it's about, and I'll speak to him, and call you back.'

'It might be better if I talked to Mr Coleman in person,' Kenyon said. 'When will he be back?'

'Why don't you put it in writing?' the assistant suggested, ignoring Kenyon's question. 'And I'll see that it's brought to his attention at the earliest possible moment.'

Kenyon thanked him, said that it was not an urgent matter, and possibly Mr Coleman would telephone him at his convenience.

Pinder sucked his teeth, as Kenyon hung up. He had grasped the gist of the conversation from Kenyon's remarks. 'How is this man Coleman involved?' he asked.

'He may be able to confirm certain small things in Miss Brooks' account,' Kenyon said. He had not mentioned to Pinder that according to Sarah, Coleman had been her lover.

'Dodgy when diplomats come into things,' Pinder grumbled. 'Don't like it. Have you made out a report form on all this?'

'No, sir,' Kenyon said.

'Don't,' Pinder said. 'I think I'd better have a word with Percy at Special Branch.'

'You know what Special Branch are like, sir,' Kenyon said, wondering if he should have mentioned his chat with Steve Rimmer. 'They're not much use at the best of times. They won't want to know.'

'You may be fishing in muddy waters,' Pinder said.

'All right if I keep it warm though?' Kenyon asked.

'So long as nothing gets put into writing,' Pinder said.

'Right, sir.'

'And don't spend too much time on it,' Pinder added. 'You've got plenty to keep you busy without this.'

'I think Miss Brooks needs protection,' Kenyon said, going rather further than he would have done on oath. 'That's our job, too, isn't it, sir?'

'Well, don't stick your neck out,' Pinder said cryptically.

Kenyon thought it was possible that Detective Superintendent Pinder knew a little more about it than he had revealed.

Mallory was waiting in Kenyon's office. From his attitude, his casual turn as he caught sight of Kenyon coming, it seemed likely that he had been glancing at any papers which might be lying around on the desk, a habit of Mallory's which Kenyon found irritating.

'Got a minute?' Mallory asked.

'You're wasting your time,' Kenyon said, shortly. 'Anything I don't want nosey buggers to see, I keep out of sight.'

Mallory grinned, unabashed, and changed the subject. 'Why should anyone still be interested in Jenny Abel?' he reflected.

'No reason,' Kenyon said.

'Someone is,' Mallory said.

'Who?'

'Don't know. But some fellow's been asking questions at the

night club, talking to the girls. Then he spoke to the porter. Slipped him a fiver, and wanted to know if he had any idea where Jenny went when she left the club, the night before she was killed. The manager got to hear about it, and thought we should know.'

'What's this merchant trying to find out?'

'Who Jenny Abel was with that night,' Mallory said. 'Or where he lives, or preferably both.'

Kenyon frowned. 'A middle-aged creep with a beard,' according to the distraught Winston Peters before he killed himself, who had taken Jenny Abel to a block of flats in Battersea. Which block had remained an unimportant mystery. Winston Peters had shaken his head vaguely, unable to remember the address. He had thought he remembered a park in the darkness, which probably made it Prince of Wales Drive, but that residential road, the former parking place for Edwardian mistresses, ran the length of Battersea Park, and large blocks of flats stood shoulder to shoulder throughout its length.

Half-hearted enquiries at the night club had produced no result. The bearded man was not known to the staff, the term 'club' was a misnomer: anyone could walk in, and since the man had paid his bill by cash there was no record of his name. In any case, it had not mattered. Winston Peters had killed Jenny Abel, no question, and the identity of the man who had sampled her delights the night before, was a matter of some indifference. So why should anyone be trying to find out now?

'Funny,' Kenyon said.

'There's something else,' Mallory said. 'I happened to notice this. Pure chance.'

He laid a folded copy of the *Evening Standard* on the desk, and stabbed his finger at the personal column. There, among the advertisements for massage parlours and pregnancy tests, was another, which began 'Jenny Abel'. Kenyon read it.

'Jenny Abel (deceased). Among Jenny's personal effects is a large sum in cash, which appears to be the property of the person she met the night before her death and who is believed to live in Battersea. To reclaim this sum, the person concerned should contact . . .' There followed a box number.

'What large sum in cash?' Kenyon enquired, rhetorically, puzzled.

'I've been on to the newspaper,' Mallory said. 'That's one of a series.'

'Inserted by . . . ?'

'Someone who prefers to give a fictitious address and phone number,' Mallory said.

Kenyon sat down, and thought back, going over that rainy November night in his mind. Mallory went on talking.

'All I can think of,' Mallory said, 'is that some of Winston Peters' mates blame this Battersea punter, whoever he is, for Winston's suicide, and fancy decorating his face with a few razor strokes.'

'Have you ever met a spook who composes prose like that?' Kenyon objected, pointing at the personal ad.

Mallory shrugged. 'Maybe not, but they could be using someone who does. Anyway, our bearded friend could be running into trouble. Do you want me to check on this box number, just in case?'

'Yes, you'd better,' Kenyon said. Inside his head, he was moving along Jenny Abel's hall, and glancing at the telephone. 'Is there anything in the *Times* personal ads?'

'I don't know,' Mallory said, taken aback. 'Should there be?'

'There was a pay telephone in the hall,' Kenyon said, staring at the ceiling, looking back. 'Tucked behind it was that day's copy of *The Times*. It looked out of place in that filthy drum, and I assumed it was bum paper.'

'It probably was,' Mallory said.

'Winston Peters said he came out of the lavatory, and found Jenny on the phone in the hall. He thought she might have been talking to the creep with the beard. I just wondered if there was any connection . . .'

'Perhaps she'd written his phone number on it,' Mallory suggested.

'No, there was no phone number,' Kenyon said. 'I looked. Oh, I don't know,' he said. 'Check it out as best you can, anyway.'

He had the vague, uneasy feeling that he was missing something. He gave it two minutes thought, which was all he could spare just then, failed to make sense of his unease, and gave up. The Jenny Abel case was closed. She did not matter any more.

Mallory checked the box number, which led him to a newsagents in Victoria where mail was held on a confidential basis. No replies to the advertisement had been received, and the newsagent could only give the barest description of the advertiser, who checked for replies by telephone, and had paid cash for the facilities provided, like the call girls who used the same facility at the same newsagents.

The newsagent was clearly alarmed by Mallory's visit, and was convinced that it had something to do with the call girls' adverts. Mallory tried to reassure him and left with a promise that he would be notified if the advertiser were to call in, but Mallory did not believe the promise would be honoured.

By the time he was able to report all this to Kenyon, things had happened and Kenyon's interest in that personal ad was nil.

After his talk with Mallory, Kenyon had some enquiries made, during the next day or two, about Harry Coleman, using only such unobtrusive sources as were not likely to check with the American Embassy. The picture which emerged was shadowy and incomplete. Coleman was a Harvard graduate. His money came from his grandfather who was a biscuit manufacturer. He had been married for twenty years and had two daughters, now aged fourteen and eleven. He lived quietly and entertained infrequently. He attended formal functions alone, but one diplomatic correspondent hinted that he was more than friendly with a fairhaired Englishwoman, and declined to say any more.

His role in the American Diplomatic Service remained obstinately vague. He was regarded as a defence expert, and, at one time, a personal friend of the Secretary of State, although gossip suggested that they had a stormy disagreement. At conferences he was not a negotiator, but he sat behind the negotiators and was referred to frequently by them.

He travelled a good deal, but to what purpose was not always clear. The word 'trouble shooter' was used as a hesitant suggestion. He appeared to be good at avoiding personal publicity. His name scarcely figured on the files of the press cutting agencies, except in the guest lists of receptions at various foreign embassies.

Kenyon found time to check those ten flats from which Sarah Brooks' penthouse could be kept under observation. He eliminated eight of them, where the residents were of long standing, and well respected. Two of the flats were let on short tenancies, furnished, and little was known about the occupants. Kenyon obtained the telephone numbers of both flats.

'Hullo,' said a husky, feminine, French-accented voice, at the first number.

Kenyon thought that he had come across that sort of voice before. 'A friend of mine gave me your number,' he said, laying odds on his thought.

'Do you want to come round, darling?' the husky voice enquired seductively. 'Do you want a good time?'

'How much?' Kenyon asked, to make sure.

'Twenty pounds?' the voice suggested.

'Make it five,' Kenyon said.

'Fuck off, sweetheart,' the voice said, and rang off.

Kenyon thought she sounded pretty genuine, but he did not know about her. He reckoned to know most of the Toms on his patch, but then he had been pretty preoccupied lately.

He asked Mallory, who did not know her either, but very soon found out.

'She's a French whore from Le Havre,' Mallory said. 'Calls herself Annette. Moved into that flat two weeks ago. Why the interest? Do you fancy a bit of flagellation?'

'If I'm going bent,' Kenyon said, 'that's my business.'

Mallory grinned, and forgot about it.

That left the other flat.

Kenyon spent the evening with Sarah Brooks. They talked casually and inconsequentially. He did not tell her about his phone call to America. 'I couldn't get through,' he said, when she asked about it. 'All the lines were engaged, and I've forgotten about it since. Perhaps I won't bother. There's probably not much point.'

She seemed pleased at that, and offered to cook him something. He accepted, and they ate lamb chops. She remembered that he had told her to keep her curtains drawn at night, and moved to the draw cord. Kenyon laughed, and told her not to bother. He was keeping an eye on the flat across the other side of the gardens. The window had been dark all evening.

Kenyon wanted to make a phone call but he did not want to alarm Sarah by saying why. He helped her wash up, and thought that sooner or later she would have to go to the bathroom. He only needed a few seconds. Eventually, she excused herself.

Kenyon moved quickly to the telephone, made sure he was out of sight of that dark unlit window, and dialled the number of the flat opposite.

'Hullo,' a man's quiet voice said.

'Is Jane at home?' Kenyon asked.

'There's no Jane here,' the man said. 'You've got the wrong number.'

'Sorry,' Kenyon said.

He moved to the sliding glass windows, picked up a table lighter, and lit a cigarette. He squinted past the flame at that flat. There was still no light in the window. Kenyon thought that someone who sat in the dark and answered the telephone without putting a light on interested him considerably.

He had exchanged a few words with Detective Superintendent Pinder since their interview, but Pinder had said nothing about Sarah Brooks or Harry Coleman, so presumably no one had imposed any veto when Pinder had had his word with Percy. On the other hand, Kenyon had received no encouragement, either, and could safely be left holding the baby, if convenient.

Sarah came back, and made some more coffee. Kenyon wondered how much to tell her about what he intended to do, and decided it should be as little as possible.

'What time do you leave for work in the morning?' he asked.

'Just after nine,' Sarah said. 'Why?'

'I'll need to see you,' Kenyon said. 'I'll come round at eight-thirty.'

Again he had that feeling that it would be normal and acceptable to kiss her, that indeed she half expected it. But he did not.

He went back to his flat, poured a large whisky, sat down at his portable typewriter, wound in sheets of paper and carbons, and lit a cigarette. He typed away busily for fifteen minutes. He took one more carbon copy than he normally would. When he had finished, he put the spare copy in his breast pocket, and the remaining copies in his brief case.

He went to bed, set the alarm for 7 am, and slept soundly.

Sarah Brooks was dressed, made up, and perfumed when Kenyon rang her door bell at eight-thirty the following morning, although the dark shadows under her eyes suggested that she had not enjoyed as good a night's sleep as Kenyon had. He accepted the offer of some coffee, and sipped it, studying Sarah as she lit a cigarette.

'Do you always start smoking this early in the day?' he asked.

She looked at the cigarette, as though surprised to find it between her fingers. 'I ought to cut down,' she said. But when she had finished that one, she lit another one.

They said little. 'I'm not very bright, first thing in the morning,' she explained, apologetically, at one point.

'Living alone,' Kenyon said.

'What?'

'Like me. You can be as morose as you like. There's no one to make an effort for. You don't get into the habit.'

Sarah looked at her watch. 'I should be going.'

Kenyon finished his coffee, and stood up. 'Will you do something without asking why?' he enquired.

'Of course. What is it?'

'When you've finished work, don't come home. Stay at the office until I contact you. Then I'll meet you somewhere.'

'Why?' Sarah asked.

Kenyon grinned at her. She managed her first smile of the morning. 'Sorry,' she said. 'All right.'

'Talk to you later,' Kenyon said.

'Why did you want to come round?'

'I've just told you.'

'You could have told me that last night. Or phoned.'

'I thought you might feel sexy, first thing in the morning,' Kenyon said. 'A fallacious idea, as it turns out, but you make good coffee.'

Sarah smiled. 'Don't forget your briefcase.'

'I shan't need it today,' Kenyon said. 'I'll leave it here and pick it up tonight, if that's all right with you.'

Her smile faded. She looked at the briefcase, which was lying behind an armchair, and then her eyes sought Kenyon's. He held her gaze steadily. She might not know what he was up to, but she had guessed that the briefcase was being left for a purpose.

'I'll come down with you,' Kenyon said.

They rode down together in the lift. 'Do you ever come home during the day?' Kenyon asked.

'No.'

'Fine,' Kenyon said.

Sarah shivered, and pulled her coat closer around her body, although it was not cold. They stood for a moment outside Cleeve Court.

'I'll stay at the office until I get your phone call,' Sarah said.

'It'll be late afternoon,' Kenyon said. 'I've got a busy day.'

He watched her slim, coated figure walk away. On the corner, she lifted her hand, hailed a taxi, and got in. Kenyon watched the taxi until it disappeared from sight, and climbed into his car. He noted the number of the cab, which was radio-controlled. During the morning, he established that it belonged to the Owner Drivers net. The driver remembered picking up Sarah. He had taken her straight to the Foreign Office.

Kenyon adjusted his driving mirror, and looked for a few moments at the window of the flat where a man answered telephone calls while sitting in the dark. The address was Flat 16, 2 Rockstone Gardens. The building consisted of standardized, furnished apartments, available on short-term lets. The rents were high.

Kenyon had preferred not to try and find out too much about the occupant of that flat, in case he took fright and left. The tenancy was in the name of Evans, which was quite as good as Smith, Brown or Jones. The owners of the building were reputable, and required good references, which were easier documents to forge than most, and meant nothing. In any case rent in advance, in cash, was still the best reference there was.

Kenyon did not know what 'Evans' looked like, or anything about him. All Kenyon knew was that he was the only slender contact with whoever was harassing Sarah Brooks, if indeed anyone was. Kenyon wished to tickle his man gently, like a trout, and see what happened. He thought it possible that, after today, his fish might do something which might make it possible to identify him. Where he went after that, Kenyon did not know. He was not a believer in too much planning, when he was about as sure of his bearings as a man in a dense fog in a strange place. One step at a time was quite enough in case something unpleasant lay underfoot.

Kenyon realized only too clearly that the person who could most easily find out why he had left his briefcase behind was Sarah Brooks. She did not even need to take time off. Her lunch hour would be quite enough. He had done his best to make sure that Cleeve Court would be kept under observation, but without very much hope of success. CID were stretched to the limit, and all he had been able to arrange, when he had telephoned early that morning, was for a couple of uniformed branch men to be placed on plain clothes obbo.

They would do their best, but there were altogether too many ways in and out of Cleeve Court for anyone who wanted to get in unseen. Kenyon had thought of placing a man in the flat itself but he had rejected the idea. He did not want to nab an intruder, he wanted to alarm the outfit concerned. If, of course, there was any outfit concerned at all.

The 'if' arose from Kenyon's reservations about Sarah Brooks, which came and went like the tide, and at the moment were close to high water mark. He had decided, after seeing her a number of times, that his first assessment of her as attractive was wrong.

She was beautiful. Since this beauty had crept up on him, as it were, Kenyon was well aware that the transition was only in his own eyes. No change had taken place in Sarah. Even had she been just a girl he had met in the normal course of events, Kenyon would have been wary of the implications which followed. That kind of attachment to any one woman was not what he was looking for.

In Sarah Brooks' case, there were more urgent and pressing reasons not to get involved, with all the consequent and inevitable damage to his detachment and judgement. Kenyon well knew that all the indications were that Sarah was not merely a victim. That she was directly mixed up in whatever was going on.

He drove his car to Bayswater Police Station and parked it in the car yard, until he should need it later in the day.

At four-fifty-two that afternoon Kenyon's car blew up. Unrecognizable fragments of flesh and bone, the remnants of what a second before had been a man, adhered to the smoking, blackened wreckage, and hideously littered the car yard.

The explosion shook the building, and shattered twelve windows. Three constables were slightly injured by flying slivers of glass. There were no further casualties.

6

Prior to the explosion it had been a busy day. The raid on the suspected Long Firm Fraud premises took place at two pm, as the lorries were leaving the empty warehouses. Meacher's information was correct. The lorries were loaded with perfume and cosmetics. Eight men were arrested, two after a chase which ended in Shepherd's Bush.

Kenyon stood beside the police car which had brought him and watched the rest being hauled into vehicles. He recognized one of them, and got in beside him.

'Hullo, Freddie,' he said. 'This is where you sing for your supper. It can't do you any harm, and it might do you a lot of good.'

Freddie considered the idea in gloomy silence.

Bayswater Police Station was a hive of activity. The arrested men were interrogated, separately, by relays of detectives. Statements were taken, cross checked, inconsistencies found, torn up, and taken again. And again. And again.

Meacher was cock-a-hoop. Kenyon found him modestly explaining the brilliance of his undercover work to an admiring and pretty young policewoman in the corridor.

'All right,' Kenyon said. 'Your holiday's over. I've leaned on Freddie until he's ready to cough his guts up. Go and take his statement.'

Meacher grinned. 'Yes, sir,' he said gratefully and with enthusiasm. Kenyon was doing him a favour, and Meacher knew it. He would figure even more prominently in the witness box when the accused men came up for trial. The judge would quite likely single him out for some words of praise. Kenyon did not begrudge the young man his present and prospective glory. Meacher deserved it all. He had done a first rate job.

Detective Superintendent Pinder was curious to know why Kenyon had handled the arrests, and not the Long Firm Fraud Squad at Scotland Yard.

'We had a piece of luck, sir,' Kenyon said. 'Meacher was on routine observation on another matter and became suspicious about the warehouse. I decided to raid the premises but we had to move fast. There wasn't time to inform the Yard.'

'Off the record, Kenyon,' Detective Superintendent Pinder said, 'you're a terrible, bloody liar.'

'Yes, sir,' Kenyon said. 'But the eight arrests are on the record.'

'On the record,' Pinder said, 'a praiseworthy piece of quick thinking on the part of all concerned.'

This was what Kenyon had anticipated. The Yard might be irritable, perhaps, but Pinder was not likely to have any objection to crime in his own manor being solved by his own men. It looked better in the statistics, and Pinder liked Bayswater to be a front runner, which it was.

It was four-fifty, when Meacher came up to them. 'Excuse me, sir,' he said to Kenyon, 'but could I borrow your car for half an hour? Mine's in dock.'

'Why?' Kenyon asked.

'Freddie's done his nut,' Meacher said. 'He says the organiser was Lennie Peters. He also claims that Lennie was robbing them on the take and he hid some receipts, which will prove Lennie's involvement, under the floorboards in the warehouse office. Apparently he was going to use them later to twist Lennie's arm. We hit the place just as he was going to fetch them.'

Lennie Peters had not been arrested, but was a man well known to the frustrated police of Bayswater, and was a prize worth having.

'Good man, Mike,' Kenyon said, handing Meacher his car keys. 'You can take it with pleasure, so long as you don't bend it.'

'I've never bent a car in my life,' Meacher said, and walked off jingling the keys happily.

'God,' Pinder said. 'What it is to be young.'

'Like me,' Kenyon said.

'You were never that young,' Pinder said. 'He's so wet behind the ears, it hurts.'

'He's done a damn good job,' Kenyon said. 'I think he deserves a commendation.'

'He'll get one,' Pinder said.

Kenyon was satisfied that he had done everything possible for Mike Meacher. If the young man did not make Detective Sergeant within a year or two, it would be his own fault. Kenyon and Pinder chatted for another few moments, and then went their separate ways. Thirty seconds after they parted, the explosion shook the building. Kenyon was opening the door to the interview room where a PC was keeping Freddie company.

Glass from the window spattered against the walls and floor. Blood suddenly streamed down the PC's face. The PC felt his cheek, and looked at his red fingers with shocked surprise. Freddie dived under the table. There was a tableau-like moment when nobody moved, and it was silent, except for the ringing in Kenyon's ears.

The car yard could have been a fragmentary glimpse of hell. Kenyon ran out with the others. Thick smoke set them coughing. Kenyon realized that the mess of tangled metal was his car. He had a momentary hope that Meacher had not been inside it. The smoke billowed aside for a couple of seconds, and the hope died.

Kenyon's foot was on something soft and sticky. He realized what he was standing on, wiped his foot savagely on the asphalt, and went back into the station.

He walked up the stairs to his office, sat down, took a bottle of whisky from a cupboard, put the neck to his mouth, and swallowed hard. He put the bottle away and sat for a while without moving, his eyes open, staring fixedly without blinking. Eventually, he stirred, picked up his electric razor, went to the wash room, and shaved carefully. He unplugged the razor. There were beads of perspiration on his forehead.

Kenyon laid his razor on a shelf, splashed his face with cold water, and dried himself on a roller towel. Sweat began trickling down his face again at once. He walked into a lavatory, slid the bolt closed, and vomited violently into the basin, continuing to retch helplessly long after he had spewed up the contents of his stomach. At last, the heaving ended. Kenyon flushed the lavatory, leaned shakily against the door, and closed his eyes, willing himself to become Detective Inspector Sidney Kenyon again, the DI who had seen it all, and not this trembling person whose eyelids burned, whose eyeballs prickled.

Kenyon had seen worse sights than that in and around the jagged wreckage of his car, far worse. He frequently attended post mortems, where the pathologist and his assistants looked like butchers from some Dantesque inferno in their rubber aprons, with their forearms running with human blood. He watched them cut those former human beings open, and extract the heart, the liver, the kidneys, the throat. He watched them dissect and analyse, and listened to the pathologist's musings on the things he found. 'Every body tells a story,' one pathologist used to reflect, as he peered and probed at the bits and pieces. 'You can tell if a man was a drinker or not, his eating habits, what his sex life was like . . .' He watched them place the organs in plastic bags and sew them back inside the body when they had finished. None of this affected him any more.

In his world, death, mutilation, shocking injuries, screaming agonies, the helpless pain of bereavement were commonplace. It was part of his job to deal with those who suffered and inflicted them, what he received his monthly salary cheque for. None of it interfered with his pleasure, or kept him awake at night. But those pieces of slippery flesh which had been Detective Constable Michael Meacher penetrated his crab-like shell and turned him into a man who wanted to cry.

Poor young, likeable Mike, always looking for some girl he could make love to. Mike, who was a good detective in embryo, blown to shreds as he set out to crown his first real triumph. Mike, who could have been a friend in a way that Mallory never could. Mike, to whom he had lent his car so casually. The car which was supposed to have ended the life of Detective Inspector Sidney Kenyon.

There was a kind of order in the car yard when Kenyon went back. Floodlights illuminated the scene. All the trades, so familiar to Kenyon, who assemble round death were there, with an additional trade with which he was less familiar – the Bomb Squad. Kenyon engaged one of them in conversation. The man was busy and not anxious to talk. At the entrance of the car yard, a uniformed Chief Inspector was telling a television news team that they could not film inside.

'What do you think?' Kenyon asked the Bomb Squad man. 'It was set to go off when the car was started, wasn't it?'

'Don't know yet.'

'Terrorists don't use that sort. And there was no warning,' Kenyon said. 'They usually telephone a warning.'

'Look, do you mind?' the Bomb Squad man said. 'I'm busy.'

'He was one of my DC's,' Kenyon said.

The Bomb Squad man was as unimpressed as Kenyon would have been, had their roles been reversed.

'It was my car,' Kenyon said.

'Bad luck,' the Bomb Squad man said.

The questioning of the Long Firm Fraud suspects had been resumed. It no longer seemed nearly so important to those at Bayswater Police Station, but it had to be done.

Kenyon found Mallory, who was pale and tight lipped. 'I want to borrow your car, Len,' Kenyon said.

'Good idea,' Mallory said. 'Check it out, and see if it blows up.'

Kenyon resisted a strong impulse to clench his fist, and knock Mallory flying. From the look of him, Mallory was even more shocked than Kenyon had been.

'Just give me the keys,' Kenyon said.

Mallory shook his head. 'The Bomb Squad have got them,' he said. 'They're making sure that nobody else is going to get a nasty surprise.'

Kenyon thought that he should have known that himself without being told. He was still not functioning normally.

'I quite liked the silly little sod,' Mallory said.

Kenyon started to walk away.

'Hey,' Mallory said, 'what are you on about, anyway? You won't be allowed to leave the station. They'll want you.'

'I know,' Kenyon said, 'I'll be around.'

Kenyon left the station without being noticed, walked to Leinster Terrace, hired a self-drive car, and drove to Rockstone Gardens. The men he had left on observation were not there. They had been pulled off when the bomb exploded. Kenyon went into Number 2, flashed his warrant card at the resident caretaker, used some harsh words, and was led to Flat 16. The caretaker opened the door with a pass key. He seemed not to know that Kenyon had no right to demand entry without a search warrant.

There was no one there, and no sign that it had been recently occupied. The mahogany veneered furniture contained nothing in the drawers, except the crockery and cutlery supplied by the owners. The caretaker knew nothing about Mr 'Evans' leaving, and was vague in the extreme about his appearance. Kenyon promised to talk to him later, closed the door on him, and searched the flat properly.

He was careful about what he touched. Tomorrow, he wanted the fingerprint people here. But there was nothing, except a polaroid film wrapper under a chest of drawers. The wrapper had probably been aimed at a nearby waste-paper basket, missed, and rolled out of sight. Apart from that, not an item of clothing, toothbrush, scribbled memo, nothing to show that anyone had visited, let alone stayed and watched Sarah Brooks' flat across the other side of the gardens.

Kenyon went round again, patiently, this time searching for any evidence that anything might have been destroyed. The inside of the waste-disposal unit was greasy. Something would have adhered to that grease. Kenyon carefully scraped it out. Nothing. There were no fireplaces, but there were several large ashtrays. One of them was slightly scorched. Kenyon stroked the scorch mark, and looked at the black dust on his finger.

He went to the bathroom, knelt down, lifted the lavatory seat, and peered into the water. There were a few tiny fragments of black material. He stripped off his jacket and rolled up his shirt sleeves. Carefully, he put his hand in the water, and groped round the U-bend for anything which might be still floating there. His fingers encountered something. Cautiously, he drew it out. It was a fragment of a photograph, half burned, blackened round the edges. It showed a section of a man's raincoat. The man's right hand hung at his side. Mostly obscured by the raincoat was another coat, in checked material, worn by someone else.

Kenyon thought that it looked like his raincoat, and Sarah Brooks' top coat. He thought that, from the curious angle, it appeared to have been taken from high up, when they were standing outside Cleeve Court that morning. But what interested Kenyon especially was that someone had circled the man's right hand with a white marker pencil. And that the man's right hand was holding nothing at all.

Kenyon carefully dried the one inch square of print, wrapped it in lavatory paper, and put it in his wallet. He washed his hands, put on his jacket, went into the living room, and picked up his raincoat. He hesitated by the telephone, but the former occupant of the flat had used it, Kenyon knew that, and he decided to leave it for fingerprints.

Kenyon went downstairs, and used the phone in the caretaker's flat. The radio was on. Kenyon listened to the news summary as he dialled. 'This afternoon, a bomb, believed to have been planted by a terrorist organization, exploded at Bayswater Police Station. One CID officer was killed. The police are not releasing the name of the dead man until relatives have been informed.'

'Hullo,' Sarah Brooks said.

'I'll pick you up in about half an hour,' Kenyon said.

'Thank God you're all right. Someone told me a detective had been killed by a bomb, at Bayswater. I've been phoning the station, but no one would tell me anything.'

'I'm all right,' Kenyon said. 'See you.'

There were newspaper placards as Kenyon drove through the West End. LATE EXTRA. TERRORIST BOMB OUTRAGE. POLICEMAN KILLED.

Kenyon wondered if the Press Office at Scotland Yard were being inefficient, or if they believed it, or if they had been told what story to put out. There were times when terrorists came in useful. You could hang anything on them, and everyone would believe it.

7

Kenyon bought a newspaper, while he waited for Sarah to come down. There was a small item in the stop press, and that was all. A car bomb had exploded, evidently in retaliation for recent raids on suspected terrorist households.

Sarah got into the car. She seemed not to notice that it was not Kenyon's. He handed her the newspaper. She studied every word of the brief report as he drove to Buckingham Palace, round Hyde Park Corner, and up Park Lane.

Kenyon parked round the corner from Cleeve Court. Sarah got out and waited while he locked the driver's door. Only then did it appear to occur to her.

' Where's your car?' she asked.

' Mine was the one that got blown up,' Kenyon said.

He was watching her face, as he had the faces of endless suspects when he had dropped some remark into the conversation, waiting to analyse the subtle change of expression, or perhaps no change at all, which would tell him how much they knew, how much they had revealed, how much they were concealing.

Sarah Brooks' eyes widened fractionally. She stared at him in disbelief.

' It needed a new clutch anyway,' Kenyon said.

She continued to stare at him, her blue eyes dark under the street lights. Kenyon took her arm. Under the material of her coat, he could feel that she was trembling. 'We'll go in the back way, if you don't mind,' he said.

Kenyon sat on the couch while Sarah drew the curtains. Kenyon had no wish to join Meacher, killed in the course of duty. Anyone who would use high explosives could equally cheerfully turn to a sniper's rifle.

Tomorrow, after the hullabaloo about the bomb had died down a little, he would place the facts before Detective Superintendent Pinder. A senior detective would be assigned to the investigation, and Kenyon, while continuing to assist with the enquiry, would receive armed protection and would feel much safer. Tonight he intended to keep his head down as much as possible. Since the police had not released Meacher's name there was a good chance that Mr 'Evans' and his friends, would believe that the dead CID officer was Kenyon. 'Evans' himself had pulled out. There might be no further danger, but still . . .

'Would you like something to eat?' Sarah asked.

Kenyon shook his head. 'Just a drink, please,' he said.

He told Sarah as much as he thought she should know, while she smoked a cigarette, and gazed at him intently.

Kenyon had marked the position of his briefcase, that morning, and since then it had been moved and replaced. It was almost exactly where he had left it, but not quite. He picked it up now. It was still locked, but it was only one of the flat, mass produced variety and keys were easy to come by. Kenyon lifted the lid, although he knew what he would find.

'There was something in here,' Kenyon said, 'which has now gone.'

'You mean you expected them to come here today,' Sarah told him. 'You wanted them to.'

Kenyon no longer questioned her use of the plural. 'I think you knew that,' he said.

Sarah looked round the flat. 'I had the locks changed,' she said, a note of despair in her voice.

'Keys can be copied,' Kenyon said. 'Your hall porter isn't the brightest man I've ever met. He holds duplicates. Professionals can get in anywhere if they want to badly enough.' Including a car yard at a busy police station, he thought. Enquiries would be going on all night to try and establish how that had happened.

Kenyon knew that he should be taking part in those enquiries, that the phone at his Gloucester Terrace flat would be ringing, that men would be sent to find him. It was his car. Pinder would want to know if there was any connection. But none of that would bring Meacher back to life. Kenyon preferred to pursue his own line, and let them get on with theirs. Tomorrow, he would be able to present more to Pinder than all the rest of them put together. He might receive a token blast of rebuke for not keeping Pinder informed, but he was used to that. Results were what counted in the Police Force, provided you got them. Otherwise, it was safer to stick to the book, but Kenyon did not have much time for the book.

'What was in there, that you wanted them to see,' Sarah asked. 'Can you tell me?'

Kenyon shook his head.

'Did you leave the office at all today?' he asked.

'Only for lunch.'

'Were you alone?'

'No. Mr Everitt took me to Simpsons.'

'Why?'

'Why?' Sarah echoed, puzzled.

'He's your Establishment Officer. Does he often take you to lunch? Or is he a personal friend?'

'Neither,' Sarah said. She seemed at a loss, and uneasy.

'I just wondered what the occasion was, if any,' Kenyon said.

'It was arranged last week,' Sarah said. 'It was just a general chat. He wanted to know if everything was all right now.'

Kenyon considered. Supposing this were true, he did not believe that Everitt was anything but what he was supposed to be. He might take instructions, in the form of delicate hints, but that upper-class creep would always make quite sure that he was never involved in anything he could not safely disclaim.

'Do you have his home phone number?' Kenyon asked. 'I'd like to have a word with him.'

Sarah looked at Kenyon. Her eyes, he thought, were like those of a trusting dog, when it has been kicked for no reason.

'We left the office at twelve-forty-five,' Sarah said, flatly. 'We walked to Simpson's. We both had roast beef. We left at two-fifteen. I was never out of his sight.'

'Fine,' Kenyon said. 'Can I have his phone number?'

Sarah gave it to him. Kenyon registered that it was a St John's Wood number.

A maid answered the telephone. Presumably Everitt had money of his own, which was no surprise to Kenyon. Lance Everitt was icily ill-humoured when he came to the phone. He was in the middle of his dinner, did not wish to be disturbed, and proposed that Kenyon should call at the Foreign Office the following day, when Everitt would endeavour to spare him a few moments.

'I'm investigating the death of a police officer,' Kenyon said. 'You can either talk on the phone, or I'll come round there, and you can shove your bloody dinner in the oven until I've finished.'

There was a period of silence. 'I don't see how this . . . event . . . can be any concern of mine,' Everitt said carefully.

'You're not required to see anything,' Kenyon said. 'Merely act like a good citizen, and answer my questions. Did you spend any time with Miss Brooks today?'

'Why?' Everitt asked cautiously.

'I wish to eliminate her from my enquiries,' Kenyon said.

Smoke trailed in lazy coils from Sarah's cigarette. An inch of ash, suspended on the end, fell on to the carpet. Sarah did not notice. She was sitting motionless, staring at Kenyon.

Everitt related his lunch with Sarah. He had wanted to talk to her informally, in pleasant surroundings. He did this occasionally, with senior staff members about whom he was concerned. The appointment had been made last Friday and was in his diary. They had walked to and from the restaurant, and were together all the time.

'Right,' Kenyon said. 'Now I want to know if Miss Brooks left the building at any time today, except during her lunch hour.'

'Good God,' Everitt said. 'I can't get that sort of information at this time of night.'

Kenyon said, 'You either make a few phone calls, and ring me back in ten minutes, or we can go and find out together if it takes all night.'

Kenyon hung up. Sarah bit her lip, stubbed out her cigarette, got up, and walked out of the room. Kenyon heard water running into the wash basin in the bathroom.

Kenyon gave himself another drink, and waited for Everitt to call back. The phone rang, just after Sarah returned. She said nothing. Her eye make up was freshly applied. There were small lines of strain at the corners of her mouth. She sat down and lit a cigarette. Kenyon thought that she had been crying, for some reason.

'Miss Brooks arrived at the office at nine-fifty-eight this morning,' Everitt said. 'She did not leave again, except with me, until you yourself picked her up this evening, Inspector.'

The last bit satisfied Kenyon, but he asked automatically, 'Are you quite sure of that?'

'Absolutely,' Everitt said. 'Would you like the names of the people I've spoken to, so that you may take statements from them?' he added sarcastically.

'Not at this stage,' Kenyon said. 'Thank you very much for your assistance, sir.' He chucked in the 'sir' for good measure. He was pleased with what Everitt had told him, and hence, for the moment, pleased with Lance Everitt.

Kenyon hung up, and sipped his drink. He waited for Sarah to say something, but for a long time there was silence in the flat. A taxi stopped somewhere nearby, its diesel engine rattling. A door slammed, and the taxi drove off.

'Nice and quiet here,' Kenyon said, conversationally. 'Like my place. Gloucester Terrace gets a bit busy sometimes. People use it to get on to Westway. But I've got a basement flat at the back, so I don't hear it.'

Sarah seemed not to hear him. She was pushing cigarette stubs round the ashtray, intently forming patterns in the ash.

'I thought you trusted me now,' she said at last. She did not look up. A whorl formed in the ash.

'I like to try and check, when I can,' Kenyon said.

'Are you satisfied?'

'That you didn't come back here? Yes. Good old true blue Lance Everitt wouldn't risk giving anyone an alibi which could be blown. He'd be in for it then and I'd take odds Lance looks out for number one.'

'An alibi,' Sarah said, wryly. 'So that's what I've got.'

'One that I can buy, more to the point,' Kenyon said.

'You'd take odds on Lance Everitt, but not on me.'

'Everitt didn't know my briefcase was here. You did. You might have come back and looked inside.'

'I didn't,' Sarah said.

'I deal in "mights" all the time,' Kenyon said. 'You might have telephoned someone, come to that.'

'I didn't,' Sarah said, again.

'You'd have been wasting your time, if you had,' Kenyon said, thinking of that scrap of photograph, showing a hand which should have been carrying a briefcase, and was not.

Kenyon finished his drink, and put it down. 'Sarah, I'm sorry about all this,' he said. 'But that's not an apology. I'm a copper, and that's the animal I am. I think differently. I behave differently. I don't trust anyone or believe anything until I've checked, and for preference twice. I didn't want to think you had anything to do with it, but that's personal. Me, I take a few coppers on trust, not all by a long way, and that's it.'

'You must be a very lonely man,' Sarah said, quietly.

'I don't think about it,' Kenyon said. 'The fact is, someone wanted to kill me.'

She moved gracefully from the chair where she was sitting, and knelt at his feet. Her hands rested on his arm. Her eyes looked up into his. 'When I heard about the bomb,' she said, 'I was afraid it was you. There was no reason, but I was still afraid. When you phoned, I was so relieved. I don't know if you believe me. I can't really tell, with you.' Her fingers touched Kenyon's face, lightly.

Kenyon leaned forward, and kissed her lightly on the lips. She straightened. Her arms went round his neck. Her lips were soft, and slightly open. She was warmth, and perfume, and soft flesh. Kenyon had intended his kiss to be no more than an indication of an armistice, a reassurance. He forgot about that now.

Slowly, her mouth opened, her tongue darted to and fro, she

clung to him. Kenyon's hand slid from her shoulder to the soft roundness of her breast. She made a small noise, her fingers caressed the back of his neck. Kenyon began to stroke her flanks and every movement of his hand brought an answering response from her slim body.

Her lips slid away from his, and she rubbed her cheek against his face. Kenyon's throat was taut, and he knew that his voice was husky when he spoke.

'Sarah,' he said, 'We can stop this and I'll leave. Otherwise, I either undress you here, or we go to bed.

'I think we'd better go to bed,' Sarah said.

Kenyon stood up. His knees seemed shaky, but he thought he could make it to the bedroom. He helped Sarah to her feet. She put her arm round his waist, and her head on his shoulder. They walked the few, necessary steps.

'I shan't be a minute,' Sarah said, and went into the bathroom.

Kenyon undressed, pitching his clothes on a chair, and got into bed. The sheets were cool and pleasant. The bedside light was on. Kenyon had ceased to think about anything except Sarah. He lay on his back, looked at the ceiling, and waited.

Sarah came in. She had undressed in the bathroom, and was wearing a satin dressing gown, belted at the waist. Kenyon turned his head, and looked at her. Slowly, she loosened the belt. The satin fell open. He saw her white flesh beneath.

He folded the bedclothes back. Sarah's eyes ran down his naked body, and then she slipped into bed beside him.

'Which side do you prefer to be?' Kenyon asked.

'It doesn't arise,' Sarah said. Her arms went round his body. He felt the gentle pull of her fingers, and rolled over on to her. She was waiting and ready, and at once he was inside her.

He knew now why Sarah Brooks spoke of making love, and not screwing. She gave everything of herself, as though craving to grant him reassurance, protection, warmth, devotion, God knows what. Later, he drifted into a doze, which would have become a sound sleep, except that he turned over, and discovered that Sarah Brooks was not there. The room was in darkness but the place beside him was empty, and where she had been the sheets had lost their warmth.

Kenyon thought he heard a tiny sound and rolled over blinking, clearing his sleep-misted eyes. The bedroom curtains were apart. The sliding window was closed. But outside on the balcony, he thought he could detect the shape of a human figure.

Kenyon's heart began to pound, and the adrenalin brought him wide awake. Stealthily, he slid out of bed, and groped for his shoes. The naked human body was too vulnerable to tackle an intruder unclothed, and unshod. But even as he was about to slip on his shoes, he put them down again. As his eyes adjusted fully he realized that the shape outside was familiar.

Kenyon opened the sliding glass window, and stepped out on to the balcony. It was nearly freezing outside, and he began to shiver at once. Sarah Brooks was barefooted. Her satin dressing gown offered little protection to her naked body.

'What the hell are you doing out here?' Kenyon asked.

She did not answer. Kenyon put his arms round her. 'Hey,' he said. Her flesh was icy. She must have been there for a long time. Her body was shaking uncontrollably, but not from the cold. She was crying, without ceasing, without sobbing, just crying, the tears running down her face, like the rain on the face of the dead West Indian girl, Jenny Abel, an age ago, wetting his fingers, as he tried to turn her face towards him. But all her muscles were tensed and rigid. All the soft warmth had gone. It was like trying to turn a block of wet stone.

'What's wrong?' Kenyon asked.

She did not answer.

'Come on,' Kenyon said. 'You're frozen.'

He forced her to go back into the bedroom. She moved unwillingly, as though she wanted to stay there and suffer the bitter cold. Kenyon released her while he closed the sliding window. She stayed where he left her. He guided her back to bed, laid her down, wrapped the bedclothes round her, and sat beside her, massaging her limp hands.

'Would you like a brandy?' Kenyon asked.

There was no answer. 'OK I'll get one,' Kenyon said.

'No,' she said, speaking at last, apparently with a great effort.

'Something else. Coffee?'

'Nothing.'

Her hands were growing warmer. Kenyon switched the bedside light on.

Sarah turned her face away from him at once. All he could see was her hair. 'No. Please,' she said. She seemed to have stopped crying, which Kenyon supposed was a gain of some sort. He switched the light off.

His former mood of euphoria had vanished, and he tried to suppress his growing irritation. What the hell was wrong with this woman to whom he had been so close, not long before? How was it possible to reconcile her smiling, eager, almost loving caresses, with this silent, removed, remote, monosyllabic stranger? All Kenyon's former suspicions about neurosis returned.

'Look, I'm pretty bloody cold myself,' he said, shortly. 'I think I'll get into bed too, unless you've any rooted objection.'

Sarah neither objected nor acquiesced. Kenyon got into the other side of the bed, and waited until it grew warm again. He wondered what he was doing here with this woman and her unpredictable moods and actions. He should be quietly sleeping, safely alone, in his basement flat in Gloucester Terrace. Instead, here he was, with some screwed-up female, whose problems were none of his concern, so far as he knew, with a situation to cope with of the kind which he disliked intensely.

Kenyon was no stranger to hysteria and neurosis in women. Apart from meeting it frequently while on duty, it had exploded in his face, like some unsuspected land mine, more than once in the course of his private life before now. Kenyon had long since lost faith in his ability to detect the possibility in advance. Some women acted up and you could never tell which, and that was it.

He still shuddered at the thought of Kate, who, like Mollie, happened to have a husband. He had met her when he was doing relief duty at Epsom, enjoyed it, and said goodbye without regret. Three weeks later, Kate had turned up at a club Kenyon often used in Bayswater, complete with suitcase, and announced that she had left her husband, and would live with Kenyon until she could get a divorce. Some highly unpleasant scenes had followed. Kenyon needed to become a corespondent in a divorce case like he needed a hole in the head. Theoretically, the Police Force recognized that in the nineteen seventies these things happened and there was no stigma attached. In practice, promotion usually and mysteriously eluded a man involved in a divorce.

Kenyon cared about promotion, and he cared not in the least for Kate. The whole thing was madness from beginning to end. Kate's husband was rich, their house sat in three acres of well tended gardens, they ran his and hers Mercedes, and kept an ocean-going yacht at Hamble. What could Kenyon offer her but poverty and squalor? He had put it to her, laying it on a bit thick.

' Love,' she had replied, weeping.

Kenyon expressed, sadly, his regrettable defectiveness in that respect. Kate replied that she had enough for both of them. It had taken many hours of earnest and tactful talking to get out of that situation. He had watched the tears flow, given her more gin, kept on explaining that he was not good enough for her, and hoped to God that her husband would not get back from his business trip to Hong Kong before he got the woman back home again.

In the end, he had managed it, and even managed also to play his required part in a prolonged and sentimental goodbye. No, said Kate. Not goodbye. *Au revoir*. Although he had never heard from Kate since, he had resolved to have nothing to do with any more dramas like that. Since then, he had hastened to walk firmly away at the first and slightest hint. And now, here was another drama going on which he could not account for, and did not wish to.

Kenyon thought about getting dressed and going home without more ado. But the bed had grown warm, and Sarah was silent, and he was comfortable. He supposed that she had some sort of sexual hang up, although her behaviour in bed would have fooled the most suspicious of men. Still, whatever it was, remorse, regret, or just plain guilt – perhaps about Harry Coleman, whom she was probably still in love with – was nothing to do with Kenyon. There was no way he could help her.

And yet he felt regret himself. He wished that what had happened between them could have continued without being soured like this. He thought about how she had been, about the way she whispered 'Darling, darling, darling,' and the recollection was enough to make his stomach turn over.

Kenyon was growing pleasantly tired again. She was not moving and her breathing was even. She must have fallen asleep. Kenyon turned over on his side, and put his arm round her now warm body.

'Don't touch me, please,' Sarah Brooks said, in a clear wide awake voice.

Kenyon recoiled, as though from some hostile animal. He groped for his jacket, found cigarettes and lighter, and lit a cigarette. The gas flame cast a brief light on Sarah. She was lying on her back. Her eyes were open. Her fine, regular features were chiselled and cold, and then she was in darkness again, as he snapped his lighter closed. He found an ashtray at the bedside, and sat up, propping himself on the head board.

'All right,' he said, wearily. 'Let's have it.' Whatever hang ups you've got, he thought, let's play the obligatory scene. Let's find out what I've done wrong. Kenyon had little doubt that it would all turn out to be his fault, in some way.

In this case, as it happened, he was wrong.

'I'm sorry,' Sarah said. 'I'm very, very sorry. I hope you'll try and believe that.'

Kenyon smothered a yawn, drew on his cigarette, and watched the red glow. So that was it. Confession time.

'I've got to tell you,' Sarah said. 'I've known that all evening. I swore I wouldn't, but I must. I've been trying to put it off, but I know I've got to do something now, and you must tell me what it is.'

Oh, it's that one, Kenyon thought. Here we go. Tell me what to do. Kate had said that, although she did not mean it. What she meant was 'tell me that you are going to do what I want you to do.' He wondered what he was supposed to do on this occasion.

Send her back to Harry Coleman? Advise her to write to Mrs Coleman revealing all? Offer to take Harry Coleman's place in her life?

'Do you remember the very first time you came here?' Sarah asked. 'How I insisted that you had to come yourself?'

'Yes,' Kenyon said.

'I had been told to do that,' Sarah said.

Kenyon's preconceptions about what he was going to hear vanished. All his suppressed suspicions returned, all the indications which he had tried to ignore blazed clear again. Thoughts flashed like lightning across his mind. He had been set up. His exploding car was supposed to be the end. Instead it had been young Michael Meacher whose body had disintegrated, but it was Kenyon who should have sat in that car, and turned the ignition key.

As fast as his thoughts, Kenyon grew coldly, bitterly angry. He wanted to wrench the bedclothes off Sarah Brooks, drag her out of bed, and beat her with his clenched fists until she told everything she knew. But that was not the way, at this moment, on this night. She had to be encouraged to talk freely and willingly.

'Who by?' Kenyon asked. His tone was considerate, understanding. There were men in Dartmoor, Parkhurst and Broadmoor, who would have recognized that kind and gentle voice.

'Everything I told you was true,' Sarah said. 'About the feeling that I was being followed, that my belongings were being searched.'

'And the flat being broken into as well?'

'Oh, yes. When I came home that night, I was terrified. But . . .' She broke off.

'But what?' Kenyon asked. 'It's all right,' he said encouragingly. 'Whatever you tell me now, it's all right.'

'Is it?'

'After tonight, yes,' Kenyon said, squeezing her hand gently.

Sarah's fingers returned the pressure. She seemed relieved, and spoke more easily. 'As soon as these things started to happen, I'd told Mr Everitt,' she said. 'He was very kind about it, although I didn't think he believed me. But he told me to let him know at once about anything that worried me. Anything at all, he said.'

'You discovered the break-in when you got home from work,' Kenyon said.

'I was to phone him at any time of the day or night.'

'I see,' Kenyon said. He was no longer pleased with Lance Everitt.

'When I found they'd been here, I phoned him. He said he'd call me back. Half an hour later, he did. He told me to ring a number, which he gave me. A man would answer, and I was to do exactly as he said.'

'What did he tell you to do?'

'I was to report the break-in to the police at Bayswater, but I was to insist on seeing Detective Inspector Kenyon.'

Kenyon released her hand, turned over on his side, and put his arms round her. She answered his embrace gladly, pressing herself against his body, as if seeking comfort. Kenyon stroked her back lightly.

'Do you know why it had to be me?'

'No. I asked, but he just said you were the right man to deal with it.'

'Who was this man on the phone? Did he say?'

'Mr Everitt had told me not to ask. He reminded me that I was subject to security regulations to the letter and that I was to maintain complete secrecy.'

'Especially from me, presumably,' Kenyon said.

'Yes.'

'So when you told me that you thought you were being investigated by your own security people, that wasn't true.'

'Yes, it was,' Sarah said. 'I'd suspected that from the beginning, and the man on the phone said he thought some outfit was setting up a private empire on their own, and were overstepping the mark.'

'Was that the word he used? Outfit?'

'Yes.'

'What else did he say? You're just an ordinary civil servant,' Kenyon said, holding her warm body close to his, and wondering if she was anything of the kind. 'You must have thought the things you were being asked to do were all very odd.'

'Yes and no,' Sarah said. 'The odd part had already happened, when I first thought I was being watched. When I was told to get the police in, I was mostly relieved. I thought at least they'd be ordinary people I could trust.'

'Even though you'd been ordered not to tell me the complete truth?'

'The man on the phone said it was a tricky situation. He said one branch of security couldn't very well investigate another. He said it would be best if the police took over, but we couldn't tell them why. You must remember that by that time I was pretty frightened. I didn't much care who dealt with it, so long as it stopped.'

'Yes, of course,' Kenyon said. He lay in the darkness, his lips touching Sarah's hair, and wondered if she was lying again. How could you tell from the softness of a woman's breasts? How could you tell from a long, velvet smooth thigh, which lay across yours? 'I didn't much care,' she had just said. But even if she were now telling the exact truth, her compliance had led, directly or indirectly, to Meacher's death.

'What time were you told what to do by the man on the phone?' Kenyon asked. 'The exact time.'

Sarah thought. 'Eight o'clock,' she said at last. 'About then. I can't be quite sure.'

Kenyon's mind ticked, unrolling what he had been doing on that day, and at what time. The dead West Indian girl, Jenny Abel, in the basement area, the rain, the underground club, Winston Peters who had hanged himself.

'Everitt gave you a special phone number,' he said. 'What was it? Do you remember?'

Sarah gave it to him. Kenyon got out of bed, went into the living room, put the light on, sat down and dialled the number.

He had not bothered to put any clothes on, and as he flicked the dial, he caught sight of his genitals, passive and forgotten now. Strange how that collection of tissue and blood could change, most of the time an appendage, mostly unconsidered, yet now and then the centre of all urgency, all feeling.

The voice answered after three rings. It was quiet and controlled, the voice of a man who was accustomed to come awake fast, the way a doctor answers the phone in the middle of the night. Although Kenyon did not think this was any doctor.

'Hullo,' the voice said. Kenyon listened intently. 'Hullo,' the voice said again.

Kenyon hung up. He would have committed perjury had he sworn it on oath, but he would take six to four on with any bookie that the voice belonged to Tom Bradley.

He went back into the bedroom, and switched on the overhead light. Sarah blinked, and shaded her eyes. 'Did you find out who it was?' she asked.

'No,' Kenyon said. The sheets had fallen from Sarah's shoulders, and he could see the rise of her breasts.

'One thing you haven't told me,' he said. 'You took me to bed tonight. You switched me on like an expert, no trouble at all. Why?'

'It wasn't like that,' she said.

'How was it?'

'The way I felt,' Sarah said, simply. 'When we first met, I didn't really see you. You were just a man in a suit. When I did see you, as a man I mean, I didn't think I liked you very much. Later, I realized that I did.'

'Do you get on your back for everyone you like?' Kenyon enquired. Unfairly, in view of the shallowness of most of his own past encounters.

'No,' she said, quietly hurt. 'Far from it.'

'Just this once,' Kenyon said. 'A couple of relaxing screws to put me in a good humour, before I'm told how I've been shopped.'

'If that's all you think it was, forget it,' Sarah said, her voice raised, flaring up. 'I knew it was my fault you were mixed up in it all, and it was my silly way of trying to show you how sorry I was. I should have known better. You wouldn't know the difference.'

She turned away from him. Kenyon reached out, gripped her shoulders, pulled her round, and slapped her face hard. Sarah cried out, once, and then lay staring up at him, shocked and startled.

'You stupid bitch,' Kenyon said. 'Whether you knew what you were doing or not, you set me up. Just before five o'clock tonight, a nice young fellow called Mike Meacher was blown apart. They had to scrape the bits of his guts from the bits of my car with a teaspoon. All you can think of is getting your precious legs open, so that I'll feel better, and you'll feel better. And then you have the bloody gall to talk about feelings worth having.'

Sarah flinched. She thought he was going to hit her again. He bundled his clothes, took them into the bathroom, locked the door, and turned the taps on. He had vented his angry grief. He had found someone to blame. Later on, he knew he might feel regret, but just now he did not.

Sarah's clothes were hanging on the bathroom door. Her wrist-watch, and the pyramid shaped ring she always wore, were on a glass shelf above the wash basin. Kenyon picked up the ring, and glanced at it idly, while the water ran into the bath. The ring was eighteen carat gold, and must be worth a great deal of money. Probably a gift from Harry Coleman, who bought original pictures, and lent money to buy flats.

Kenyon was about to replace the ring on the glass shelf, when he became interested in it. Perhaps because his perceptions were heightened by his renewed doubt and distrust of Sarah Brooks. Perhaps because he was a policeman again without the distraction of desire for an attractive woman. Perhaps because he recalled the Edgar Allan Poe short story in which the best hiding place for an important letter was in full view of everybody. He never knew quite why, nor did he much care.

The bath was nearly full. He turned off the taps and sat down on the bathroom stool. He rotated the ring, examining it care-fully. It was just a gold, pyramid-shaped ring. There was a strip light over the mirror above the wash basin. Kenyon took the ring over there and tried again, peering at it closely, watching the glint of the precious metal, catching the reflection in the mirror.

It was in the mirror that he first saw it – the tiniest of hair-lines, tucked beneath the tiny mock stones of the small mock pyramid. Kenyon sat down again, spread a towel across his knees, and worked intently on the ring. It took him ten minutes. Once you knew the trick, it came apart like a Chinese puzzle. He placed the various small pieces carefully on the towel, as he managed to detach them.

When he had finished, he was left with a small hollowed out portion. Inside the hollow a microfilm fitted snugly. Kenyon felt excitement, the same excitement he always felt when the fog of a difficult investigation momentarily cleared, but not surprise. As soon as he suspected that the ring came apart, he had guessed what he would find. It took five minutes to get the ring together again. Now that he had the knack, it would take less another time.

Kenyon draped a towel round his waist, wrapped the microfilm in a tissue, and put it in his jacket pocket. The bedroom was in darkness, and Sarah seemed to be asleep. He switched the light on.

'Who gave you the ring?' he asked.

The hunched figure under the bedclothes did not move.

'You're not asleep,' Kenyon said. He gave the humped bedclothes a push. 'Where did your pyramid ring come from? Harry Coleman?'

Sarah turned over. 'Leave me alone,' she said. 'I'm tired.'

'What did that cost him? Another five hundred quid?'

'You think everything's got a cash value, don't you?' Sarah said.

'What was it for? Services rendered?' Kenyon asked, needling her deliberately and cold-bloodedly.

'You really are the original, complete bloody shit, aren't you,' she said.

'Good heavens,' Kenyon said, 'the lady does know the four letter words after all.'

'I know a few more I could apply to you,' she said.

'Go on,' Kenyon mocked. 'Tell me it was a keepsake. A farewell gift.'

'You probably wouldn't understand such a thing,' Sarah said with quiet, patient contempt, 'but that's exactly what it was. What's more, I treasure it.'

'And wear it all the time,' Kenyon said, grinning without humour. 'Because that's what he said, "Darling Sarah, never take this off your finger. In that way, a little part of us will always be together".'

'His choice of words was a good deal superior,' Sarah said. 'And it was given with kindness and gentleness and love. All the things you wouldn't know about.'

'I suppose you took it off tonight because you were going to screw around with me,' Kenyon said.

'Something like that,' she said. 'We all make mistakes.'

'I think I feel like a drink now,' Kenyon said.

'You hit me,' Sarah said. 'I believe that's an assault. I think I'm entitled to send for the police, and I think I shall.'

'Do,' Kenyon said. 'Then we can both sit here with a couple of boot-faced coppers, while you explain that after a couple of good bangs, you got fed up with me.'

He had been obliged to push her, to make her feel genuinely furious, but there was always a risk that he would go too far. *In vino veritas* was a good motto, but some men and women always retained sufficient control to avoid giving anything important away. Kenyon believed that real anger brought out the truth more efficiently. Unless Sarah Brooks was a much better actress than he thought she was, she regarded that ring as a sentimental memento, not as a hiding place for something important.

He wandered into the living room, poured the drink he had promised himself, and dialled Bayswater Police Station. He asked if Sergeant Downs was still there. Sergeant Downs was one of the two men who had kept observation on Cleeve Court during the day. He did not give his name, saying that it was a personal call. Sergeant Downs came to the phone.

'Hullo, Bill,' Kenyon said. 'Still at it?'

'Aren't we all?' Downs said. 'They'll be paying out a fortune in overtime. Where have you been anyway? Your guv'nor's been screaming for you. He's threatening to have your balls for billiards practice.'

'I'm just on my way to see him now,' Kenyon said. 'I wondered if you'd had any joy at Cleeve Court.'

'No one suspicious, and no one answering Miss Brooks' description, before the bomb went off,' Downs said. 'Can't answer for after that, though.'

'After that doesn't matter,' Kenyon said, and hung up.

He went back to the bathroom. The water had grown tepid. He ran the hot tap, and lay in the bath for a long time, thinking. Mostly, he was thinking about Jenny Abel and Winston Peters.

Eventually, he got out of the bath, and dried himself. In the bedroom, he switched the bedside light on, and got into bed beside Sarah. She had been only half asleep, and her eyes opened watching him. Her fingers clutched the sheets, pulling them up under her chin.

'I'd like you to go, please,' she said. 'I thought I'd made that plain.'

Kenyon looked into her eyes, without speaking. He did not have to. After a few moments, she understood, and turned swiftly to get out of bed. Kenyon moved faster. His weight clamped her down. She struggled silently and savagely. She was dry, but he pushed inside her. She became a little moist, and then more so.

Kenyon kissed her. Her lips were cold and closed. He lifted his head, and looked at her. She turned her face aside. Kenyon began to move, driving to and fro, methodically, continually. Her head remained averted, her hands stayed at her sides.

Kenyon did not stop. He felt the fluttering, unwilling response in her belly. He went on and on, forcing her to have an orgasm, until she groaned and cried out as if in pain, and only then did he come inside her.

As soon as he had finished, he rolled off her, and lay on his back. Both were breathing hard. Neither said anything for a long time.

At last, Sarah said, in a matter of fact voice, 'So that's what it's like. Being fucked.'

'That's what it's like,' Kenyon said. 'And what's more, you deserved it.' He was emptied and tired, and ready for sleep. 'Also,' he added, 'you liked it.' His eyes were closing. He felt her lift herself.

'Which do you prefer?' she asked softly. 'Sid or Sidney?'

'Sid,' Kenyon said. He opened his eyes with an effort, and turned his head towards her. 'Why?'

For a woman with such slim arms and shoulders, there was a surprising amount of power in the blow, when she hit him across the face. His head spun sideways, his cheek flamed, and he thought his teeth rattled.

'Right, Sid,' she said. 'I think that's what you have coming to you.'

She was kneeling. That was how she had got such a good swing, when she hit him, Kenyon thought. Even now, when he felt no desire, he still admired the lift and beauty of her breasts, that powder puff of hair, those long slender thighs.

'Agreed,' Kenyon said. 'No question. Are we even now?'

'I don't know,' Sarah said.

'Don't count on getting it three times a night,' Kenyon said. 'I'm not that virile. I'd be a debilitated wreck.'

'I'm not looking for any encores, thank you,' she said.

'I am,' Kenyon said. He took her hand, kissed it, and drew her down beside him.

'How's your face?' he asked, touching her cheek.

'Bruised,' she said. 'How's yours?'

'Let's say we both ran into the same lamp post,' Kenyon suggested.

'I've never been hit before in my life,' Sarah said.

'It won't happen again,' Kenyon promised.

She switched the light out, and settled down. 'I'm tired,' she said.

The sheets rustled for a while, and then there was stillness.

8

Kenyon woke up to find a trolley at the side of the bed. On the trolley was fresh orange juice, coffee, bacon and eggs, and toast. He drank the orange juice before trying to speak. Sarah poured a cup of coffee for herself and buttered a piece of toast.

'The rest is yours,' she said. She wore her satin dressing gown, and looked none the worse for wear.

'Your face looks fine,' Kenyon said.

'I've put a lot of make up on. Under this goo, there's a distinctly battered-looking female.'

'Sorry,' Kenyon said, sincerely.

'I bruise easily. And I'm not used to sadistic rapists in my flat.'

Kenyon wondered whether to invite her back to bed. 'Come back to bed,' he said.

'Now you're bragging,' Sarah said.

'You may be right. Let's find out.'

'Do you know what the time is?'

Kenyon looked at his watch. 'Jesus,' he said, forgot about finding out, and started to eat fast.

'If you want to shave, I've got a razor here,' Sarah said. 'And yes, Harry left it behind, to forestall any sarcastic comments.'

'I'll shave at the nick,' Kenyon mumbled, his mouth full. He swallowed. Sarah was wearing her pyramid ring again. Kenyon speared his last piece of bacon, and pointed at the ring with his fork. 'Talking of Harry . . .' he began.

'Don't start again,' Sarah said. 'We had quite enough of that last night.'

'I'm jealous,' Kenyon explained, apologetically.

'I doubt if you've ever cared enough about anyone to be jealous,' Sarah said, with reasonable insight.

'No,' Kenyon said. 'Not until now.'

He was surprised to realize that this bit of play-acting contained a germ of truth. He did feel an unfamiliar twinge of jealousy when he thought about that good-looking American who had possessed this woman for years, travelled abroad with her, shared her bed as a matter of course.

'You're just trying to make up for your disgusting behaviour,' Sarah said, although she did not appear to be all that disgusted.

'I've been given the odd present as a keepsake, now and then,' Kenyon said. 'I've always lost them.'

'I was in love with him, for a long time,' Sarah said. 'I didn't want to accept it, but . . .' She broke off, and studied the ring with affection. 'Harry said . . . well, never mind what he said, exactly. I promised him I'd always wear it. And I shall.'

'Even if anything happens to him?'

Sarah stared at him. 'Why did you say that?'

Kenyon shrugged. 'I don't know. He's quite a bit older than you. Something might happen. He might have a heart attack.'

'He said something very much like that,' she said, slowly.

'Well, there you are. Great minds. What did he say?'

'If he died, he made me promise to take it to be valued. Somewhere in Chancery Lane. Claythorpe's.'

'Why?'

'He did explain. Something about a valuation being necessary under American inheritance laws. I told him not to be so morbid, but he was insistent.'

The ring was certainly valuable, but Kenyon did not know if there was any such requirement under American law.

'Why this particular place in Chancery Lane?'

'He's made arrangements with them to handle his UK property in the event of his death.'

'I thought he'd gone back to America for good,' Kenyon said.

'He's got investments here,' Sarah said. She fiddled with the ring, in a troubled kind of way. Then her eyes searched Kenyon's face. 'You never ask anything without a reason,' she said. 'I'm beginning to realize that. I think you staged everything last night for some purpose of your own.'

'Not all of it,' Kenyon said. 'I liked young Mike Meacher. I hit you, because I couldn't get at the people who killed him. You were within reach. They weren't.'

Sarah nodded. 'A substitute whipping post,' she said. 'It's my lifelong ambition.'

Kenyon took another look at his watch. He was late now. He might as well be good and late.

'I'll tell you this,' he said. 'You're easy to fancy, and that gets in the way. I spend my life trying to judge people who may or may not be telling the truth. As a rule, I'm about ninety per cent right. The percentage drops if I'm wondering what some female looks like without any clothes on.'

'Well, you don't have to wonder about that any more in my case,' Sarah said.

'I have the nasty feeling that you're addictive,' Kenyon said. 'Since we met, I've done it all. I've believed you, written you off as a hysteric, and suspected you of cold-bloodedly setting me up. I've not been sure if you were an innocent victim, an unknowing pawn, or a dangerous lady I should handle with tongs. That's why I've pushed you pretty hard sometimes, one way and another. There's been nothing personal about it,' Kenyon said, adding with a faint smile, 'except a recurrent desire to get your clothes off.'

'So where do we stand now?' Sarah asked.

In the face of those round, bottomless blue eyes, there was only one answer Kenyon could give. 'I like to sit on the fence as long as I can,' he said. 'But the time always comes when you've got to get off, of your own accord, before you're pushed off by events. I'm on your side.'

Sarah extended her hand towards him. 'What's wrong with this ring?' she asked, directly.

Kenyon took her hand, and pulled her on to the bed beside him. She came willingly, and put her arms round him.

'There's nothing wrong with it,' he said. 'I check on everything, but nine times out of ten it means nothing. That ring's one of the nine. Do as Harry asked, and wear it. Apart from that, forget it.'

He did not think she would be able to disentangle that Chinese puzzle of a ring, even if she tried. There was some risk to Sarah, of course. That microfilm was presumably what 'they' were looking for when they searched her flat. On the other hand, Kenyon himself seemed to have replaced Sarah as the centre of their attentions. Besides, it was only for a few hours. Kenyon knew that the case was now too big for a DI to handle. Detective Superintendent Pinder would decide what to do, once the microfilm had been blown up, and they knew what it contained.

Sarah seemed reassured. Her fingers caressed his naked back.

'I said last night,' she murmured, 'that you'd have to tell me what to do. You didn't.'

'Do what any innocent civil servant would do, who'd got caught up in a thing like this,' Kenyon said. 'Go to Lance Everitt. Tell him that the man on the phone had told you to ask for me to handle the case in person, and now my car's been blown up, you want to know what it's about. I think I can guess what he'll say, but I'll be interested to know.'

'What will you be doing today?' Sarah asked.

'Getting my balls chewed off,' Kenyon said.

'I don't think I approve of that,' Sarah said.

Nothing was going to stop the storm of Pinder's anger, and Kenyon stood in the Superintendent's office, waiting for the verbal battering to come to an end. Pinder's voice was raised well above its normal growl, but Kenyon did not bother to take in every word, although the occasional peaks succeeded in penetrating his mind.

'. . . no bloody right to slope off without a word . . . every man in this station worked half the night except you . . . and it was your bloody car, for Christ's sake . . . you know better than that . . . the Commander was here, asking to see you . . . I had to tell him a pack of bloody lies . . . you finally condescend to turn up at bloody noon, with a week's growth of bloody beard . . .'

It was 10.15 am, and Kenyon had not succeeded in getting to the wash room to shave, before being intercepted. But he did not think it tactful to correct Pinder, who was prone to hyperbole, when annoyed, and disliked being interrupted at the best of times.

There was much more concerning Kenyon's failings, but in the end, the storm blew itself out. Kenyon prepared himself for his turn. He was, in fact, quite pleased with himself. He was obviously the only one with a genuine lead, which would account for the explosion. He said as much, by way of a beginning.

Pinder interrupted. 'We know who planted the bomb.'

Kenyon stared at him. 'Who?'

'It was in the papers this morning, for Christ's sake. Can't you read?'

Kenyon brushed that aside. 'The Press Office don't know their arses from their elbows. The explosion had none of the hallmarks of any terrorist organization.'

'Do you know better than the bloody Bomb Squad?' Pinder enquired, dangerously. 'The Press Office didn't invent this morning's news story out of thin air. A lot of men worked all night – unlike you – to establish exactly what happened. That's what was printed.'

Kenyon had developed a sense of unease. Pinder was by no means the trampling bull which he sometimes appeared. That was a useful act, which he also happened to enjoy. Underneath the pose, was a shrewd, experienced and able detective. Anyone as good as Pinder had an open mind, or he would never have got there. It was not like him to be unwilling to question a conclusion.

Kenyon decided to play his cards in a different order, just in case. He showed Pinder the scrap of photograph. He related how he had deliberately left his briefcase in Sarah's flat. That something was missing. He drew the conclusion that it was because of this that his car was blown up.

'What was in there?' Pinder asked.

'Report forms on the Sarah Brooks case.'

'I distinctly told you that nothing was to be put in writing,' Pinder said, in a deadly voice.

'Well, it wasn't really, sir. It was bait. I wanted to see what they'd do, if anything. I must admit, I didn't expect them to go quite so far. Anyway, I took an extra carbon copy.'

Kenyon handed the copy to Pinder, who read it in silence.

The Report Form was light on facts, since Kenyon did not have too many at his disposal at the time, but heavy on innuendo. The reader would glean that Sarah Brooks possessed valuable information, although she was not aware of it. That the signatory ('Sidney Kenyon, Detective Inspector') had drawn certain conclusions as to what this information might be. That Sarah Brooks was being kept under observation by unknown persons. That an American diplomat, Harry Coleman, was involved. That the case was one of the utmost seriousness, with a recommendation that it should be handled at the highest level. That the writer would prefer to commit no more to paper, but requested the opportunity to report verbally to Scotland Yard, as soon as a copy had been forwarded to them.

Pinder looked up. 'How much of this is fact, and how much is fiction?' he asked.

'Well, quite a lot's guesswork,' Kenyon admitted. 'But it did the trick.'

'How do you mean?'

'They tried to kill me, sir,' Kenyon said. He felt that he was banging his head against a brick wall, and Pinder was not that thick.

'Look,' Pinder said, patiently, 'there are people in and out of that blasted car yard all the time. We even get members of the public trying to use it as a bloody car park. Someone slipped in and wired up a car at random. We're still trying to trace and interview any unauthorized persons who entered the yard yesterday.'

'The car wasn't chosen at random, sir,' Kenyon said. 'It was mine.'

'Well, dammit,' Pinder said, 'if they were going to do it, it had to be somebody's.'

' I see,' Kenyon said. ' Coincidence.'

' I can quite understand you thinking there was some connection,' Pinder said, generously. ' But in the light of the Bomb Squad's report . . .' he shrugged.

Kenyon had never felt so alone before in his life. He had been led by the nose into Sarah Brooks' life on someone's orders. He had been used. He had been set up. And now they were doing a snow job. He was being fixed. Kenyon did not imagine that it was Pinder himself who was doing the fixing. Pinder was doing as he was told. How high up did this thing go? Loyalty in the Police Force was strong. Pinder would not like doing this, it would be against all his instincts. Someone with a lot of weight must have leaned on him hard. All for one lonely DI who had kept his nose to the ground and sniffed around a bit.

Kenyon considered himself to be something of a nonconformist, but he knew that, in fact, the latitude he gave himself was relatively slight. The police were a disciplined force and, as such, were necessarily conformist. A man could take a flier, as Kenyon often did, but if he wanted to stay a copper he remained within the boundaries, even if he winked at the rules. For the first time, Kenyon felt genuine rebellion. He did not like being pushed around, he did not like being told nothing, he did not like being conned. Right, he thought, if they're going to play it that bloody way, so will I.

The spare carbon copy of the report form was lying on Pinder's desk.

' What about that, sir?' Kenyon asked.

' I can't accept this unsubstantiated bull,' Pinder said. ' Any copper'd know that.'

' They weren't coppers, sir,' Kenyon said. ' I'll do a fresh one that you can accept, including an account of dummy documents being stolen from my briefcase.'

' Don't bother,' Pinder said. ' I'll assign the case to someone else. He can do it.'

Kenyon stared at him. ' Do you mean I'm being taken off it?'

' No, of course not,' Pinder said. ' You just won't be handling it any more.'

'Why not?'

'Because you've been transferred,' Pinder said. 'You'll be in Police Orders on Friday.'

For some reason, Kenyon had not been expecting that, although it was obvious, if they wanted to make quite sure.

'Where am I going?'

'Potters Bar,' Pinder said. 'Report for duty on Monday.'

'Potters Bar.' Kenyon was appalled. For a moment he forgot that he was being ruthlessly fixed. Bayswater was where the action was, and that was the way he liked it. Potters Bar was the dismal back of beyond as far as Kenyon was concerned.

Pinder launched into a eulogy of Potters Bar. There was plenty of crime in Potters Bar. A different kind of crime perhaps, but a good man like Kenyon could soon make a name for himself. He should be a Chief Inspector within a year or two, and he could easily become a Superintendent by the time he was forty.

'You never know,' Pinder said affably, 'you might come back here, and take over my job. You'll still be a young man. You could make Commander, or Assistant Commissioner in the end, if you're lucky.'

All by the simple process of being transferred to Potters Bar. Kenyon wondered why the exceptional merits of Potters Bar as a launching pad for the highest ranks were not more widely known in the Police Force.

'And you'd better think about moving, too, Sid,' Pinder said. 'You're not a married man. You're liable to be there for three or four years. You'll find it a hell of a drag travelling from Gloucester Terrace to Potters Bar every day.'

'I suppose so, sir,' Kenyon said, diplomatically.

They were really pushing it, he thought. They wanted him out of the area, and well away from Sarah Brooks. Well, they could transfer him with the stroke of a pen, but even the Police Force could not dictate where he lived, so long as he did his job.

'Is that all, sir?' he asked.

'Except for a word in your ear, Sid,' Pinder said. 'The Sarah Brooks case. Drop it. That's from me to you, as a friend. But it's official as well. Got it?'

'Yes, sir,' Kenyon said.

Like hell, I'll drop it, he thought. Kenyon knew more than they thought he did, and he could guess at some of the possible implications. Apart from being offended at the treatment he had received, his professional pride came into it too. He did not like abandoning a job which was only half completed. And there was Sarah Brooks as well.

Kenyon found Mallory, and briefed him on outstanding cases so that Mallory could cope until the new DI took over. Mallory's manner was a little too natural and normal to be true. The word had got around that Kenyon had been banished to the sticks, and everyone supposed that he had put up some sort of black, although they did not know what it was.

Mallory did some gentle probing, over a drink in the pub, but Kenyon did not enlighten him. Sometime, perhaps, he would need a man he could trust implicitly, but he did not think Mallory qualified.

'I suppose you'll be going to Mike's funeral,' Mallory said, changing the subject.

'What are they burying? Odds and ends?' Kenyon asked curtly.

There were a few things Kenyon wanted to do that afternoon. He went to his insurance company, and reported the destruction of his car. It would be a while before they paid out the write-off value. Kenyon wondered whether to buy another car at once, but decided against it. He had enough money in the bank to get something reasonable, even if not the Volvo he wanted, but he thought he would rather continue to hire a car.

It was by no means certain that 'they' would not have another go, and self-drive cars could be changed frequently and without question. He would rather not be driving a car, for the time being, which anyone could get to know. He was not sure if someone in a Ford Escort was following him, or not. He tried a couple of quick back doubles, just in case. The Escort did not reappear.

He drove to a firm in Holborn, and paid to have the microfilm blown up. They were doing this sort of thing all the time, and Kenyon knew they would not even bother to glance at whatever was on it. He took the large envelope to his car, and read the result. There were several typewritten pages, double spaced. He decided that a quick glance like this was no use, and left it for more careful study later.

A traffic warden strolled by. Kenyon smoked a cigarette, and when the man did not reappear, got out and fed the meter. He did not fancy his chances of parking near Chancery Lane. It would be simpler to walk.

Claythorpe's was a firm of valuers. Kenyon went in, and made some enquiries on behalf of an elderly relative, who lived abroad. Yes, indeed, they would be glad to assist. Including investments, and jewellery? Kenyon enquired. Of course. And yes, indeed, their valuations were accepted by the revenue departments of most Western countries.

The office was a small one, and Kenyon spun out the conversation, while he tried to check the staff. There appeared to be three men and a girl, as far as he could tell. He wondered if the whole firm was a front, but if it was, it appeared to be in a legitimate way of business. More likely, just one of the staff was a plant. That pyramid ring was very distinctive. If it were brought in for valuation, someone who knew the trick could get that microfilm out much faster than Kenyon had been able to do. But what was supposed to happen to it then?

Kenyon was outside, and had turned up Chancery Lane, when sweat suddenly broke out on his forehead. What if one of those three men were Mr 'Evans'? Any one of them would fit the loose description which the caretaker had given Kenyon. And 'Evans' knew Kenyon, and had photographed him.

Kenyon did some fast walking, and took a circuitous route back to Holborn, frequently crossing, and recrossing the road. But no one was following him after all.

Kenyon got in his car. At first, he was relieved. But of course, there was no need to follow him. They probably knew where he lived. They knew where to find him. Kenyon cursed himself. If anyone in Claythorpe's had recognized him, they would guess from his presence that he knew about the microfilm. He could have blown the whole thing. However, the odds were that he was worried about nothing. There had been no flicker of recognition from any of them, and Kenyon was good at spotting such tiny symptoms.

Kenyon was beginning to appreciate how a villain on the run must feel, not knowing who was liable to turn into an informer or a plain clothes policeman – the isolation, the feeling that nowhere was safe – and Kenyon did not like it at all. He was used to being one of the hunters, not the hunted.

He picked Sarah up at the Foreign Office when she finished work. It was rush hour, and they had plenty of time to talk during the intermittent traffic jams. Christmas displays were appearing in shop windows. Winking lights on Xmas trees, and jolly cut-out Santa Clauses attempted to impose the appropriate spirit for the forthcoming festive season.

'What did Lance Everitt have to say for himself?' Kenyon asked.

'He was full of apologies,' Sarah said. 'He already knew the general drift, of course, from your phone call to him last night. He said that he'd checked at once . . .'

'Who with?'

'A higher level. That's all he said. Had it been the case, he said, that one of his staff – meaning me – had become involved in any way in causing a man's death, he would have demanded the strongest possible action.'

Jesus Christ, Kenyon thought, they dish out the same meaningless jargon, whether it's missing paper clips or a man's death.

'Happily,' Sarah went on, 'he said he was able to reassure me. There was indisputable technical evidence that the bomb was planted by a terrorist organization, in which case it could foreshadow a change in their methods. The stilted language isn't mine,' Sarah apologized. 'I'm trying to quote him word for word.'

'I gathered,' Kenyon said. He quite liked that bit about a change in method. Everitt had been more subtle than Pinder. When it came to really high-class hypocrisy, you could not beat a top civil servant from Eton and Oxford.

The traffic lights in front of them had changed twice, but a bus was broadside on across Kenyon's bonnet, and he could not move.

He looked at Sarah. The street lights shadowed her face, and he thought he could detect a bruise on her left cheek. He could also detect uncertainty in her face.

'It wasn't terrorists,' he said. 'That bomb needed an electrical device to trigger the explosion when the car was started. It's conceivable they might try it, if they were after a particular man, but why me? I haven't done anything to them.'

'Mr Everitt said you'd taken part in a number of raids on suspected premises. He thought you'd become known to them, and they'd chosen you for retaliation.'

'The next thing you know,' Kenyon said, 'there'll be a phoney claim planted in the press.'

This proved to be an accurate prediction. That afternoon, the *Daily Mirror* received an anonymous phone call from a man who used the appropriate codewords, and said that the terrorists intended the bomb as a lesson to the London Police. Convinced by the codewords, the *Daily Mirror* published the claim, having checked with their contacts at Special Branch. It did not occur to them, although it occurred to Kenyon, that Special Branch, and some of the informants they used, knew those codewords perfectly well and a man willing to make one phone call for perhaps fifty pounds, was not exactly the hardest thing in the world to lay your hands on.

'You can't be absolutely certain though,' Sarah said, doubtfully.

The bus in front of them finally made its exit into the road to their left, and Kenyon managed to get across the lights on the amber. The road ahead was reasonably clear.

'It's a cooked-up cover story,' Kenyon said. 'They don't believe it. I've been taken off your case, and transferred to Potters Bar.'

'Oh.' Sarah seemed put out.

He dropped her outside Cleeve Court, and explained that he had some work to do at his flat, and would call her later. Sarah said that she would get a meal ready.

Kenyon switched his electric fire on, gave himself a whisky, and read Harry Coleman's document slowly and carefully, three times. He wound paper in his typewriter, and copied the document. Like most policemen, he was a self-taught typist, and used only his two forefingers on the keys. The uneven result would have horrified a trained touch typist, but Kenyon was accurate and that was all he cared about.

That gave him the microfilm itself, and two copies. He should be able to make sure that one of them was in a safe place against any contingency, although he grappled for some time as to how to achieve it. His flat would not do. It was small; under the fitted carpet the floor was of concrete. And they seemed to be good at searching flats.

Tomorrow he could make arrangements, although he was still not sure what. Neither his bank nor his solicitor would serve. Among the things which Kenyon did not know was just who thought he was so damned important. If it were the British, any safe deposit could be winkled out and never mind the so called legalities. If it were the Americans, they could lean on the British to achieve the same result. If it were someone else, then he ought to have friends somewhere, but Kenyon thought they seemed to be bloody few on the ground so far.

Still, that was tomorrow. Tonight was the problem. Kenyon wanted them dispersed, just in case. He decided against posting anything to himself or Sarah. Nothing was easier than to intercept a person's mail. In the end, although not too happily, Kenyon used a coffee table book on cars, which had been an unwanted Christmas present once, and which he had always meant to get rid of. Carefully he unstuck the glossy cover, slipped in the photocopies, and sealed the cover again. He thought it looked pretty good, and he replaced the book where it always lay.

He considered the idea of repotting one of the dilapidated plants on his patio, and hiding the microfilm in the soil, but rejected it at once. Any good professional would spot that the soil had been recently disturbed. It occurred to him that Sarah's flat had already been searched. But they might go back. He forgot that one. In the end, as a temporary measure, he took tobacco from a cigarette, inserted the micro-film and tamped the tobacco back again. He spoilt four cigarettes before he was finally satisfied with the end result. He put the cigarette in a packet. He hoped he would remember and not light the damn thing.

The typewritten copy he placed in a sealed, stamped envelope and addressed it to his father in Saffron Walden. He had no intention of posting it unless he was obliged to, but if his father, who had lived alone since his mother died, ever received it, he would read the brief, handwritten note inside and hold the document without telling anyone. He could at least trust his father, Kenyon thought. But since he was a retired taxi driver, growing old and slow, his usefulness was limited.

It was nine o'clock before Kenyon finished what he recognized were decidedly rough and rudimentary precautions. He was not used to being without the back-up which the Police Force provided. It made him feel very exposed. He dialled Sarah's number.

'Hullo,' she said. 'I'd practically given you up. I thought you'd changed your mind.'

Her voice was clear. She sounded as close to him as though she were standing beside him.

'I promised to come and have a farewell meal with you,' Kenyon said.

There was a brief pause. 'Is that what it is,' she said. The warmth had gone from her voice.

'I'm being transferred,' Kenyon said. 'I've got a lot to do. I don't suppose I shall be able to see you much after tonight. Be round in ten minutes.'

He hung up before she said anything else which could be studied when the tape was played back.

All CID officers were paranoid about their private telephones being tapped. They never knew when it was going to happen, or why. It could be some totally unjustified allegation which was being investigated. They would not be told. So men like Kenyon were always alert to the possibility, and made every phone call with instinctive wariness and caution.

Sarah's lips were compressed. She was not in the least pleased to see him. 'I'm surprised you bothered to come at all,' she said.

'There's a tap on my phone,' Kenyon said. 'Call one of your friends, and have a chat. It doesn't matter who.' She stared at him. 'Jesus Christ,' Kenyon said, 'will you do as I ask, without looking at me as if I've gone potty?'

Lucille was surprised to hear from Sarah after so long, but only too willing to bring her up to date. Kenyon put his ear to the phone, listened to Lucille's chatter briefly, and then sat down and smoked until Sarah promised faithfully to keep in touch this time, and hung up.

'There's a tap on yours as well,' Kenyon said. 'Did you hear that pristine, crystal clarity? You won't get any trouble with it going out of order either. Some bastard'll be poised to fix it in no time flat.'

There had been the normal static like noises when he spoke to Everitt last night. They must have slapped a tap on both phones today.

Kenyon tried to shake off the feeling of helpless, growing depression. He was going to need to make phone calls. The police station was no good. He loathed public telephone boxes which were even more unreliable anyway. The sods are closing in from all sides, he thought. Well, tomorrow, he would try a counter attack.

'Come on, let's eat, and to hell with them,' he said.

He enjoyed the stew which Sarah took out of the oven, and finished his meal before putting something to her. 'Officially, I'm off the case,' he said. 'But someone's been screwing me, and before I've finished I'd like to return the compliment. You can step out now, if you want to. It might be the most sensible thing. I can't swing any weight any more. I'm just trouble.'

'I'd as soon see it through,' Sarah said. 'Provide moral support at least. There's nothing I can do.'

'Do you have any leave you can take?'

'Yes. There's some owing to me.'

'Arrange to take it as from Monday, that's what you can do. Give the impression you're going away.'

'Where am I supposed to be going?'

'Christ knows,' Kenyon said. 'Away from tapped telephones.'

Sarah seemed to take it for granted that he would be staying the night, and Kenyon had no wish to be anywhere else.

This lousy situation had its compensations, he thought, as he climbed into bed beside her. Very pleasant compensations they were, too.

9

In the morning, Kenyon took his self-drive car back, and complained of lack of power. He was given another one. He drove to Hyde Park underground car park, found a space and parked. He sat in the huge, shadowy cavern for ten minutes, watching people arrive and go. Satisfied, he used a screwdriver, taking care that he did not attract any attention.

Then he walked across the park to Queen Anne's Gate. No one followed him. He filled in a form at reception, and waited. There was some discussion behind a glass screen, and the head porter came back with his form.

'I'm afraid you're under a misapprehension, sir,' the head porter said. 'There's no Mr Tom Bradley here.'

'Try sending it up to the first floor,' Kenyon advised. 'They'll know.'

The head porter pursed his lips, and shook his head. 'No, sir. I've checked our personnel list to make quite sure. You must have the wrong building, sir,' the head porter said. 'People often make that mistake. Try three doors along.'

Kenyon snatched the form back. 'Give me an envelope,' he said wearily.

Using a fibre tipped pen, he wrote JENNY ABEL in block capitals across the form, sealed it inside the envelope, and addressed the envelope to Tom Bradley.

'Give him that,' he said.

'I can't sir,' the head porter said. 'We've no Mr Bradley here.'

'I'll be back in half an hour,' Kenyon said.

He walked to the nearest pub, bought a large Scotch, sat down, and lit a cigarette. A tall, well dressed man of about forty crossed to his table, and said, politely, in a New England accent, 'Would you mind if I joined you, sir?'

'Since you've just followed me from Queen Anne's Gate,' Kenyon said, 'I don't see why not.'

The American smiled ruefully, and pulled up a chair.

'You wouldn't be Harry Coleman's assistant, by any chance?' Kenyon enquired.

'No, Mr Kenyon,' the American said. 'My name is Mark Fisher. How do you do, sir.'

He extended a friendly hand. Kenyon ignored it. 'Let's cut out the time wasting crap,' he said. 'Just tell me where you fit in.'

Mark Fisher said, 'You worried Mrs Coleman, you know. She couldn't understand why you should make a transatlantic call over a traffic accident. The Embassy knew it was official of course, since you also contacted them, but they were somewhat surprised when they didn't hear from you again.'

'We now know that Mr Coleman wouldn't be able to assist us after all,' Kenyon said.

'Someone claiming to be a police officer gained access to Mr Coleman's apartment,' Mark Fisher said. He gave Kenyon a friendly smile. 'The man concerned could not have been genuine, naturally. A real policeman would have known that he needed a search warrant.'

'No real copper should be without one,' Kenyon agreed.

Mark Fisher's smile was replaced by a look of soulful sadness. 'If the Embassy chose to lean on Scotland Yard,' he said, 'a real policeman could be busted. It was a mistake for you to become involved, Mr Kenyon.'

'I agree,' Kenyon said. 'My car got blown up, and a nice young fellow was killed. Any inspired guesses on who did that?'

'Some terrorist organization, as I recall,' Mark Fisher said.

'Balls,' Kenyon said. 'Any good hit men in your lot who might have let their enthusiasm run away with them?'

'We don't go around killing friendly allies,' Mark Fisher said.

'Who's we, exactly? Just as a matter of interest?'

Mark Fisher leaned forward, and spoke softly and earnestly. 'Mr Kenyon,' he said, 'this is not something you should be concerned with. It's not your line of country, you don't know what you're doing, and you don't understand what harm you could cause. You've been blundering about,' Mark Fisher went on, an unexpected hardness tightening his clear face, 'digging away, trying to uncover something which, if you succeeded, could do serious damage. I want you to appreciate how important it is that you stop interfering. Please. Think about it carefully, I beg you.'

'I don't have to think about it,' Kenyon said. 'I gave up the moment young Meacher was killed. I've no intention of joining him. I want to know what it's like to grow old.'

Mark Fisher's eyes searched Kenyon's face for a few moments. He appeared to be satisfied, and moved away.

Kenyon had found Fisher's final speech an impressive one. He wondered why he had lied, and not accepted Fisher's good advice.

He waited until Mark Fisher had left, and then walked back to Queen Anne's Gate by a roundabout route. Mark Fisher was not in sight, but someone else was tailing him. He wondered who. He was beginning to find this constant watchfulness exhausting.

This time, he was shown straight to Tom Bradley's office. The same, young, well-educated, armed porter accompanied him along the long corridors.

The form lay on Tom Bradley's desk. Kenyon could see his fibre tipped block capitals, upside down: JENNY ABEL. He was relieved that his guess had been right. It had been little more than a hunch, even though logical.

'Well, Sid,' Tom Bradley said, with a big, friendly grin, 'you're an even better copper than I took you for.'

'I ought to ram your bloody teeth down your bloody throat,' Kenyon said.

'*Mea culpa*,' Bradley said, holding up both hands apologetically. 'Though I'm not sure you could. I might just kick your balls in for you.'

'Commander Bradley,' Kenyon said, 'today you're going to talk straight for a change. For a start, you can drop the act. Stop being one of the lads because you're talking to an ordinary copper. It jars, I find it mildly offensive, and what's worse, it bores me.'

Bradley was put out. His smile went. 'I'm sorry,' he said. 'My apologies. Please sit down.' His accent had reverted to that which he had acquired at Dartmouth, long ago. 'As a matter of fact,' he said, 'I'm not sure you're right. Does a chameleon know what colour he is? Still, I don't mean to patronize you, I can promise you that.' He fingered the block capitals, JENNY ABEL. 'You're the last bugger who'd qualify,' he said with feeling. He grinned slyly. 'Sorry,' he said. 'No condescension intended. It just kind of slips out.'

Kenyon's lips twitched. No matter what, he could not help liking Tom Bradley.

'Who's Mark Fisher?' he asked. 'CIA?'

'Never heard of him,' Bradley said.

'He followed me from here to a pub, and warned me to lay off.'

'Good advice,' Bradley said. 'But I still don't know any Mark Fisher.'

Talking to Tom Bradley was like one of those party games in which any of the participants may lie at will. He could only use his wits to try and pick out truth from half truth from blatant untruth.

Kenyon said, 'Now you can show me Sarah Brooks' real security file.'

Bradley had it ready. He sighed, and handed it over. Kenyon skimmed through it rapidly. Much of it resembled the dummy file he had read before. The principal difference, as he expected, lay in a number of references to Sarah's affair with Harry Coleman.

'Information exchanged with the CIA?' Kenyon asked.

'Some,' Bradley said. 'Not all.'

'In other words, you trust them about as much as they trust you.'

'I'm dying for a drink,' Bradley said. 'Suppose you join me in a snort.'

Bradley took a bottle of whisky from his desk drawer, and poured two drinks while Kenyon read the relevant passages again. At first, the affair had preoccupied security considerably. Sarah had been kept under close observation for six months until Bradley, apparently satisfied, had scribbled and initialled 'No action required.' Thereafter, there were periodic reviews, each ending in a tersely initialled 'No change.' Only recently had the relationship become a big deal. Bradley had authorized an 'urgent and full investigation.'

Kenyon looked up. 'Did your people break into her flat, and search it?'

'No,' Bradley said. 'If we had, it'd be in that file.'

'In my limited experience,' Kenyon said, 'your records are on the patchy side, when it suits you.'

'That's Sarah's file, full and unabridged,' Bradley said. 'I'd swear it on my mother's grave, except that the old girl's fighting fit, and living in Torquay.'

'Supposing you ever had a mother,' Kenyon said. 'If it wasn't your lot, who was it? The CIA?'

'Could be,' Bradley said. 'Anyone like the CIA who think they can make and break governments – and have done what's more – aren't going to worry about keeping me informed, the bastards. But it could have been someone else. I don't know.'

'So you told Sarah to ask for me, by name, and hoped I might put the odd bird up for you.'

'The lady has been telling you things she shouldn't,' Bradley said.

'The lady was impressed when someone tried to blow me up. So was I.'

'No one foresaw that,' Bradley said. 'You shouldn't be so bloody efficient.'

'And what damn fool shoved that story in the *Daily Mirror*?' Kenyon asked, digressing for a moment.

'A keen type who got carried away,' Bradley said, apologetically. 'The silly bugger's been dealt with.'

'Commended and promoted, you mean,' Kenyon said. 'You

fixed Lance Everitt, you fixed Scotland Yard, you arranged for the Bomb Squad to lie in their teeth. Is there anyone you can't fix?'

'Provided they're of British nationality, not a great many,' Bradley admitted, modestly.

'Including me,' Kenyon said. 'Right? You put me together with Sarah. But only after Jenny Abel had been murdered.'

He pointed at the girl's name, in block capitals, and waited. Bradley sucked on his pipe, and produced a cloud of smoke.

'You know, Sid,' he reflected, 'I don't have to tell you a damn thing.'

'You're going to tell me anything I want to know,' Kenyon said.

Bradley's crinkled, friendly eyes were, Kenyon appreciated, those of a cold and heartless professional. Well, he thought, that makes two of us. Let's see what happens.

'You're not dealing with some villain in the detention room at Bayswater, Sid,' Bradley said. 'You're playing away from home where you don't know the rules. I could have you framed and broken, no trouble at all. I shan't, of course,' he added, gently, 'but I could.'

'I'm a bit pissed off with the Police Force, Commander Bradley,' Kenyon said. 'Or may I call you Tom?' Bradley nodded, warily. 'I don't like being chucked out to Potters Bar. I'm thinking of resigning.'

'Never cut off your nose to spite your face,' Bradley advised.

'I'm the sort of bloody-minded idiot who's liable to do that,' Kenyon said. 'I'm sore, Tom. Sore with you, for one. But if I resigned, I'd need to make a few quid. I've learned quite a lot, thanks to you. I think it would be quite a good story to sell to the newspapers, don't you?'

'Forget it,' Bradley said promptly. 'Any paper daft enough to deal with you would have a D notice slapped on them before they could turn round.'

'What a blessing it is to have a free press,' Kenyon sighed.

'We only intervene when security's at stake,' Bradley said. 'Don't be naive, Sid. You can't blackmail me that way.'

'You're a high-powered fellow,' Kenyon said. 'It's quite possible you really don't understand how many people a working DI like me gets to know. Apart from journalists and television producers in this country . . .'

'Forget TV too,' Bradley said. 'They know what a hot potato is.'

'You have a tendency to interrupt, Tom, if I may say so,' Kenyon said. 'I also know some American, Canadian and German reporters. I think they'd be interested in a really hard, knocking piece, which it would be. OK, you could stop it being reprinted in this country. But even you have superiors, Tom. I wonder if they'd like it? Or if you'd find your arse full of tintacks all of a sudden.'

Bradley knocked his pipe out, giving the operation his intent attention. Half a minute later, he said, 'I don't think you really know very much.'

'Which gives me plenty of room to embroider,' Kenyon said. 'Come on. It's a great yarn. How I was set up by the mysterious Tom Bradley, who was therefore responsible for Detective Constable Meacher's death.' Bradley winced. 'I describe his office. Where he operates. Chuck in a beautiful lady and an American diplomat. Mix, boil, strain, casserole, and you're cooked, Tom.'

'You're the sort of man who's a copper in his cradle,' Bradley said. 'You wouldn't resign.'

'Listen,' Kenyon said. 'I've had you and everything you're mixed up in, right up to here. I was lucky, and Meacher wasn't but I should be dead. I take that personally. Don't push me any more, Thomas. If you go on being clever, I'll screw you any way I can.'

'Deep down, you're a savage, nasty bugger, aren't you,' Bradley said.

'We're brothers under the skin,' Kenyon said. 'Jenny Abel. And try not to lie too much. I can probably guess enough to trip you up anyway.'

'Well,' Bradley said, cautiously, 'the lady was known to us, in a way.' He wagged his dead pipe apologetically. 'There are things I can't tell you, Sid. You must know that.'

'I didn't make myself clear,' Kenyon said. 'You owe me half an hour off the record. I'm calling in that debt. Otherwise, I'll create the biggest stink that's ever clogged your nostrils. I'll throw all the shit in the fan I can. Maybe it would do me a lot of no good, but you've got more to lose. There wouldn't be any smell of roses around this office, and I think you'd be junked and disowned. I could be wrong, but that's my gamble.'

'I think you could be bluffing,' Bradley said.

'That's your gamble,' Kenyon said.

He wondered if he would really do it. He thought he would. He was feeling peevish and vindictive.

It was possible that Bradley was telepathic, or, more likely, simply highly perceptive. At any rate, he partially succumbed. 'You're probably right, Sid,' he said. 'I do owe you. But after this, we're even. In fact, you'll be overdrawn, in my book. And if you make a nuisance of yourself again, if you cross me, if I even see you around, I'll have you. I think that's a fair bargain.'

'You would,' Kenyon said. 'But I'm on the side of the angels, because my heart is pure. How's yours?'

'I'm more concerned about my liver,' Bradley said. He poured two more generous whiskies, which emptied the bottle. He threw it into a wastepaper basket. 'Jenny Abel,' he said, 'was one of ours.' He glanced at the girl's printed name on the form. 'Which I presume is no great surprise to you.'

'Just keep talking,' Kenyon said. He had not been sure, in point of fact, whether Jenny Abel had been one of 'ours' or one of 'theirs'. She had to be one or the other.

'Not a very important lady,' Bradley said. 'Just one of those people we have around at various levels. I never even met her. She'd worked at various clubs. Some people from Eastern Europe – trade delegates, diplomats, even KGB men – find London night life exciting, Christ knows why. Also lovely coloured ladies. She'd come up with a few interesting items. Sometimes from drunken indiscretions, sometimes from wallets and briefcases. She was a good whore.'

'Winston Peters thought she was a good girl gone wrong,' Kenyon said.

'Winston Peters was a harmless ponce,' Bradley said, 'who thought with his prick. He was part of Jenny's cover, and I expect his cerebral activity was a bonus. At the time of her death Jenny had been asked to be alert for information which might be related to a certain matter. She wasn't selected in any way. All the troops had the same message. None of them knew what it was really about. Very few people did know. Or do now,' Bradley added.

'Harry Coleman,' Kenyon shrugged. It figured, in the circumstances, and Bradley did not deny it.

'On the day she died,' Bradley said, 'Jenny telephoned her contact. She said she'd been with someone the night before, and she had something, and documentary evidence to back it. She was excited and pleased with herself. She apologized for not being able to phone before . . .'

'Since Winston Peters had been having jealous fits,' Kenyon said.

'In any case, she couldn't talk on the phone, of course,' Bradley said. 'Her contact made an appointment to meet her, and then she said she had to ring off.'.

'That would be when Winston Peters came out of the bog and found her,' Kenyon said.

The scruffy hall, the pay telephone, the whole layout, were in Kenyon's mind, as clear and accurate as a photograph.

'She didn't keep her appointment,' Bradley said, 'and then we heard the silly bitch had got herself killed. By that time, half the bloody flatfoots in London were swarming all over the place. Jesus, we'd hit a bloody disaster,' Bradley said, with feeling. 'Imagine it. A woman who's been level-headed and accurate in the past, claims to have something. And instead of a nice quiet handover on the top deck of a bus, she's lying dead, and your shower are trampling all over the place, rigging up lights, photographing everything like maniacs, and carting all things portable away for examination and analysis. Including, one assumed, Jenny's piece of information.'

Kenyon laughed. He could not help it.

'It wasn't funny,' Bradley grumbled. 'It was a bloody shambles. We couldn't just move in, there were too many members of the public hanging around, and it would have needed too muc.. explaining. For all we knew, some thick constable was busy filing a titbit I was dying to get my hands on. I knew you were the officer in charge of the case, and in the middle of trying to arrange a salvage job, Lance Everitt phoned to say that Sarah Brooks' flat had been broken into. I decided to see that you got that case as well.'

'Because you suspected there was a connection,' Kenyon said. 'Also, it put the same copper handling both cases, and on the same rein.'

'That rein's proved bloody slack in your case,' Bradley complained.

'We weren't positive about the connection, but I thought you might turn it up, if there was one. We thought we'd need to get close to you at some time. If Jenny had something in writing, you had it, or perhaps Winston Peters, and you hadn't arrested him when I told Sarah Brooks what to do. We needed that bit of paper, and we needed to talk to Winston Peters. He might know who Jenny had been with the night before, and he might have told you.'

'A white man with a beard,' Kenyon put in. 'That's all he said.'

'I know,' Bradley said. 'I read his statement. But before we could get to him, he hanged himself.'

'Are you quite sure Winston Peters wasn't a plant?' Kenyon asked. 'Someone might have had him killed.' Including you, he thought. You could gain access to police cells, no trouble at all. Kenyon was only buying with caution.

Bradley shook his head. 'That seemed only too likely,' he said. 'And we gave the history of Winston Peters the works. By the time they buried him, I knew more about him than his mother did. No, the silly bugger really did hang himself.'

Kenyon thought that Bradley's annoyance sounded genuine. He was irritated that Winston Peters had been so inconsiderate as to take his own life before he could be grilled about important matters. Not about Jenny's murder, but about who she had slept with the night before.

'And no piece of paper turned up,' Bradley said. 'It should have been in Bayswater Police Station, and it wasn't.'

'That's not what the bloody Flying Squad were doing there?' Kenyon enquired, remembering those registration numbers, which he was always on the look out for.

'We borrowed a couple of their cars a few times,' Bradley admitted. He studied Kenyon speculatively.

'And made enquiries at the club, and shoved adverts in the *Evening Standard*,' Kenyon said. 'You wanted to know who Jenny had been with.'

'You ignore the book, when it suits you,' Bradley said. 'I suppose you didn't pop some interesting bit of paper in your pocket, on the off chance, and forgot to mention it?'

'No,' Kenyon said truthfully. 'I had Winston Peters wrapped up in a few hours. I hadn't even met Sarah Brooks then. He was just a spook with a knife, as far as I was concerned. I had no reason to conceal anything. Besides, that's hard to do, when you're part of a team.'

'Yes,' Bradley agreed reluctantly. 'All the paper work double checks. There's nothing that doesn't fit.'

'All right, now for the big question,' Kenyon said. 'Who tried to kill me?'

'I don't know,' Bradley said. 'As far as I was concerned, half your usefulness had gone, once we drew a blank with Jenny Abel. You seemed to be sniffing around like a diligent hound dog, using your friend Steve Rimmer from Special Branch, and so on. You were on the wrong track, but you might find the right one and it seemed worth leaving you alone. Then you pulled that daft stunt with the fake report form.'

'Someone didn't think it was daft,' Kenyon said. Meacher's mangled remnants testified to that.

'You frightened somebody,' Bradley agreed, 'but you hadn't turned up anything we didn't know already. People who run the risk of being murdered in this game, should be volunteers. There was no point in risking your life, for no end result.'

'Thank you,' Kenyon said. He noted the qualification.

'Best to have you pulled off,' Bradley said, 'and transferred to somewhere safer, like Potters Bar. Since the bomb, someone's been supposed to guard you, but if you will lose every tail that's slapped on you, that's your look-out.'

'I always assume that anyone following me is not well disposed,' Kenyon said.

'Well, I've gone through the motions,' Bradley said. 'I've got more things to worry about than your personal safety.'

There was a long silence. There were signs of strain in the network of tiny lines, at the corners of Bradley's eyes. Eventually, he sighed. 'And that's it,' he said. 'I'm sorry you were used. It was a hasty decision which didn't work out. I'm also very sorry about your young colleague. I wish I could say that it served some purpose, but I'm afraid it didn't.'

'Harry Coleman,' Kenyon said. 'A rich American diplomat, who takes part in disarmament talks. Why does he frighten you?'

'High-class amateurs always frighten me,' Bradley said. 'They're unpredictable. No one ever quite knows what they're up to.'

'The CIA should know,' Kenyon said.

'If they do, they're not saying.' Bradley gestured at a map of Europe which hung on the wall. 'The Eastern bloc and NATO,' he said, 'with certain neutrals like Sweden, Switzerland and Austria. At the bread and butter level, it's a perfectly simple situation, as far as I'm concerned. They have people here, and we have people there. Some do it because they're paid, some do it from so called principles or idealism, some do it because they're mad. We nail theirs, if we can, or feed them false information. When they nail ours, we make sure the press carry indignant stories about innocent men and women being arrested. We sift the information we get back, and try and work out what might be true, and how much is misleading bull, which they're feeding back to us. Now, that's good straightforward work and doesn't keep anyone awake at nights. We all know what we're doing, we all know the rules, we can all behave like perfect gentlemen and lie our heads off. But a man like Harry Coleman, intelligent, literate, honest, and upright worries the shit out of me. He's liable to get bright ideas. He's liable to think he's the only one who can achieve some messianic purpose. What's worst, he's liable to keep it to himself.'

Bradley fell into a brooding silence. Kenyon considered prompting him, but decided against it. He had the feeling that Bradley was quite glad to get some of his frustrations off his chest.

At last, Bradley stirred, and looked at Kenyon. 'You know the situation,' he said. 'A blind man could see it, although I sometimes think we now live in a country of the blind. We worry about inflation, the cost of holidays abroad, pensions, and raising the standard of living. We cut down on the armed forces, and any politician who was lunatic enough to talk about re-introducing conscription would be hounded out of office, although even neutral Sweden has it. The West has got fat, and it likes it. No one chooses to remember that the fat boy at school was in no shape to defend himself. The politicians clutch at detente. It's the magic word. OK, I'm all for giving it a try, but I like to keep an eye on what the other fellow's doing.' Bradley waved vaguely at the map. 'Europe. NATO and the Eastern bloc. While we negotiate about detente, we cut down, and they don't. They build the biggest submarine fleet the world has ever seen. They outnumber us four or five to one in guns and tanks and planes, and three to one in fighting men. While the talking goes on, they go on building up their armaments, which are already vastly superior to ours. Me, I may be a nasty suspicious bugger, but I wonder why. In effect, they're on the borders of West Germany. They could sweep across Europe and reach the Channel within seven days any time they wanted to, and we couldn't do a damn thing about it. I'm not at all sure there'd be much fighting. We'd be too busy trying to pull back, and every well-meaning world figure from the Pope to the Secretary General of the United Nations would be calling for a cease fire. There'd be a cease fire all right, in seven days flat.'

'The Americans are supposed to intervene with their hydrogen bombs,' Kenyon said. He had listened to Bradley, fascinated. Kenyon was not a political animal. He was too busy trying to deal with the enemies he came across in his job – the rapists, the murderers, the thieves – to devote overmuch time to international affairs. He had once attended a conference at Stockholm, where the Russian police were present as observers. He remembered discussing the problem of drug addiction with the Russians over a long and alcoholic meal in a restaurant one night. The Russians seemed very concerned about drugs. Later they had swapped stories, as among fellow professionals, about robberies, and multiple murders, and clever frauds. Kenyon had come away feeling that he had a lot in common with the Russians. He supposed that the pros in any trade, in any country, had a lot in common.

'We've lived under the so called nuclear umbrella since the Second World War,' Bradley said. 'But times have changed. History's moved on, although it's more comfortable to believe that it's magically come to a stop. That kind of blackmail worked over Cuba, but since then the Russians have achieved superiority in missiles as well. Europe doesn't seem inclined to defend itself. I wonder if the Americans would really start exchanging thermonuclear missiles with Russia, and commit national suicide because we'd rather have our welfare services than enough tanks? I know I wouldn't, so why should I expect them to? Fortress America, in one form or another, has its attractions if you happen to be American. Do they really owe us the destruction of all their cities? Doesn't it make more sense to do a deal with the only other world power that matters yet? We think Europe's so bloody vital only because we live here. We worry about regulations being imposed on us from Brussels and forget that laws could be imposed on us from Moscow. We're proud of our standard of living as compared with the Russians, and ignore the fact that they could supply their people with all the refrigerators and colour television sets they liked, except they prefer missiles, Mach 2 fighters, nuclear submarines, and tanks that outgun ours. Europe has no special immunity, and from a satellite you can't see any frontiers. It's simply a land mass containing good farmland, and a highly concentrated area of efficient units of industrial production. It can be defended, absorbed, or bargained away. We may act like the chosen people, but we're not. There are bigger boys than us, and they might decide to do a swap.'

'You make it sound a pretty gloomy prospect,' Kenyon said.

'Most of recorded history,' Bradley said, 'has been mostly unpleasant, for most people, for most of the time. We bend our energies now to making life more pleasant for more people, which is legitimate enough provided you don't ignore the simple truth that dogs who can't bite get bitten themselves. If you believe that within the last few years – the blink of an eyelid in human history – we've acquired so much wisdom and forbearance that, suddenly, it's all different, then you may conceivably be right, but you're an optimist. Me, I'm a pessimist. I think we live in a dangerous world, and what we can't defend, we lose. There is no idealism in me, by the way,' Bradley said wryly, 'as you may have gathered. I'm not talking about the superiority, or other-wise, of one social system over another. I'd make a perfectly good senior KGB officer, and I know it. I'm talking about simple, crude, brutal power politics.'

Kenyon sat there, thinking. There was no mention in Harry Coleman's document of the possibility of a military invasion of Europe. He tried to recall the exact phrases used, but Bradley started again and Kenyon concentrated on what he was say-ing.

He had no intention of telling Bradley about the document. Bradley's interest in world affairs seemed to express itself in practice at a much lower level, where Kenyon was pushed around and fixed, and Meacher was blown to bits. Kenyon intended to use Bradley, if he could, for his own personal aims, which were unpleasant and vindictive. He did not think Bradley merited much trust even though he generated liking, and Kenyon was not dis-posed to give away the few cards he possessed. This talk with Bradley had been well worthwhile. Kenyon now knew that he did have some cards after all. He did not yet know whether they included any trumps, but he was not about to resign from the game.

'In point of fact,' Bradley said, 'I don't really think that the Russians will invade. They could, and get away with it, and we know it, and that's probably enough. I think they'd rather spend time than lives. They're a patient people and very cautious in some ways. With the exception of Cuba, every move they've made since the war – Hungary, Berlin, Czechoslovakia, the Middle East – has been carefully designed to fall well short of the point of any likely response. If you nibble for long enough, you've no need to take a damn great bite. It's more likely that gradually, and one by one, various countries will acquire governments which will be responsive to Russian pressure and direction. Austria's a possible. So is West Germany, where the reunification thing is a big emotional factor. France came within two per cent of getting a President dependent on Communist Party support. Italy's in trouble, with an inefficient bureaucracy and constant, ruthless bomb outrages, responsibility for which is claimed by a Fascist group which probably doesn't exist, and which leaves their huge Communist Party as the good guys and looking more and more like the only hope for any kind of stable government. Now there's Portugal. As usual the British are more subtle. Everyone's afraid of seeing reds under the bed and being held up to ridicule. Meanwhile, kind and warm-hearted fellow travellers in politics, the unions, and the media, who don't actually know which way they're travelling, work ever more closely with efficient and clear-sighted gentlemen who know perfectly well where they're going. Between them it's just possible they could deliver us without a shot being fired, or a single act of violence, into the delights of a People's Democracy, where I'm sure we'd still have a House of Commons, although the elections might not be quite what we're used to. It could take ten years, twenty years, or thirty years, but if you're prepared to keep working at it, and you believe it's going to happen, why not wait and pluck the fruit without any boring bomb damage, or blown-up factories to repair? The only requirement is that America should not intervene. The Americans don't want to be turned into radioactive ashes. Who does? But perhaps they could be sold a bill of goods which would leave them with a clear conscience.'

'Is that what you think Harry Coleman's doing?' Kenyon asked. 'Agreeing a bill of goods?'

'I don't know,' Bradley said. He held up his fingers and ticked them off one by one. 'He's supposed to have had a quarrel with the Secretary of State. That could have been staged and deliberately leaked. But Washington's like a bloody sieve at the best of times. You never know whether a leak's inspired or not. We thought he'd been posted away from London, but after a happy family holiday he comes back, and promptly disappears. We can't very well demand to know where an allied diplomat is. But we've gone as close as we dared, and all we get are re-assuring noises about private business activities. What we don't get is sight or sound of Harry Coleman.'

'Mark Fisher, the American who warned me off,' Kenyon said. 'If he was CIA, they're worried about something too. He hinted that security was at stake.'

'It depends what you mean by security,' Bradley said, 'and that depends on which capital you park your arse in. Fisher may have been CIA. But he may have been from the Committee for American Security Overseas, CASO. We received a report that Harry Coleman had links with them.'

'What's CASO?' Kenyon asked, never having heard of it.

'At this stage, a semi-private organization.'

'What the hell's a semi-private organization?' Kenyon enquired, baffled by the juxtaposition of words.

'One to which government and private funds go by a circuitous route,' Bradley said. 'The CIA has been pretty much discredited. They've burnt their fingers too often. CASO is using intellectuals, academics, industrialists and diplomats, instead of the beefy red necks who used to go around stirring up revolutions. They may be a big improvement. We'll have to wait and see. But I worry about one thing. The Americans are simple souls at heart. They yearn for simple solutions, like the good guys always being able to outshoot the bad guys against overwhelming odds. I've always found that the bad guys shoot pretty well too, and if there are more of them than there are of you, you're going to end up dead. Anyway, one elegant and refined simple solution that seems to appeal to the Americans is the *fait accompli*. That was the basis of the CIA philosophy, really. If you once got an invasion of Cuba going, even if your government didn't know about it, they'd have to tag along. And they even managed to drag President Kennedy into the Bay of Pigs thing. We don't know enough about CASO yet. We've infiltrated a little, but at too low a level to be much use. Maybe they'll turn out to be just an arm of diplomacy. And maybe they'll be just as wedded to the *fait accompli* for their own high moral purposes as the CIA were. That's what worries me. But then I'm a worrier by nature.'

Bradley got up, and searched a filing cabinet. He found another bottle of whisky and poured two more drinks. He took a good swig. 'I know we're only a minor power these days,' he said, 'but my arse belongs in London, and I like it the way it is. They can change it all after I'm dead. I shan't care then.' He finished the rest of his whisky and poured another. 'I've levelled with you, Sid,' Bradley said, 'partly because you twisted my arm, and partly because I wanted you to know that you've wandered into a big league by mistake. The game's too rough and too important for any one man, no matter how good a DI he is. I'm showing you off the pitch, here and now. I'm not sure how much I've told you that you didn't know already?'

'Not a lot,' Kenyon said. 'I'd guessed at some, but most of it was about right.'

'Then is there anything you know that I don't?' Bradley asked.

'No,' Kenyon said. He held Bradley's cold, assessing eyes for what seemed like hours. Kenyon was a good card player, and as a copper he had bluffed some of the best con men in the business. But Bradley's eyes seemed to excavate his mind.

In the end, Bradley nodded. 'All right, Sid,' he said. 'Nice to have met you. Have a ball at Potters Bar.'

Kenyon was walking along Knightsbridge before he allowed his exhilaration to come to the surface. He stopped, winked at his reflection in one of Harrod's windows, and noted that the man who had strolled along behind him from Queen Anne's Gate paused, and made as if waiting for the traffic to clear before crossing the road. Kenyon did not care about him. The only question was where to sell him a dummy, and lose him.

He felt good. In his mind's eye was that hall and the telephone which Jenny Abel had used, a photographic reproduction of the way he had seen it. And Kenyon knew that now, at last, he was ahead of the game. For the first time, he knew something that those bastards did not know.

10

Kenyon walked into Harrods, took an escalator up two floors, a lift down again, and lost his would-be shadow so easily that he thought he would complain to Bradley about the low boredom threshold and lack of enthusiasm of the man assigned to follow him, and protect him.

A taxi delivered him to the offices of *The Times*, where he asked for and obtained a back copy. He had last seen that back copy tucked behind the pay telephone which Jenny Abel had used to make the last telephone call of her foreshortened life. Kenyon settled down to read with excitement and anticipation. An hour later, depressed, he began again. He had started with the personal ads. Without knowing what he was looking for he had expected that, with the information at his disposal, the connecting item – whatever it was – would leap to his eye and provide the final key. The endless words had done nothing of the kind. Something in that newspaper, or so Kenyon had assumed, had caused an admittedly low-level British agent to make an appointment with her contact. He began to think that he was wrong, that the newspaper had only been destined for emergency use in the lavatory after all.

Kenyon was not under the illusion that he could crack a professional code but he thought he could probably recognize one. Another close study of the personal ads convinced him that he was either overrating himself, or they were as dull and harmless as they seemed. He tried the news pages again, searching for some throwaway item of any conceivable significance, and failed to find it.

He was sitting staring at the open newspaper, and wondering, searching his mind for where he had gone wrong, when he was jolted into the realization that he was not wrong at all. He had been combing for an apparently insignificant message of some kind. But what he wanted was staring him in the face. He had overlooked it because it was too big.

The special feature was over three thousand words long. The heading read: WEST GERMANY LURCHES TO THE RIGHT. A sub-heading stated: ANTI-DEMOCRATIC GROUP READY TO SEIZE POWER.

The article itself was cogent and factual. It related the frightening speed with which members of a neo-Nazi group had gained positions of power, especially in industry and the armed forces. Their aim was the speedy re-unification of West and East Germany, the creation of a Greater Germany which would be a bastion of Western values. The group had lost faith in the normal political processes and regarded the parties in Bonn as corrupt, time-serving, and infiltrated by Marxists. Chancellor Brandt's resignation had been merely the tip of the iceberg. The policy of detente was delivering West Germany into Russian hands. Germany must stand on her own feet and rally her people against the menace from the East. Germany must reassert itself and lead NATO in the defence of civilization. The German people had been misled, but were now deeply uneasy and ready for genuine leadership. There was much more in the same strain about the volunteer crusaders of the Right, and the stark warning they were putting to the world: that, if action were not taken soon, the Communists would seize power in West Germany – using so called democratic methods – which would, in effect, advance the borders of Soviet Russia to the banks of the Rhine. The extent of the activities of this group and the seriousness of their intentions had come to light after the leaders had met in secret to plan their strategy on the Swedish island of Gotland. One of the leaders, intoxicated by prospective power and possibly Aquavit, had said more than he should in an exclusive interview.

The article went on to review in sober terms the imminent

threat to world peace which a resurgent, warlike Germany would present. Soviet and American officials were equally worried, and feared the agreed policy of detente and the limitation of nuclear arms would be seriously damaged, if not destroyed. Cautious hopes were expressed that the political parties in West Germany would recognize the menace and act together against the threat of these aggressive, undemocratic neo-Nazis gaining power. The feature had been written by an agency correspondent in Stockholm, who was not named.

Kenyon wondered if there had been any follow up and skimmed through the next few weeks' issues. There were no more articles, although a certain amount of correspondence had ensued. He found the letters predictable and of little interest. Most were from well known left-wing personalities, in and out of politics, who were universally appalled by this new Nazi threat. Some went on to point out that Germany could drag America and Great Britain into a nuclear war, and called for the peace loving nations of the world to unite against this ghastly prospect. Britain herself should get her priorities right and renounce her nuclear armoury, which was useless anyway, and build more schools and hospitals. America should cease to threaten the East, and recognize where the real danger to peace lay.

A handful of letters from addresses in places like Tunbridge Wells, Gerrards Cross and Bath tried to agree with the dangers of Soviet aggression, while disclaiming the neo-Nazis and their solution, and were pretty half-hearted as a result. But as a debate the correspondence had never really got going, and it had petered out in a few days.

It occurred to Kenyon that the item might have been picked up in the American press, and he visited the London offices of some American newspapers to find out. The reaction over there surprised him. In the USA this authoritative report from a neutral source had been taken very seriously indeed, and much space was devoted to the subject. Liberal commentators and semi-official spokesmen vied in expressing their fears of a German nationalistic revival. Many and various were the kinds of advice urged upon the American and German governments. But by then, he noted, the original feature from Stockholm was never referred to. The debate in the US press had become self-generating, and could be going on yet, for all Kenyon knew.

Kenyon had things to do and he gave up reading the reams of heavy prose after a while. He needed to make a phone call from an untapped telephone, and he thought he might as well do it in comfort, and to hell with the expense.

He took a taxi to the Hilton Hotel in Park Lane, and checked in as Mr Smithers from Portsmouth, explaining that his luggage was on the way. The receptionist was not entirely happy about that, but when Kenyon paid for the room in advance she was reassured. In his room he ordered a large whisky and placed a phone call to Stockholm. The whisky arrived while he was waiting to be connected to Lars Hagner.

Lars Hagner was a detective in the Stockholm police with whom Kenyon had become friendly during the conference there. Lars had introduced him to the Swedish speciality of cold herrings.

'Do you want to eat it the Swedish way?' Lars had enquired.

'Tell me,' Kenyon had said, looking at the herrings and the various sauces into which he was to dip them.

'You take a little piece of herring,' Lars had said, 'dip it into one of the sauces, put it in your mouth. Then you take a sip of Aquavit. If you find that makes your mouth hot, swallow some beer. And then again. And so on. All right?'

It was not only a pleasant dish, but the combination of the fiery liquor and beer, followed by wine later, proved to be a civilized way to get slightly pissed.

During his short stay in Stockholm, Kenyon had abandoned his preconceived notion of the gloomy Swede. Those he met had been outgoing, entertaining and amusing, and Lars Hagner was no exception. He was also a good copper, Kenyon thought, having been involved in that spectacular affair in Stockholm when the staff of a bank were held hostage.

'Your party in Stockholm in on the line now,' the operator said.

'Lars?' Kenyon enquired. 'It's Sidney Kenyon.'

'You're a bloody liar,' Lars Hagner said, down the line. 'An imposter. They'd never let Sidney Kenyon into the Hilton Hotel.'

'I told them to send the bill to you,' Kenyon said. 'Since I'm still having weekly interviews with my bank manager after buying you that bloody dinner.'

Prices in Sweden had shocked Kenyon. Starting with dry martinis at one pound fifty each, it had cost Kenyon over sixty pounds to entertain Lars and two of his colleagues to a meal one evening. Lars had tried to pick up the tab, but Kenyon had been determined to make some gesture of generosity in return for the Swede's hospitality. Although the expenses allowed by the Metropolitan Police did not run to sixty pound meals.

'You can blame your lousy exchange rate for that. But OK,' Lars said good humouredly, 'so I owe you. What is it?'

'A murder enquiry,' Kenyon said. 'I'm trying to short-circuit the red tape.' Kenyon told him what he wanted.

Lars Hagner promised to ring back as soon as possible.

'Don't ask for me,' Kenyon said. 'Ask for Mr Smithers.'

'My God,' Lars Hagner said, 'are you screwing someone else's wife again?'

'I'm off all that,' Kenyon said. 'It all got too complicated.'

'You must be getting old and tired,' Lars Hagner said.

Kenyon rang off. He thought about phoning Sarah, but decided against it. Someone would be listening in on her extension, and there was no point in a guarded conversation. He would meet her from work.

He was glancing anxiously at his watch, and wondering if he would be in time to do so after all, when the phone rang at last. Kenyon told the operator to put the call from Stockholm through.

'I have contacted the correspondent here in Stockholm,' Lars Hagner said, 'who filed that story, but he did not write it himself.'

'Where did it come from?'

'London,' Lars Hagner said. 'The correspondent here was told that his London man had the story on good authority, but to protect the source, the story should emanate from Sweden.'

'Who, in London?' Kenyon asked.

'A freelance journalist,' Lars Hagner said.

'His name,' Kenyon said.

'I hope you really are conducting a murder enquiry,' Lars Hagner said.

'Yes,' Kenyon said. 'I am.'

'You know what the press are like about revealing sources,' Lars Hagner said. 'And protecting their own kind. I had to bully him a little. I would prefer something on paper.'

'Come on, Lars,' Kenyon said urgently. 'I need a favour, and I need it fast. I haven't got time to bother with bumph. I'll keep you out of it, and that's a promise.'

There was a pause. 'OK,' Lars Hagner said. 'The man in London was called Arthur Kale.'

'Was he,' Kenyon said, with an inflection he did not intend. 'Do you know him?'

'Yes,' Kenyon said. 'As it happens I do.'

He thanked Lars Hagner for his help, and they promised to look each other up some time. Kenyon went down to the foyer, paid for his whisky and phone call, and handed the key of the room back again. He had been called away to an urgent meeting, he explained, and would not need the room overnight after all. The receptionist asked what they should do about his luggage, when that arrived.

'It won't,' Kenyon said. 'It's been intercepted.'

He took a taxi to the Foreign Office and sat inside the cab, waiting for Sarah to come out.

Arthur Kale was a middle-aged journalist, who had failed in television, and reverted to being a freelance. Kenyon had first met him when he was front man for an 'in depth' television show. Kale had persuaded the police to send along some representatives for what was to be a factual look at the role of the police in modern society. Kenyon had been one of the row of policemen among the studio audience, the remainder of whom, it transpired, were anti-police to a man. The word 'pigs' was used frequently.

Kale had affected neutrality, while yet managing to turn the whole occasion into an inquisition. Every allegation of brutality, corruption and planting of evidence from incoherent young men and women was treated as an accusation founded on solid fact, demanding an immediate answer. Every attempt by the police to ask for substantiation was treated as an evasion. Any suggestion that the police spent most of their time dealing with violent criminals, was brushed aside.

Kale smirked and insinuated his way through the programme and ended with a solemn summing up which warned about the weight and abuse of police powers.

'I thought that went very well,' Kale said to the producer afterwards.

Kenyon did not think he was the only copper there who would have loved five minutes alone with Arthur Kale. The programme hit the headlines, and was the high point of Kale's television career. After that, his sneering, snide technique began to repel the viewers, and when his contract expired it was not renewed.

For a while Kale then ran a television column in which he gave vent to his bilious envy of his more successful former colleagues, but no one offered him the chance to return and put things right, and despairing of the recognition he deserved, he reverted to conventional journalism.

Kenyon had seen him a number of times since in one club or another. Kale's taste in girls ran to the exotic, or the very young. He wore a beard. Kenyon wondered if he lived in Battersea as well.

Sarah Brooks walked towards the cab, got in beside Kenyon, and kissed him.

'I'll drop you off at your place,' Kenyon said. 'I want to go home and see if there's any mail. I'll come back later.'

As soon as he walked into his flat, Kenyon knew that it had been searched. It had been conducted neatly and cleanly. Everything had been put back in almost the same position. But not quite. Cautiously, Kenyon made sure that no unwelcome intruders were still in the flat. Then he examined his coffee table book on cars. It did not appear to have been tampered with. He slit the cover open. The photocopy of Harry Coleman's document had gone.

Kenyon opened a fresh packet of cigarettes, lit one, and smoked it thoughtfully. For a day which had begun with such promise, this one had gone badly wrong. He had noticed an unfamiliar car parked on the other side of Gloucester Terrace. The man behind the wheel had not looked at him, as he opened his street door, but Kenyon thought he was one of Bradley's men.

Kenyon stubbed out his cigarette, left his flat, checked that the door locked behind him, and climbed the stairs which led to the ground floor. A fire door was at the top. Kenyon pushed it open, as he did every time he left his flat.

This time, there was someone there. Kenyon caught a glimpse of him and reacted, but too late. He felt the stunning, head-splitting blow on his skull. He remembered hitting the banisters as he began to fall down the stairs. After that, he remembered nothing.

11

The phone was ringing. Through waves of purple pain Kenyon struggled back to consciousness. He was lying on the floor of his own flat. Above him towered a stool beside the breakfast bar. Beside that was the telephone. It went on ringing.

Kenyon tried to stand up, and fell over bringing the stool down as well. He groaned and cursed, and managed to kneel. Reaching up for the telephone he got the receiver off.

'Hullo,' Sarah Brooks' voice said. 'Hullo.'

Kenyon manoeuvred the receiver to his ear. 'Hullo.'

'Are you all right?' Sarah asked, worried. 'You were so long . . .'

'I'm fine,' Kenyon mumbled.

'I've been ringing for ages. I couldn't think where you were.'

'In the bathroom,' Kenyon said.

'Oh, sorry . . .'

'Give me another half an hour,' Kenyon said, and tried to hang up.

He missed the telephone rest, and brought the whole unit down on to the floor. The cover cracked, and a corner of plastic fell off. 'Shit,' he said uselessly. 'Sod the thing.' He jammed the receiver on to the rest, and left it on the floor. He sat where he was, and leaned back against the breakfast bar.

He was dizzy, and his head was not aching, it was pounding like a demented pile-driver. His back and shoulders were bruised. Every time he tried to move, some part of him hurt. Gingerly, he felt his scalp. There was a lump like a hen's egg, but no blood as far as he could tell.

His vision remained blurred and he wondered if he had concussion. People only got hit over the head and shook it off a few moments later in films. The human brain did not like being battered around like a jelly and unpleasant things were liable to happen. He closed his eyes, and waited. He did not think it conceivable that he could feel worse. Some time he must feel better.

A few minutes later Kenyon opened his eyes. He did not feel better, but some small vestige of thought process was returning. He groped in his pocket for the packet of cigarettes, and came up with the wrong one, the fresh packet. But the contents were a mangled mess, and he knew then. He found the other packet. The few remaining cigarettes were broken and shreds of tobacco fell on the carpet. The microfilm had gone.

When Kenyon felt that his legs would carry his weight, he stumbled into the bathroom and looked at himself in the mirror. He was as pale as death, but his hair covered the egg-like lump. He splashed cold water on his face and took two codeine tablets. He felt like being sick, but he repressed it, swallowing saliva, and forcing himself not to vomit. He wanted to keep those tablets down.

Eventually, he felt that he could just about face the walk to Sarah's flat. The same strange car was still parked on the opposite side of Gloucester Terrace. Kenyon got in beside the driver, who looked at him in surprise.

'I haven't got the time or inclination to fart about,' Kenyon said. 'Are you one of Bradley's people? If so, did you see anyone suspicious going into my building?'

'I don't know what you're talking about,' the driver said, huffily. 'I'm waiting for my girl friend. Who are you, anyway?'

'Jack,' Kenyon said, 'who fell down and broke his crown.'

'You're drunk,' the driver said. 'Get out before I call the police.'

'You've got the police already, mate,' Kenyon said, fishing for his warrant card. The driver looked at him warily.

'I'm entitled to park here,' the driver said. 'I'm not on a

double yellow line, and there are no parking restrictions in the evening.'

Kenyon said, 'Just tell Bradley that if he knows who did my flat, I'd like to know too. Unless you did it,' he added.

Kenyon did not think that was very likely. Whoever it was had got what they were after. They would not hang about.

Kenyon got out of the car and walked away. One copy left now, concealed in the self-drive car parked in Hyde Park underground car park.

It seemed a long way to Sarah's flat, and when he got there, he collapsed into an armchair.

'What's wrong?' Sarah asked. 'You look ill.'

'Tired, that's all,' Kenyon said. 'I'll feel better after a drink.' He did not explain, not because he wanted to conceal it from her, but because he could not be bothered.

The drink improved him a little, but not much. 'I'll have another one,' Kenyon said, holding his glass out for a refill, 'and then I have to go out.'

'You look as though you're out on your feet already,' Sarah said, with more accuracy than she knew. 'Why don't you have an early night?'

'Tomorrow,' Kenyon said.

He tried the Pickwick Club and Gerrys without success, but finally found Arthur Kale in a small, dimly-lit club off Shaftesbury Avenue. Kale was sitting with a girl, talking to her animatedly. His hand was stroking her thigh. The girl was very pretty despite her make up and false eyelashes. Kenyon guessed that she was perhaps sixteen.

He sat down opposite them. 'We have things to say to each other, Arthur,' he said. 'We'll go to your place.'

Kale's beard twitched, indicating a smile. 'This,' he said to the girl, 'is one of our pillars of law and order. Protects property. Very keen on protecting property. That will tell you who he really works for. He is of course a public servant, and exhibits the true qualities of the servant. Servile to the establishment, who are his masters. An aggressive bully boy to those weaker than himself.'

The girl giggled. Kenyon thought that Arthur Kale was stoned out of his mind, which was par for the course, for him, at this time of the evening.

'Christ, Arthur,' Kenyon said, 'what a crashing bore you are. Come on. Let's go.'

'You're suffering from delusions, Kenyon,' Arthur Kale said. 'You're so used to pushing people around who can't stand up for themselves, that you really believe you can push anyone around. Go away my man.'

'I'm Detective Inspector Kenyon,' Kenyon told the girl.

'This is a private club,' Arthur Kale said. 'And I doubt if they'd have you as a member. So kindly disappear before I ask them to show you the door.'

'I have reason to believe,' Kenyon said, 'that this young lady is under age. So for a start, we'll talk to the barman about serving minors with alcohol. I also think she may be under the age of consent. You can both accompany me to the police station while we sort that one out.'

'You really are beneath contempt,' Arthur Kale said. He conferred with the girl in a whisper. She shook her head vigorously. 'Hard luck,' Kale said to Kenyon. 'You've guessed wrong.'

'Could be,' Kenyon admitted. 'Let's go to the police station, talk to her parents, and check it out.'

A look of alarm crossed the girl's face. She clutched Kale's arm, and whispered in his ear again. Kenyon guessed that she had parents in somewhere like St Albans, who imagined she was being safely chaperoned by several flatmates of her own sex, and who would view a night out with a fifty-year-old man with something this side of delight. Or perhaps she was an escapee from Borstal who had no wish to go near a police station. He did not much care what she was afraid of, so long as it worked.

'Your place now,' Kenyon said. 'The little lady can make coffee, or something, while we have a private chat.'

Kenyon's head was thudding excruciatingly. He felt the urgent need to get outside, and breathe some fresh air.

The taxi drove south across the Thames, turned into Prince of Wales Drive, SW 11, the district of Battersea, and stopped outside a mansion block. Kale's flat was a large one, and Kenyon liked it. The lobby opened into a dining hall, off which was a long, pleasant living room-cum-study. Other doors led to what Kenyon presumed were bedrooms, kitchen and bathroom.

'Very nice,' Kenyon said. 'Do you own it, or rent it?'

'Rent it,' Kale said. He appeared to have recovered his composure. 'I've been here for years, so it's still pretty reasonable. The owners keep trying to get everybody out so that they can break it up and sell it, but we're fighting the bastards.'

Kenyon wandered over to the large bay window which Kale had converted into a study area. A desk, an IBM golf-ball typewriter, sheaves of typescript, files, books, newspapers lying around. He glanced at some of the typescripts and newspapers, while Kale and the girl talked quietly behind him. Kale was telling her where the kitchen was, and when she left the room, he closed the door behind her. 'I've told her that you'll be leaving in twenty minutes,' he said.

Kenyon was comparing a typescript with a newspaper. 'What do you do?' he enquired. 'Check your original article against the published version?'

'I like to know how much my work gets mangled by some bleary idiot of a sub-editor,' Kale said.

'How much does it get changed?'

'It depends,' Kale said. 'The heavies aren't too bad; they've got the space. Why this interest in my technique? Are you looking for a ghost for your tedious, self-justifying memoirs? If so, I'm too expensive. You couldn't afford me.'

Kale gave himself a large brandy.

'I won't thank you,' Kenyon said.

'I wasn't going to ask you,' Kale said. 'Most policemen, in my experience, would have fitted happily into the Gestapo and are not my ideal choice of company. I also find them limited, petty, and boring. I'm not anxious to prolong this interview whatever it's about.'

Kenyon admired the way the man held his drink. He still thought Kale was smashed, but he remained as lucid and articulate as ever. Only the red patches on his cheeks and the brilliance of his brown eyes testified to his alcoholic intake that night.

'You may be able to assist us with a murder enquiry,' Kenyon said. 'Jenny Abel.'

'Never heard of her,' Kale said.

'You screwed the lady,' Kenyon said. 'You picked her up in a night club, brought her back here, and spent the night with her. I'm surprised you ever find it necessary to pay for it judging from tonight's willing little filly. Do coloured ladies do that much for you?'

'When was this?' Kale asked.

'November,' Kenyon said. He had intended to add the date but was shocked to find that it eluded him. The thudding inside his head threatened to burst his skull wide open. He was finding it increasingly hard to concentrate.

'Not me,' Kale said. 'As you so cleverly perceived, I don't have to buy it. Is that all?'

'Don't be a prick, Arthur,' Kenyon said. 'Jenny kept a diary,' he went on, lying. 'Your name was in it. She told her fellow, a spade called Winston Peters, about you,' he said, lying some more. 'Didn't you stop on the way home, and buy a copy of *The Times*?'

Kenyon knew that he was taking a terrible chance in adding that last question. Normally, he would have played his hand more carefully, leading off with a low card first, protecting himself against being trumped, working gradually, taking his time, until he knew what Arthur Kale's cards were. But that meant sorting out the order of play, and in his present condition his mind would not cope with that. It was the grand slam, or nothing.

But Arthur Kale seemed, luckily, to be impressed. He sat down and stared at Kenyon warily while he lit a cigarette. Kenyon knew that Kale too was groping with a certain fuzziness, drink induced in his case.

'I think I dimly recall something about it,' Kale said, at last. 'She was killed by the coloured man she was living with. He hanged himself in his cell.'

'I'm in charge of the case,' Kenyon said. He was walking right out on a limb now, but he had gone too far to protect his rear any more. 'Winston Peters wasn't tried and convicted. I was never certain of his guilt. Other matters have since come to light, which lead me to believe that some other person may have been involved. I'm now interested in anyone she may have seen the night before she was murdered.' He stared at Kale's bearded face. 'That is, you, Mr Kale,' Kenyon said, softly.

Kale did not like it one little bit, which was precisely the way Kenyon liked it. 'This is utterly ridiculous,' Kale said.

'Convince me,' Kenyon said. 'Or alternatively, we could go to the station, if you prefer,' he offered, trusting sincerely that Kale would rather not take up the offer.

Kale wet his lips, and jerked his head in a gesture of reluctant assent. 'What do you want to know?'

'How it happened,' Kenyon said. 'How you met her.'

'I'd been working very hard,' Arthur Kale said. 'I don't usually go to that night club. I was supposed to meet some people there. I sat and waited, but they didn't turn up. To pass the time I was talking to this girl.'

'Jenny Abel,' Kenyon said. 'Let's use her name. Had you eaten? Were you drinking a great deal?'

'We ate together much later,' Kale said. 'And I'm not a tee-totaller.'

'Nor am I,' Kenyon said. 'So you had a lot to drink. What was Jenny like to talk to?'

'Surprisingly intelligent,' Kale said. 'She was very interested in my work. We talked mostly about that. I knew she was a whore, of course, but if she wasn't feeling randy, she gave the best imitation I've ever seen.'

'She turned you on,' Kenyon said. 'And you were drunk enough to think it would be money well spent.'

'Something like that,' Kale admitted. White teeth showed in the middle of his beard as he smiled. 'She had certain physical attributes which I find it hard to resist.'

'Like she was black,' Kenyon said. 'And you like either very young tits, or coloured tits. Why did you buy the newspaper? I should have thought your mind would be on something else by then.'

'Jenny was interested,' Kale said. 'The article was a very good one, written by a Swedish journalist I know. I'd been talking about it. We came back here and, for the record, I'm very sorry she's dead. It was worth the money. She left, and I never saw her again.'

'Ah, but can you prove that?' Kenyon asked. 'Can you establish where you were when she was murdered?'

Kale thought about that for a while, and then got up, put on a pair of large, horn-rimmed spectacles, and consulted a desk diary.

Kenyon watched him. Jenny had heard something which interested her. But Harry Coleman's name was not mentioned in that article. And how had she known that Arthur Kale had written it? Possibly, they had had a night cap in this room. Perhaps Kale had gone to the bathroom, and Jenny had glanced at the typescripts which were lying around and noticed a carbon copy on Kale's desk of a feature which had supposedly emanated from Sweden. But it did not matter how she had worked it out; somehow, she had. Jenny Abel had been a pretty bright girl, Kenyon thought. He got up and moved noiselessly to Arthur Kale's elbow.

'I see from my diary,' Kale said, 'that I was with friends during the afternoon and evening when Jenny was killed.'

Kale closed his diary, took off his glasses, and started as he found Kenyon beside him.

Kenyon took the diary, and opened it. The relevant page was blank. 'Let me give you a small, friendly word of warning, Arthur,' Kenyon said. 'Don't try any phoney alibis, because they're liable to be checked. Don't rely on making a phone call to some old mate, asking him to back you up. Old mates like that get frightened when they suddenly find they're mixed up in a murder investigation.'

'You're not a fool, Kenyon,' Kale said, paying what was possibly the first compliment in his life to a policeman. 'You must know that I'm in no way involved in Jenny's death.'

'It's not me, Arthur,' Kenyon said, apologetically. 'It's my guv'nor. I keep trying to tell him that a man like you couldn't be concerned, but he's got it fixed in his head that it was you. Or at the very least, that you know something.'

'I've told you everything I know,' Kale said, agitated.

'Not quite,' Kenyon said. 'Not about Harry Coleman.'

Kenyon had seen the exact equivalent of the expression on Arthur Kale's face once before in his life. That was on television, years ago. It was the way Cassius Clay looked, as he sprawled with no dignity across the ropes, after collecting a left hook to the jaw from Henry Cooper.

Like Clay, Arthur Kale recovered. 'Harry Coleman,' he said, 'is an American diplomatic adviser who I've met a few times. Like all Americans of his type, he looks as though he takes hourly shower baths, and changes his shirt six times a day.'

'His name came up that night,' Kenyon said, 'possibly in connection with the article which you wrote for *The Times* on the neo-Nazi movement in Germany.'

'That was sent in from Sweden,' Kale said, agitated. 'I didn't write it. I always get a by-line.'

'You had to forgo the privilege that time,' Kenyon said. 'It was supposed to be from a neutral and dispassionate observer, not a committed fellow like you. I doubt if you could even get a visa for the United States. Their serious newspapers wouldn't pick up anything signed by you, and that was the idea wasn't it?'

An echo of his former shocked expression crossed Arthur Kale's face, swiftly joined by anger and resentment. 'I'm beginning to grow curious,' he said, 'as to how my work is supposed to be related to a murder.'

'Take my word for it,' Kenyon said. 'Who told you to write that article?'

'No one tells me what to write.'

'OK, you were only too willing,' Kenyon said. 'But someone suggested the contents, the slant, and what to do with it, and I want to know who.'

The door opened, and the girl came in. 'I've had my cup of coffee,' she complained. 'Haven't you finished yet?'

'No,' Kenyon said.

'Go to bed,' Kale said. 'It's the first door on the left.'

The girl pouted, and slammed the door after her.

Kale studied Kenyon, as if seeing him in a new light. 'Have you been transferred to Special Branch?' he asked. 'I've had those bastards on my back, off and on, for years. Your interest in my politics intrigues me, Kenyon. This is laughingly called a free country. I think I'll get on to the Council for Civil Liberties tomorrow.'

'Listen, chum,' Kenyon said, his voice low and quiet and deadly. 'I don't give a shit about your politics. Jenny Abel wasn't the only one who died. A nice young copper called Michael Meacher got blown to shreds too. You know how worked up the police get when a copper's murdered, and I'm bloody worked up about it, I can tell you.'

Arthur Kale retreated. He seemed to think that Kenyon was on the brink of hitting him, which was near enough the truth.

'I sat and listened to you telling a nationwide television audience how the police plant evidence, and frame innocent people,' Kenyon said. 'Well, those words of yours are going to prove self-fulfilling, little man, unless you give me some answers. You smoke pot. I can see the bloody stuff from here,' he said, pointing to the mantelpiece. 'That'll do for starters. That'll give me time to cook up a really good frame that'll keep you in prison for years, writing letters to the Home Secretary, protesting your innocence. Now, who gave you the information for that article, and told you what to do?'

'You wouldn't know him,' Kale breathed, still retreating.

'Try me.'

'Mark Fisher,' Kale said. 'He's had staff collecting material on this German thing for a long time.'

'Staff employed by whom?' Kenyon demanded.

'CASO. The Committee for American Security Overseas.'

'I think you're lying,' Kenyon said. 'I think it was Harry Coleman.'

Kale was astounded. 'Coleman? That Fascist? You must be mad. He's probably got money in Krupps.'

Kenyon had suddenly lost his mental bearings. Kale's astonishment carried conviction. 'You use the word Fascist like a bloody insect spray,' Kenyon said. 'You've applied it to the police force before now. You say Mark Fisher's CASO. Harry Coleman has links with CASO.'

'Every organization gets the wrong people in it, who want to use it for their own ends,' Kale said. 'Coleman's just a new-style Cold War Warrior.'

'His name came up when you were talking to Jenny Abel in that night club.'

'If it did, I don't remember,' Kale said.

'You'd better remember,' Kenyon said. 'You talk about my political interest. Doesn't it occur to you that Jenny Abel's murder may have been politically motivated?' he asked, improvising for the last time that night.

'How?' Kale was puzzled, and also rather frightened.

'Never mind how. How is my business not yours. Harry Coleman, if you can recall your drunken ramblings of that night.'

There was a long pause, while Kale racked his brains. Finally, he said, 'I'm honestly not sure. I think I may have said something about Coleman not liking the article from Sweden.'

'Which you wrote yourself. Why shouldn't he like it?'

'Because he was in Gotland when that conference took place,' Kale said.

'And you think he took part in it?'

'If he didn't,' Kale said, 'what the hell was he doing there?'

Kenyon felt like a tennis player who had failed to see his opponent's return. He tried to cover his bewilderment. 'You must have seen the advert in the *Evening Standard* about Jenny Abel,' he said. 'Why didn't you answer it?'

'I didn't want to get involved,' Kale said, tiredly.

'You are involved,' Kenyon told him.

When Kenyon left the flat, he thought he could hear Kale and the girl arguing about something. He took no notice. He was confused. It was four o'clock in the morning as he stood in Prince of Wales Drive. It was cold, and the road was empty of all traffic, let alone taxis.

Kenyon grew more confused when the girl came out of Kale's block, crossed the road and joined him. 'If you're waiting for a taxi,' she said, 'can you give me a lift?'

'I thought you were staying the night,' Kenyon said.

'I don't know him very well,' the girl said. 'He had some things in his bedroom. I didn't know he had that in mind.'

Kenyon thought that Jenny Abel had stayed, but then she was presumably used to variations from the normal.

A lone taxi appeared twenty minutes later. Kenyon dropped the girl off in Chelsea, where, as he had guessed, she shared a flat with four other girls.

'You're very young and very pretty. Leave people like Arthur Kale alone,' Kenyon said, by way of parting advice.

'I can look after myself,' the girl said.

Famous last words, Kenyon thought. He had seen what could happen to confident kids like her often enough.

Sarah had given Kenyon the keys to her flat. He let himself in, undressed, and crawled wearily into bed beside her. Sarah was fast asleep. He tried to shake her into wakefulness.

'Hullo,' she said, drowsily. She slid her warm arms round his neck. 'What time is it?'

'Late,' Kenyon said. 'Wake up. I want to know something.' Sarah yawned and then kissed him. She smelt of sleep and woman. 'When you were in Gotland with Harry Coleman,' Kenyon said, 'did he attend a conference of some kind?'

'I don't know,' Sarah murmured. 'He said he had some private meetings he couldn't take me to, but I shouldn't think it was a full-scale conference. I mean he wasn't away from nine to five every day, or anything like that.'

'Who did he see?'

'I don't know,' Sarah said. 'He went out for three or four evenings. Something like that. Dinner with someone I should think. Why?'

'I don't know why,' Kenyon said. 'I wish I did.'

He lay in bed, trying to think. Coleman's document; Arthur Kale's article; things which had been said to him by Sarah, by Bradley, by Arthur Kale. But his head was hurting more than ever. It was some days since he had read Coleman's document, and try as he might he could not bring it back to mind.

Sarah said, 'I'm wide awake now.'

But her tentatively exploring fingers did nothing for Kenyon. 'I'm too tired for all that. Sorry,' he said. 'Or else I've turned into a eunuch.'

'Sunday tomorrow,' Sarah said. 'We'll have time to check that out.'

They made sure, and by the time Kenyon had bathed and dressed, and was on his way to Bayswater Police Station, it was after three o'clock.

A man was washing an unfamiliar car, across the gardens from Sarah's flat. The man did not follow Kenyon as he walked to the station, but someone else did. Kenyon decided not to try and get to the car in Hyde Park underground car park. There were too few people about on Sunday, and it would not be easy to lose a determined shadow. God willing, they were Bradley's men, and presumably meant him no harm. He still did not wish to lead them to the copy of Coleman's document.

He spent the rest of the afternoon and half the evening clearing up the loose ends at Bayswater Police Station. Mallory was around, and they had a farewell drink together.

'Good luck in the cesspool of Potters Bar,' Mallory said.

'Watch it,' Kenyon told him. 'Or I'll ask for you to be transferred there as well.'

'No, sir, please don't,' Mallory groaned. 'Have mercy. Good men have passed away of boredom in Potters Bar.'

'Then buy a bloody round for a change,' Kenyon said. 'After that, I'm going.'

Kenyon let himself into Sarah's flat. The lights were on, but she was not in the living room. 'Sarah' Kenyon called. 'I'm home.'

Sarah came in from the bedroom. She was wearing her satin dressing gown. 'I thought I'd slip into something more comfortable, as they say.'

'Very nice too,' Kenyon said, and kissed her on the lips.

'The supper's been in the oven for an hour, you're late, and what's more you've been drinking,' Sarah accused. 'You'd rather go boozing with your friends than come back to me.'

'Any time,' Kenyon said. His hands caressed her soft form. She was now growing familiar to him, and yet was just as interesting as when he had wondered what she would look like with no clothes on. He held her close to him. He could smell the freshness of her hair. 'Freudian slip,' he said. 'Saying I'm home. But it feels like that.'

There was silence from Sarah for some moments, and then she kissed his ear lightly. 'We'd better give that one some thought,' she said.

On Monday morning, Kenyon caught the train to Potters Bar, reported to his new guv'nor, and asked permission to take accumulated leave at once.

'I've got twenty-three days owing to me, sir,' Kenyon explained. 'I have some personal matters to see to, and also I'll have to find somewhere to live in Potters Bar. So if it's not inconvenient . . .'

Kenyon had not the slightest intention of ever living in Potters Bar, nor of working there for long. He meant to pull every string he could think of to try and get back to Central London. Unless he had put up a permanent black, he thought he might achieve that within a year or so. Meantime, he would claim that he had failed to find anywhere to live, and commute.

His new guv'nor raised no objection to Kenyon taking immediate leave, but suggested that since he was on the spot, he might as well meet his future colleagues. He spent the morning in various offices, and lunched at a pub. A lady had phoned when he was out. He called Sarah, but there was no answer.

Dusk was falling as he rode back on the train. He thought about Sarah and felt comfortable and relaxed. She was taking her own leave as from today. They would be together all the time. Kenyon had not quite decided what they would be doing, but he liked the idea just the same.

He let himself into Sarah's flat. 'Sarah,' he called. There was no reply. 'Sarah,' he called. 'Sarah.'

But the flat felt and sounded empty, and he decided that she had gone shopping. He went into the kitchen, and made himself a coffee. The breakfast dishes were still piled, unwashed. 'Bloody slut,' Kenyon complained to himself, grinning. He ran hot water, washed them, dried them, and put them away. He thought she would be pleased and looked forward to seeing her reaction. He sat and smoked a cigarette with his coffee, waiting for the sound of her key in the door.

For the next three weeks plus it would be like this, waking with her, talking to her, waiting for her. No, it would not, he told himself. He had taken his leave in order to pursue his un-official enquiries. But somehow he felt lethargic about that, today. He would of course. But it would do no harm to take a day or two to work out what to do next. Meanwhile, Sarah would be around. He could see her whenever he wanted to, by opening a door and walking into a room.

He wondered again, as he had done many times, about his auto-matic, unthinking use of the words 'I'm home', last night. Home. Not a flat, but a woman. A woman to whom it was good to come back. Did it mean nothing? Or did it mean more than he cared to decide?

Kenyon wandered into the living room, sat down, and read the *Evening Standard* which he had bought at the station. He turned to the television programmes. There was a film which might be worth seeing. He looked at his watch. Time for the early evening news soon.

The flat was silent, save for the rustle of the newspaper. A vague sense of unease began to envelope Kenyon. Where the hell was she? Growing restless, he went into the bedroom. It looked slightly different. It took Kenyon a fraction of a second to realize why. The dressing table was clear and uncluttered. Sarah's make up and creams had disappeared.

For a moment he stood, staring, and then he banged wardrobes and drawers open viciously. After that he controlled himself, and searched the entire flat as a good copper should. When he had finished, he sat down, gave himself a whisky, and lit a cigarette.

Two large Antler suitcases, which should have been standing in Sarah's wardrobe, were not there. Many of her dresses, suits, and clothes had gone. Most of her underwear drawers were empty. Even her toothbrush and toothpaste were missing. It had taken time to pack as thoroughly as that, but there was no message left for him, no note.

And Sarah's passport was nowhere in that flat.

12

The number which Sarah had been told by Lance Everitt to ring, back in November, was evidently a hot line to Tom Bradley, day or night. Bradley listened, and said he would be there as soon as possible.

Kenyon smoked three cigarettes while he was waiting, and had another drink. The door bell rang. Kenyon let Bradley in.

'Mind if I look round?' Bradley asked.

'Help yourself,' Kenyon said. He sat back, and closed his eyes. Bradley was thorough. It was an hour before he stopped moving around the flat, and sat down opposite Kenyon.

'No sign of a struggle, nothing suspicious,' Bradley said. 'She's on leave. Nothing more natural than to go abroad on holiday somewhere.'

Kenyon shook his head. 'She'd have told me.'

'Perhaps she chose not to,' Bradley said.

'Listen,' Kenyon said. 'She's missing. I want to know where she is.'

'You know as well as I do where she is,' Bradley said. 'She's with Harry Coleman.'

Kenyon had resisted that logical deduction since the moment when he had first seen the bare top of Sarah's dressing table. Bradley's factual sounding statement made it much harder to resist, somehow.

'There's no reason to suppose,' Bradley said, 'that she didn't leave of her own free will. And some good reasons why she would.'

Kenyon took a deep breath. 'I think Coleman may be in Gotland,' he said.

Bradley raised his eyebrows. 'Oh? Why?'

Kenyon told him about the article, supposedly from a neutral source, which Arthur Kale had planted. How, according to Kale, he had mentioned Coleman's name, saying he would not like it, which presumably had made Jenny think the article was important. And how, again according to Kale, Coleman and Sarah had been on holiday in Gotland when the conference was being held.

Kenyon did not mention the microfilm. He would wait until he had laid his hands on the typed copy hidden in his self-drive car. He had thoroughly cocked that one up, he thought.

Bradley knew about the article, and how seriously it had been taken in the United States, but not that it had originated with Arthur Kale. 'So that's what the bastards are doing,' he said. 'You should have told me this at once.'

'I only found out Sunday morning,' Kenyon said, truthfully.

Bradley stood up. 'I must go. There are people I have to talk to. Not that it'll do much good.'

'Suppose Jenny had got this through to you before she died? Would it have been any use?'

'I doubt it,' Bradley said. 'There may have been a conference in Gotland, or it may be pure invention. I think there's a bloody great fix going on which this little offshore island can do damn all about.'

'Arthur Kale regards Coleman as a Fascist cold war merchant,' Kenyon said.

'Arthur Kale is an envious little pseudo-intellectual,' Bradley said, 'who believes what he's told, provided it comes from the right quarter, and repeats it like an obedient bloody parrot. This is like no game you've ever known, Sid. Nothing's what it seems, and no one's what they appear to be. I'm only guessing because London's not important any more, and we don't get told what it's thought we shouldn't know. I just hope I'm a bad guesser.'

'If Coleman's in Gotland,' Kenyon said, 'you could find him.'

'What do I do then?' Bradley enquired. 'Send in a gunboat? Use your loaf, Sidney. Gotland is a Swedish island in the Baltic, which is a Soviet sea for all practical purposes. The Swedes are nervous about their neutrality, and I don't blame them, since they've got a frontier with Finland and Russia as a near neighbour. Harry Coleman's an American diplomat. Mix that little lot up and I can imagine no faster way to cause an international incident than to salt the stew with British agents.'

Bradley went to the door, turned, and looked at Kenyon. 'And why?' he asked. 'To find your girl friend who's decided to graze in other pastures.' He pointed at Kenyon. 'You don't give a damn about what's going on, or about Harry Coleman either. You've fallen hook, line and sinker for a woman, Sidney, that's all. Forget it. She'd be here in this flat if she wanted to be. You were told to lay off. Bloody do it.'

'She could have been forced to go,' Kenyon said.

'Nothing's impossible,' Bradley said. 'But there are varying degrees of probability. You're a copper who's seen a bit of life. Work it out for yourself. Good God, what's so important about one woman? My wife left me ten years ago, and I don't blame her. I'm a cold-hearted phoney, wielding a lot of power in a very small pond. I'm like a compulsive gambler. I'm hooked on a game I'm not going to win. I think you're a bit like me, Sidney. You're an obsessive copper. Going home to the little lady isn't your style, so don't kid yourself.'

Kenyon walked slowly to his flat in Gloucester Terrace. No unfamiliar cars caught his attention, and no one was following him. Bradley did not think he needed protecting any more. No one else thought he was worth watching. Both sides, or however many there were, had written Kenyon off. He was no longer important. It was over. Bradley was right about one thing. Kenyon had been dabbling in matters he did not understand. At one time he had thought he did. But the jig-saw puzzle which, when assembled, should have provided a picture, instead only displayed another enigma.

In his flat Kenyon packed a bag. He would go and pick up the self-drive car and read Coleman's document again. Then he would decide what to do with it. Possibly post it to Bradley. Possibly not.

The telephone rang. Kenyon leapt for the phone thinking it might be Sarah. The crackling on the line was so bad that he could hardly hear his father's voice. The tap had been removed from his phone as well.

'Look, Dad, not now,' Kenyon said. 'I'm sorry. I'm just going out.'

'It's about that thing you sent me, it arrived this morning,' his father said.

'What thing? What are you talking about? Speak up,' Kenyon said loudly. 'I can hardly hear you.'

'You said in your note that I was to keep it until you contacted me,' his father shouted. 'But it doesn't make sense.'

It did to Kenyon. Quite suddenly. 'All right, Dad,' he said, flatly. 'What was in it?'

'The centre pages from the *Evening Standard*. I mean, if you say it's important I'll keep it,' his father said. 'But I thought I'd better ring you, just in case.'

'I'm sorry, Dad,' Kenyon said. 'I put the wrong thing in the wrong envelope. My fault. Forget it.'

'You're as bad as me,' his father said, chuckling, pleased. 'You shouldn't be getting absent minded yet. Not at your age.'

Kenyon enquired after his father's health, promised to come and see him soon, and hung up.

He was not getting absent minded, Kenyon thought, he was plain incompetent. For Christ's sake, a copper should be able to keep a piece of evidence safe and sound. But these boys were a higher-class lot than the men he was accustomed to deal with. Even good villains were not capable of this sort of thing.

Kenyon appreciated, as a pro, the ironic gesture of sending the envelope to his father with substitute contents. His father had been supposed to do exactly what he had done. Kenyon had been given a message. OK, fellow, that's it. You're wiped off the board. They were painstaking, these people. A microfilm and a blown-up copy should be enough to satisfy anybody. But they had wanted to make sure.

Kenyon could guess how. The keys to the self-drive car in his pocket, had the registration number stamped on an attached disc:

they had seen those keys when they searched him. Perhaps that was enough. Or perhaps they had found out what make the car was first. Even grubby little private detectives had informers in the Licensing Department. This lot could get the details, no sweat at all.

Kenyon had not been seen using a car for several days. It followed it must be parked somewhere. They had had Saturday night and Sunday. Kenyon groaned as he thought how conspicuous that car must have been in the nearly empty cavern of Hyde Park underground car park on a Sunday. If only he had gone and moved the damn thing. Or if he had hidden the copy in Sarah's flat. Although it would probably have been found in that case, when Sarah was picked up. Kenyon clung to the idea that force of some kind had been used. If she had gone because she wanted to . . . well, he would face that if necessary, when he knew.

He took a taxi to the car park. The driver's door had been forced. The interior door panel had been removed, and lay on the seat. Kenyon threw it in the back, started the engine and drove to London Airport where he parked the car and went to the terminal. He had just missed the last direct flight to Stockholm that night. So he decided to go via Copenhagen rather than wait until the following morning. He used his credit card to buy a ticket, and trusted he would be able to use it in Gotland. He had twenty pounds in English money on him, but no foreign currency or traveller's cheques.

There was a five hour wait in Copenhagen, before the early-morning flight to Stockholm departed. Kenyon spent that time sprawled out, his eyes closed, apparently asleep. He was not. He was patiently trying to recall all that he could of Harry Coleman's document. Like all good DI's, Kenyon was accustomed to remembering words on paper. It was necessary. The file on quite an ordinary case could run to many thousands of words. But this was not so easy. He tried to see himself again, as he typed the copy. In his mind he watched himself tapping the keys. Some of it was clear; he could 'see' the paper as he pulled it off the platen. But there were a lot of gaps. Too many gaps.

'On reflection, I have become concerned . . . it seemed a proper and straightforward course of action . . . as I look ahead now, I see dangers . . . right to take this precaution . . . achieved a close, personal relationship with General Grauer . . . mutual liking, certainly, but whether we should bank on mutual trust is another matter . . . we may both be playing in different ball games . . . inevitable grave risks attached to this kind of delicate negotiation, to which the US Government cannot and must not be a party and yet from which, given a successful outcome, such great advantage would flow . . . General Grauer hinted at a bargain which he will put to me when we meet again at our previous neutral location . . . General Grauer will have shown his hand . . . I am acting independently of the State Department, but it would be my duty to report any unacceptable quid pro quo . . . Grauer will know this . . . should our negotiations fail, he may not wish that report to be made . . . I have become uneasy about some of the aspects of CASO . . . do not mind being disowned, but do not wish any story General Grauer may originate in the event of failure to be used by your enemies in the Cabinet and the White House staff to discredit you . . . why it was vital our connection be severed, and I act independently as a private citizen . . . in the event I do not return to London on the due date . . . taken these precautions well in advance . . . a trusted member of my staff will announce that I have been involved in an accident and am presumed dead . . . this will be delivered into your hands . . . under no circumstances will I depart from the possible and acceptable brief . . .'

Kenyon opened his eyes. His flight was being called. On the plane he endeavoured to fill in the gaps. But whoever that document was intended for knew what it was about, and Kenyon did not.

At Stockholm, he had to go to another airport for his flight to Gotland. He caught the 10.10, arriving in Gotland at 11.00. On the way, he read about Gotland. The island was bigger than he had imagined. The coastline was five hundred kilometres long. As far as he could judge from the inadequate map, the place was shaped very roughly like a lozenge, and was about seventy-five miles long and twenty-five miles wide at its extreme points. He began to feel somewhat foolish. Apart from the difficulty of finding Sarah, suppose she was not there at all? He was guessing like a lunatic. No, Kenyon told himself firmly. Gotland kept coming up: the neo-Nazi so-called secret conference there; the holiday which Sarah and Coleman had spent there; the reference in Coleman's document to a previous neutral location where he had met with General Grauer. It had to be Gotland. All right, suppose it was? What was so special about the place?

According to the guide he had bought, Gotland had been an important trading centre where many well-to-do merchants had lived, due to its position as a kind of half-way-house between two land masses. That was several hundred years ago in the days of sailing ships.

Looking at the map again, Kenyon guessed that it was about a hundred miles from Stockholm and about ninety miles from the coast of Latvia, an independent country before the Second World War, now the Soviet Republic of Latvia. Kenyon studied the tourist map of Gotland and was relieved to find that part of Northern Gotland was a restricted area, where aliens could only stay for seventy-two hours. He did not think that two people conducting private and delicate negotiations would bring attention to themselves by trying to stay there. That lessened the possible area a little, but not a lot.

He hung around at Gotland Airport while a self-drive car was arranged for him. The terminal building was quite small, and soon there were very few people left in it. One of them had stared at Kenyon briefly and was now making a telephone call. Possibly he was being too suspicious. Then again, it might be routine to have someone watching arrivals at the airport. If Mr 'Evans' was involved in all this, he knew what Kenyon looked like, very well indeed.

It was only a few yards walk to the self-drive car, but the weather outside was foul, a high, bitterly cold, driving wind, carrying occasional flurries of snow. Kenyon had looked down at the Baltic as they came in to land and thought what a grey, icy-looking sea it was. But this wind tore through his clothes and chilled his bones. He was glad to get into the car and gain the warmth of its heater.

The nearby town of Visby proved to be a tourist's delight, a walled mediaeval place dating back to the Hanseatic era, a mass of twisting, narrow lanes, lined with ancient buildings. Kenyon chose the Visby Hotel in Strandgatan, which appeared to be the largest. As the lack of a night's sleep was slowing him down, he got into bed, placed a call, and woke up two hours later when the phone rang, feeling better. The hotel boasted a sauna, and after indulging in that, he felt ready to face the elements outside.

There was no point in driving round Visby and Kenyon made his calls on foot. The snow-clad roofs of the mediaeval buildings made them look as sweet as icing sugar, and the wind was as cold as eternity. He thought he saw the man who had been at the airport, diving for shelter into a shop doorway, but he was not certain. He turned a couple of corners, and the man did not reappear.

Kenyon was enquiring for large, well appointed houses, which could be rented furnished at this time of the year. He did not think that a General and a rich American would be meeting in any log cabin. Nor did he think that private, delicate, and, according to Coleman, potentially dangerous negotiations, would be carried on in a hotel.

Everyone spoke English to Kenyon's relief. The only other language he spoke was French, and that badly. There were three houses on the island, of the type Kenyon was looking for, available now. He expressed polite thanks and said that he was interested in something in a few days, or possibly weeks time. He ended up with a list of six houses in various parts of the island. He went back to his car and drove out of Visby. Once outside the town, he realised that the island was a huge, snow-covered pancake with not a hill or a rise in sight, bitterly burnished by that biting wind off the Baltic Sea with its disconcerting gusts of snow.

The first house was near Horsne, half way across the island. Kenyon made no attempt to conceal his approach. He wanted to be seen. A group of young people looked at him through a window, and raised their glasses to him. There was a party going on. Kenyon turned round and drove away again.

There was practically no traffic: he drove for miles without seeing another car. He turned North for Tingstade. At that house a couple of Swedes were getting into a Volvo with two handsome women. Kenyon drove on and turned east. The remaining houses were on or near the coast.

Nothing seemed to be happening at the house near Gothe. Kenyon hung about, but there was no sign of life, and when he drove off, no one took any notice, if there was anyone there at all. He turned south, along the coast. The light was failing, the early darkness induced by the lowering, threatening clouds. He had some trouble finding the next house on his list. It was approached by a private road, and sat close to the sea with what would have been, in summer, its own private beach, now covered in snow, nibbled away at the edge by the vicious, windlashed waves of the Baltic. A small jetty ran out into the sea and a large, modern, sea-going cabin cruiser bobbed in the half shelter of the jetty. Kenyon thought that if the wind and sea got up any more, someone was going to lose an expensive cruiser.

A black Saab was parked outside the house, and smoke rose from the chimneys. Kenyon thought that if he was staying in this remote spot and some strange driver came snooping round, he would want to know who he was. But no one here appeared to care.

Kenyon drove back to the road and turned left. After a couple of miles a signpost told him that he had lost his bearings in the network of narrow roads. He should have been heading for Asklog, and he was not. He pulled in and was checking his map to discover where he had gone wrong when he saw a black shape in his mirror, far behind him.

The black Saab was not moving. When Kenyon drove on, the Saab followed. Kenyon took some turnings. So did the Saab. But it hung well back all the time. Kenyon was being observed. If he went back to Visby, he thought, they would be satisfied.

Kenyon now knew where to go, but he wanted to arrive alone, not accompanied by a black Saab with two occupants. He had taken the police driving course at Hendon and he knew he could drive in a way that most people never dreamed of, if he was obliged to. But this network of twisting snow-covered lanes was not ideal, to put it mildly. He drove on, watching for a shielded corner. The Saab followed patiently. Then Kenyon saw what he wanted, coming up ahead: a right turn with a clump of bare trees and bushes on the corner which served to obscure oncoming traffic.

Kenyon took the corner in low gear, spun the steering wheel savagely, skidded the car round in its own length, gunned the throttle until the tyres bit into the snow, turned on his headlights, and accelerated straight at the Saab as it rounded the corner. He caught a glimpse of two shocked faces, blinded by his headlights as he braked into a controlled skid which avoided the lurching Saab, corrected the skid, and came to a stop.

Kenyon got out. The Saab was on the wrong side of the road, nose down in a ditch. He walked back to it and opened the driver's door. The passenger was unconscious. The driver was merely dazed. A gun in his hand was moving round to point at Kenyon. Kenyon knocked the gun up, and hit the man hard. His head swung round and blood trickled from his mouth. The bullet went through the windscreen.

Kenyon took the gun and checked the passenger who was also armed with the same unfamiliar kind of automatic. He pocketed that one.

The driver groaned, and straightened himself up.

'Out,' Kenyon said. 'And then get your mate out.'

The words did not seem to make much sense to the driver, but Kenyon's gestures with the automatic did. The driver stumbled round the car sullenly. His passenger was coming round anyway.

'Back,' Kenyon said. 'Further back. Go on.'

The two men moved until they were ten yards from the Saab. Both were fit-looking men in their thirties, both were wearing suits, and both began to shiver in the agonizing wind.

Kenyon put a bullet into the Saab's petrol tank. Petrol fell into the snow but did not ignite. He wet a corner of his handkerchief in the stream of falling petrol, retreated, and lit the edge of the handkerchief with his lighter. The cloth burst into flame, and he threw it into the pool of petrol under the Saab. The petrol exploded, and the car burned.

Kenyon moved back from the heat. 'That'll keep you warm, he told the two men.

If they did not get a lift, it would take them well over an hour to get back to the house. Kenyon needed all the time he could get. They might call the police, of course, but somehow Kenyon doubted it. Men whose instinct it was to bring in the police, rarely carried guns.

He got into his car and drove towards the house. By the time he got there it had begun to snow in earnest, and it was dark. He left his car in the road, skirted the house, and went down to the beach and on to the jetty. From here he could see the lights of the house. He hoped that the swirling clouds of snow would obscure him from anyone looking out. He hoped to walk into that house and walk out peacefully, but he preferred to take precautions.

There was a rail to one side of the jetty, covered inches thick in frozen snow. Kenyon spent two minutes removing handfuls of snow, placing the fully-loaded gun in the cavity, spreading snow on top, and tamping it down. New snow soon covered any traces of his handiwork. He carefully memorized exactly where that gun was. He hoped that, in the event of any difficulty, that cabin cruiser had the significance he thought it had.

Kenyon rang the doorbell. A manservant opened the beautifully polished oak door.

'I'm here to see Miss Brooks and Mr Coleman,' Kenyon said.

'Come in, sir,' the manservant said in good English, 'and I'll enquire.'

Kenyon stepped inside. The next moment he was rammed powerfully against the wall and expertly frisked. He did not resist.

The manservant stepped back, holding the gun which he had taken from Kenyon's pocket. 'If I may take your coat, sir.'

'Thank you,' Kenyon said.

It was agreeably warm inside the house. Stairs led up from the large, panelled hall. Double doors leading to a living room were slightly open. Kenyon caught a glimpse of the welcoming flames of a fire.

'I'm sure they'll see you, sir,' the manservant said. 'This way, if you please.' He indicated politely that Kenyon should go first. The gun added weight to his politeness.

Kenyon went into the living room. It was magnificent and must have been forty feet long. Paintings and stuffed fish alternated on the walls. The bottles on a bar at the far end winked invitingly. Kenyon gave up taking an inventory and concentrated on the group which was spaced round the fireplace.

He knew all of them but one. Sarah was gazing into the flames of the fire. She did not look at him. Harry Coleman turned his head and stared at Kenyon with curiosity. His good looks were drawn with the weariness of a man who had not slept well for days. Mark Fisher smiled pleasantly and said, 'Hullo there, Mr Kenyon.' The dark haired man in his late thirties, who was lighting a cigarette, Kenyon thought he had glimpsed briefly just once in his life, and spoken to on the phone once.

The man sitting in a wing armchair to one side of the fire, Kenyon had never seen before. He assumed he was General Grauer. He was about sixty years old with grey, thick hair, cut short. He wore a grey suit, a white shirt, a grey tie. The corners of his eyes were cobwebbed with the small lines of a man who had spent a lot of his time out of doors, but otherwise, he could have been the chairman of a board of directors.

The manservant crossed to the General, spoke to him softly, handed him the gun, and withdrew, closing the double doors silently.

The General checked the magazine. 'Two shots fired,' he said. 'I hope the obvious deduction is wrong, Mr Kenyon.' General Grauer's English was thickly accented, but the inflections were vaguely American.

'They're walking back,' Kenyon said. 'They were involved in an accident. The car caught fire.'

'How goddamn careless of them,' General Grauer said, amused. 'But I'm glad there was no real violence.'

'Tell them that,' Kenyon said. 'One of those shots was meant for me.'

'Then you must have done something silly, Mr Kenyon,' General Grauer said.

'It wouldn't be the first time,' Harry Coleman said. 'He makes a habit of it.' He continued to study Kenyon with no liking at all.

The dark-haired man brushed some ash from his lapel. Kenyon said, 'You bloody near split my skull open. Mr Evans by any chance?'

'Come on,' Mark Fisher said to Evans. 'What's your real name?'

Evans smiled, drew on his cigarette, took the gun from Grauer's outstretched hand, and pocketed it.

'Normally,' Kenyon said, 'I'd ask the Swedish police to arrest you, while I applied for an extradition order on the grounds that you are suspected of murdering, or conspiring to murder, Detective Constable Michael Meacher, in London.'

They all seemed to think this was a good joke, except Sarah and Harry Coleman.

'Your business here is none of my concern, General Grauer,' Kenyon said. 'If you'll allow me to phone the police in Visby, I'll leave with this man, whom I know as Evans.'

'I think he's great,' Mark Fisher said. He directed his pleasant smile at Kenyon. 'Is that why you came all this way? To find him?'

'Partly,' Kenyon said. Sarah looked up, held his eyes, and shook her head helplessly.

'I admire your devotion to duty, Mr Kenyon,' General Grauer said, 'and I mean that sincerely. In other circumstances I'd be happy to oblige you. But there are other, overriding matters of great importance which make it impossible to grant your request. I'm sorry.'

Whatever the matters of great importance were, Kenyon thought, they all seemed to be just sitting around, killing time.

'Then I'll leave,' Kenyon said. 'Sarah? Are you coming with me?'

'I'm afraid neither of you can leave,' General Grauer said.

The manservant came in and began to lay plates on a long sideboard.

'We'll eat shortly,' General Grauer said. 'It will only be a cold buffet but we shall need something for the journey.'

'What journey?' Kenyon asked. He did not really expect to get an answer, and his expectations were fulfilled. He sat down where he could look at Sarah, and lit a cigarette. She was sitting next to Coleman on a couch. Her fingers played mechanically with her pyramid-shaped ring. She stared at Kenyon. Her eyes said, 'You shouldn't have come.'

Coleman rubbed his face tiredly, and leaned forward to the General. 'I've marshalled all the arguments I can think of,' he said.

'Mine are better,' General Grauer said.

'You're wrong. The US won't buy this,' Coleman said urgently. 'It'll mean nuclear war.'

'I don't think you believe that yourself,' Grauer said. 'Mr Fisher agrees with me. Provided it's handled properly, it will mean the beginning of a new era of real peace and genuine friendship. There may be some slight initial problems but . . .' Grauer broke off, realizing the intensity with which Kenyon was studying him. 'Is something wrong, Mr Kenyon?'

'I like to be able to follow conversation,' Kenyon said. 'I believe you're a General. Commanding what?'

'I have the honour to serve with the armed forces of the German Democratic Republic,' Grauer said.

'East Germany?' Kenyon said foolishly. 'I thought you were West German.'

'You've got it wrong, Kenyon,' Coleman snapped. 'Just as you've had everything wrong. General Grauer is Chief of Staff at Command Headquarters of the armies of the Warsaw Post.'

'The ones that outnumber us so much. I've heard of them,' Kenyon said. But he felt bruised and humiliated. All his theories had collapsed one by one. He was left with a vacuum.

Coleman ignored him, and turned back to Grauer. 'Economically,' he began, 'it would lead to the collapse of the Common Market . . .'

'The member nations,' General Grauer said, 'will be faced with a new reality. They will adjust. A new and much larger trade group will be formed embracing both East and West. If that is your prime problem, there is no difficulty.'

'All right, let's get back to basics,' Coleman said. 'There are American troops stationed in West Germany, armed with nuclear weapons. We can't accept a Communist government in West Germany, any more than Russia was able to tolerate a free Hungary or Czechoslovakia.'

'It will not be a Communist government,' General Grauer said patiently. 'The government will be composed of all democratic and freedom-loving parties, to crush the neo-Nazi menace once and for all. There will be a Communist element to ensure the support of the workers in the struggle. The people of West Germany will decide their own future, as now.'

Kenyon thought that the people of West Germany did not seem to be conspicuously represented at this meeting.

'Too many people remember Czechoslovakia just after the war,' Coleman said, 'when a Communist minority in the government turned into a Stalinist regime. It seems to me you're hoping to use that as a model.'

'Russian armies on the banks of the Rhine,' Kenyon said, recalling the phrase from somewhere.

'You may be a good policeman,' General Grauer said, disdainfully, 'but you should try to avoid banal over-simplifications. Once the risk of a new, aggressive Germany has been averted, there will be no obstacle to the re-unification of East and West Germany. There will be no threat to peace, and no Russian armies will be necessary. The advantages are enormous, and our soundings lead us to believe that much of American opinion shares that view,' he ended, looking at Mark Fisher.

'Taxes,' Mark Fisher said to Coleman. 'Taxes to pay for overseas commitments. Taxes which nobody likes, to provide armies stationed in countries which prefer not to spend their own money on defence. Trade restrictions,' he said, 'between the two most powerful nations on earth. Why the hell do we need to be on this side of the Atlantic? What are we doing here? Czechoslovakia after the war, you say, but it's now some thirty years later. Stalin's dead, times have changed. If we can avoid presenting this thing in terms of black and white, turning it into the old red menace bogey, we've got a bill of goods the USA can accept. Bring the boys home. Lower taxes. Reduced risk of war. Trade opportunities with the East we've never dreamed of. A stable balance of power that would last for generations.'

'And all we have to do,' Coleman said, 'is to say OK to a coalition government which would mean a Communist Greater Germany in five years, and you know it.'

'Oh, come on,' Mark Fisher said. 'That's cold war stuff. You'll start talking about the domino theory next.'

'I don't imagine that France, Austria, Holland, Italy and the rest would remain unchanged,' Coleman said. 'Do you? Switzerland might be left as a kind of latter day Hong Kong, but otherwise . . .' He shrugged.

'The people the Committee are in contact with,' Mark Fisher said, 'believe it's time we put America first. What did Europe do when we stumbled into the Vietnam disaster? Nothing. Do you think Europe would come to our aid? You only have to put the question to realize how fatuous it is.'

'No one wishes to encroach on any areas vital to America,' General Grauer said. 'But a warlike West Germany bent on revenge would turn against the East. We cannot permit that.'

'A neo-Nazi movement certainly exists in West Germany,' Coleman said. 'But whether it's as dangerous as you would like us to believe, I take leave to doubt.'

'According to our information,' General Grauer said, 'an attempted right-wing coup will take place in January. I've given you details. The coup must be averted. What would you have us do? Send armies in? No. If the parties of the Left combine together, they will defeat this threat. They will be encouraged in this action by the USSR. We do not ask America to join with us. Simply to understand. Mr Fisher believes that the Committee for American Security Overseas will support us.'

Coleman said, 'I'd remind Mark that the Committee is not an elected body.'

'That's why we've met together,' General Grauer said. 'Your influence is needed.'

'You overrate me,' Coleman said shortly.

'I doubt it,' General Grauer said. 'You are trusted and respected in your seat of government. Your advice will carry great weight.'

'My advice to you,' Coleman said, 'is to drop the whole idea. You should inform your government that any attempt to take advantage of right-wing activities – whether genuine or inspired – to impose a quasi-puppet government on West Germany, would be met with the maximum resistance by the USA, diplomatically, and, if necessary, militarily.'

'I note your advice,' General Grauer said. 'But in an attempt to secure your support, you have been told a great deal in confidence. It would not be desirable for you to use it to oppose us.'

'You'd made up your mind I wasn't going back the minute I started arguing against you, days ago,' Coleman said, wearily. 'If I'd had any sense, I'd have told you it was great, I was on your side, and flown home.'

'It was always envisaged that, if you felt able to offer support, it should be from the East,' General Grauer said, quietly. 'I see the time is getting on. Let's eat now, shall we?'

13

Kenyon realized that, whatever the apprehension in his mind, his stomach wanted food. He enjoyed the smorgasbord. So did General Grauer and Mark Fisher. Coleman and Sarah merely picked at their plates. Evans ate silently, removed from the group, his eyes on Kenyon. Evans was a pro who preferred action to words, Kenyon thought.

He moved until he was alongside Harry Coleman. He wondered if Evans would object if they talked, but he did not.

'I've gathered what General Grauer's here for,' Kenyon said. 'You seem to have had something different in mind. What was it?'

Coleman seemed disinclined to speak to him and turned away. Kenyon was annoyed. 'Come on, Coleman,' he said. 'Enlighten the ignorant innocent abroad. You've got nothing else to do.'

'I thought I'd established a good relationship with Grauer,' Coleman said, distantly. 'We talk for years about reducing armaments. We agree on detente. America sure to hell isn't going to invade Russia. NATO is a defensive organization. So why are the Soviet forces in Europe so large? Why this enormous concentration of conventional armaments? I always believed the Russian armies were there to deter any American response in Europe short of outright war. To back up a carefully calculated risk. I think this German thing is that risk. I came to try and dissuade Grauer, perhaps work out a deal. We could agree a mutual, phased withdrawal if they drop this move in Germany...'

'Mr Coleman,' General Grauer said, as he poured himself a glass of wine, 'we were afraid of a resurgent Germany, and we have been proved right. Once that threat has been resolved, and American forces have been withdrawn from Europe, there will be no need for large Soviet armies in the West.' Grauer smiled cordially, and moved on.

'Will it happen?' Kenyon asked. 'Taking Germany into the Eastern bloc, in effect? Grauer sounded very matter of fact about it, but it's a big thing to try.'

'The biggest yet,' Coleman said. 'And they may very well bring it off. Thanks to you,' he ended viciously.

Kenyon stared. 'Me? I'm just an innocent bystander.'

'You've blown it personally, Kenyon,' Coleman said. 'You're an interfering dumb copper, and you've really screwed it. This had to be a personal meeting. Only one man in Washington knows why I'm here, and he is not universally liked. He's regarded as too clever. When I had that ring made for Sarah and put the microfilm inside, I wasn't protecting myself. I was walking into the unknown here and I wanted to make sure I wasn't used. It was safe. And what do you do? Dig it out, and let them get it.'

'They knew she had something,' Kenyon protested feebly. 'They searched her flat.'

'And found nothing. They didn't know, they were guessing. They'd have given up. But you let them see a police report saying that Sarah had vital information, which you knew about. What the hell did you think you were playing at?'

'They keep you very well informed here,' Kenyon muttered.

'There's damn little they won't use,' Coleman said. He was looking at Sarah. Kenyon followed his eyes.

'Did you send for her?' he asked quietly.

'Don't be a fool,' Coleman said. 'Mark Fisher took her a phoney message, saying I was ill. She's supposed to make my enforced residence in the East more comfortable. And also, if I'm concerned for her safety, to encourage me to do the right thing.'

The double doors opened, and the two surly, cold men from the black Saab walked in. Grauer spoke to them and then crossed to Kenyon. 'Only one gun was found on your person, Mr Kenyon,' he said. 'The other is not in your car. Where is it?'

'In some field,' Kenyon said. 'I threw it away.'

General Grauer gazed at him thoughtfully. 'They seem to bear you something of a grudge, Mr Kenyon,' he said. 'Where was this field?'

'On the way back,' Kenyon said. 'Come on. What would I want with two guns? I don't like the things anyway.'

Grauer nodded, moved away, and spoke to the driver, who touched the manservant on the arm. They left the room. A few moments later, Kenyon saw them passing the windows. They were studying places like window ledges. Kenyon trusted that it was too cold outside for them to generate any real enthusiasm for the task. He turned back to Coleman.

'You're going to be reported dead,' he said, 'if you're not back in London by a certain date. That'll stymie them, won't it?'

'It would have done, except for your bulldog idiocy,' Coleman said. 'No microfilm of a document bearing my signature will now find its way to Washington, remember? And since I shall probably be seen in public somewhere with the General, a report of my death isn't going to carry a lot of conviction, would you think?'

Kenyon winced. He thought of trying to explain. That he had not been interested in secret meetings and undercover negotiations. That in the first place it had been about Sarah, and later about Michael Meacher: an attractive, frightened woman whom he had suspected and desired, and a dead young man whom he had liked. But that would sound irrelevant to Coleman, and indeed it was, now.

For now, General Grauer was being helped into a heavy overcoat, with a fur collar, and he was donning a fur hat.

'I don't see why you had to do all that cloak and dagger stuff with the microfilm,' Kenyon said. 'Why not just lodge the document with your Embassy, or your State Department?'

'God, you must live a straightforward, normal life,' Coleman said. 'Documents can be intercepted and abstracted. If you think that diplomatic services and governments are cheerful, united bands of happy brethren, you're crazy. It's dog eat dog. I want to reach an understanding with the Soviets, but slow and careful and easy. That gets me called names by people and powerful organizations who want to move faster. Whose real ideal is Fortress America. Who want to carve up the world into spheres of influence between America and Russia, and who don't believe that Europe matters a damn to the United States.' He was looking at Mark Fisher, who had fallen into a smiling conversation with General Grauer. 'I've been under surveillance ever since I began to disagree with CASO,' Coleman said. 'Sarah was a long-standing relationship. They accepted my meetings with her, but anyone else . . . they knew what was happening. I didn't want to use her but I had no choice. I tried to protect her. I pretended to break it off, and I still think that would have worked, if you hadn't stuck your nose in.'

Coleman was engaged in self-justification, Kenyon thought. Just the same, one sentence echoed in his mind. 'I pretended to break it off.'

The manservant brought an armful of coats. Kenyon put his on. Soon everyone was standing around wearing overcoats, but no one was going anywhere. Evidently the time was not yet.

'They're taking a terrible chance,' Kenyon said. 'A British copper may be dispensable. Even a lady translator. But kidnapping an American diplomatic adviser, that's going to cause one hell of a stink.'

'I hate to labour the point,' Coleman said, 'but since you so cleverly discovered the microfilm, and then lost it, there'll be no evidence I've been kidnapped. I'll be on a private visit, or a defector, depending on how they want to play it. Either way they'll use me to support their operation.'

'That depends on you, doesn't it,' Kenyon said.

'The British police consider they're handicapped by all kinds of rules and regulations when dealing with suspects,' Coleman said. 'That's so, isn't it?' Kenyon nodded. 'Suppose there was no limit,' Coleman said. 'Suppose you could do anything you liked, and no one would interfere. Would you say that you could get any statement, from any man, any time you liked? Their secret police have had a lot of experience. They're good at it.' Coleman stared out of the window. The wind had dropped. Curtains of thick snow were falling. 'I'll try,' Coleman said quietly. He turned his head and looked at Sarah. 'But I'm not sure I can handle it. I'm afraid they'll get from me exactly what they want.'

Kenyon craved for a cigarette, but he had run out. It was hot in this room with his overcoat on, but no one was moving. He voiced another thought which was in his mind. 'What about Sarah?'

'The General pointed out that in the East, we could get married,' Coleman said.

'I hope you'll be very happy,' Kenyon said.

The manservant came back into the room and spoke to General Grauer, who nodded, and led the way out. They crossed the hall, went through the front door, and tramped along the side of the house. The manservant closed the door from within. Kenyon supposed that he had been left behind to shut up shop. The fresh snow was slippery, and they slid and stumbled. Flakes accumulated on coats and hats and eyebrows and clung there.

General Grauer led the way, walking with Mark Fisher. Coleman followed with Sarah and Evans. Sarah had taken Coleman's arm once when she slipped and was still holding it. The two goons followed behind Kenyon. He caught sight of the house before it was obscured by the snow. He had seen it from that angle before. They were heading for the beach.

The sea was still restless. He could hear the waves splashing on the space they had cleared for themselves on the sand. He saw the jetty. Sarah slipped as she climbed on to it and Coleman steadied her. Grauer came to a stop and stared out to sea. Kenyon strained to see what he was peering at through the falling snow. Yes, there it was. A dark shape riding out at sea. Navigation lights were distant spots of colour.

Grauer was satisfied, and moved forward along the jetty towards the point where the cabin cruiser was moored. He trod carefully. The planks of the jetty were as slippery as ice, under the snow. At one point, Kenyon slipped and nearly fell. He grabbed the rail of the jetty, and saved himself from falling. One of the goons took his arm roughly. Kenyon clung to the rail. His fingers had failed to grip the gun properly.

Evans looked back and said, 'Come on. Move.'

'I wrenched my bloody knee,' Kenyon said, massaging his kneecap with his free hand, while he groped desperately with the fingers of the other.

'Help him,' Evans said.

The goon straightened Kenyon up. Kenyon leaned on him. 'Thanks,' he said. The hand on the goon's blind side slid the gun into his pocket.

Grauer was waiting by the cabin cruiser with the others, as Kenyon limped up. 'I'm all right now,' Kenyon said. The goon let go of him in response to a nod from Grauer.

'We shall soon be warm and comfortable,' General Grauer said.

In a fast patrol boat, Kenyon thought, they would be in Soviet Latvia in hours. General Grauer must be a very important person at this moment in time. The cabin cruiser was a shuttle. The patrol vessel was too large to come in close to the shore.

'Miss Brooks first,' General Grauer said, politely. Coleman helped her on board. The snow fell steadily. Kenyon wiped his eyes clear.

'I'll say goodbye, Mr Fisher,' General Grauer said. They shook hands. 'Your friendship will not be forgotten, I promise you.'

'Everybody stand exactly where they are, please,' Kenyon said, disturbing the farewell courtesies.

There was a moment of shocked silence as they all looked at the gun in his hand. Coleman was as shocked as the rest. The navigation lights of the fast patrol boat, winked placidly through the snow, out at sea.

'Get that bloody boat started, Coleman,' Kenyon said. Coleman stared at him frozen into immobility. 'I'm going home,' Kenyon said. 'If you're coming too, get a move on.'

Coleman jumped on board the cruiser, and fumbled around, looking at switches. There was an agonizing wait. Kenyon filled the silence with practical matters.

'One by one,' he said, 'you will take out your guns, very carefully, and drop them in the sea. Evans, you first. You're coming with me.'

Evans began to take his gun out very slowly. Then it came out very fast. Kenyon shot him. Evans fell back, slid sideways across the jetty, and splashed gently into the Baltic.

'General Grauer,' Kenyon said, 'if your men do anything like that, I'm quite prepared for a repeat performance.'

The engines of the cruiser rumbled into life at last, behind him. Grauer nodded. 'You first,' Kenyon said, to the left-hand goon. He was ready to shoot again, but the goon took out his gun as though handling eggs and, following Kenyon's gestures, laid it on the jetty and slid it into the sea. His colleague followed suit. Kenyon was aware that, out at sea, a powerful engine had come to life. They were wondering what the delay was all about. He backed carefully on to the cruiser. Coleman was ready at the controls. He looked pale and tense. Kenyon cast off. Coleman opened the twin throttles gently. The cruiser slipped away from the jetty.

'I assume you can handle one of these things,' Kenyon said.

'In bad visibility, on a strange coast, I can pile it on the rocks as well as the next man,' Coleman said.

'Get off and go back, if you want to,' Kenyon said.

Coleman manoeuvred the cruiser away from the shore. Soon, they lost sight of the jetty. The cruiser purred quietly through the waves, pitching and rolling steadily. The navigation lights out at sea disappeared. Kenyon peered through the falling snow, straining to glimpse the vessel which was waiting out there. Coleman had turned starboard, and was heading diagonally, leaving both the coastline and the ship behind.

A powerful searchlight suddenly snapped on out at sea. Judging from the line, it was aiming at the jetty. Presumably someone out there had checked the time, become anxious about the delay, and was trying to illuminate the jetty through the drifting sheets of snow. Apparently, they succeeded, although the cruiser was now far enough from the jetty for the snow to blank off Kenyon's vision. Grauer would be signalling.

The searchlight swung slowly round towards the cruiser. Kenyon could see the source of the light, but not the beam itself now. He tried to put himself in the position of the men on that patrol boat. He hoped that it would be like driving a car through a heavy snowfall. The falling white flakes would reflect the light, and make it impossible to see very far. The light rotated, sweeping through an arc, paused, swept back again.

'They've missed us,' Kenyon said.

'They'll have radar,' Coleman said. 'And twice the speed of this thing. We've only got an echo sounder.'

'Are we in deep water yet?' Kenyon asked.

'Deep enough,' Coleman said. 'Provided there aren't any rocks, reefs, or sandbanks.'

'I think I'd rather take a chance on those than that ship,' Kenyon said.

Coleman evidently shared Kenyon's opinion. He opened the throttles wide. The engines roared, the cruiser vibrated, surged forward, gathered speed, and lifted on to the plane, her bow banging and thumping into the waves.

Sarah was clinging on to a grab rail beside them in the wheelhouse.

'Why don't you go down below,' Kenyon shouted into her ear. 'You'll be more comfortable there.'

Sarah shook her head. 'I'd rather be able to see what's happening.'

None of them could see anything very much, except the falling snow which encircled them and blinded them. Kenyon thought that if that patrol boat had picked them up on its radar, and was thundering after them in pursuit, they would know nothing about it until its bows appeared out of that curtain of snow, a few seconds before they were sliced in two.

And then, abruptly, without warning, they cleared the snow storm, and left it behind them. A white curtain seemed to move backwards from the stern. The snow-covered coast line of Gotland was clearly visible, about half a mile to the right.

'Can we get closer inshore?' Kenyon asked. 'That boat must draw a lot more water than we do.'

'I'd rather not,' Coleman said. 'Too risky.' He glanced over his shoulder. The sea was empty. 'We may be all right.'

They roared on, battering and bouncing across the sea. Kenyon wedged himself into the corner of the wheelhouse, facing the stern, his knees flexed to absorb the constant, up and down, thudding, thumping motion of the cruiser. He stared back across the widening, white V of the cruiser's wake, searching the blackness beyond with such intensity that his eyes watered.

But when it appeared, he had no difficulty in seeing it. A black shape, no navigation lights on now, thrusting into an enormous bow wave, with awesome power. It must have been doing forty knots or more.

Kenyon touched Coleman's shoulder and indicated. Coleman looked round, and his face collapsed into folds of despair.

'They're in range already,' he said. He began to zig-zag, throwing the cruiser into one abrupt, jarring turn after another.

This had the desired effect. When the first burst of red tracer curved, with deceptive gentleness through the air towards them, it was yards wide. They could not hear the sound of the machine gun above the roar of their own engine, but they could see the bullets lash viciously into the water. But zig-zagging also slowed them down. The patrol boat was pursuing an arrow-straight line, gaining on them like a galloping racehorse after a rumbling horse and cart.

Kenyon twisted round, desperately scanning the white shore of Gotland to their right. He thought that it was uneven up ahead, that there was a small bow shaped headland projecting into the sea. He grabbed Coleman's arm, and pointed. 'Round there. The beach,' he shouted.

Another burst of tracer arced across the deck, inches above their heads. Like bloody clay pigeon shooting, Kenyon thought.

Coleman ducked instinctively, and swung the wheel wildly in the wrong direction.

'No,' Kenyon yelled. 'That way.'

'What?' Coleman followed Kenyon's pointing finger, but did not seem to understand.

Kenyon shoved him aside unceremoniously and grabbed the wheel. There was no time to explain. They were nearly past that curving outcrop of land already. Kenyon hurled the cruiser into a ninety degree turn to the right. The boat heeled and lurched and bounced. Sarah staggered, off balance. Coleman grabbed her.

'Get down,' Kenyon shouted. 'Down.'

Coleman pulled Sarah to the deck. Another burst of tracer fire, but it was well wide.

Kenyon saw that the promontory was part of a claw, which embraced a small bay, now about two or three hundred yards away, directly in front of their bows. He drove the boat as hard as he could at full throttle towards that bay. He prayed silently that there were no unseen rocks. At this speed they would shave the bottom of the cruiser off as cleanly as an axe through firewood.

Glancing over his right shoulder he located the patrol boat. His manoeuvre had evidently taken them by surprise. The bow wave had fallen away. The patrol boat had slowed, but it was turning. In a few seconds they would have a perfect shot at close range. Kenyon feinted a turn to the left as they neared the bay, and then swung, savagely, hard right. Red tracer bullets looped round them. And then the cruiser was roaring at twenty-five knots towards the tiny beach on the claw of the promontory which formed the right hand side of the bay. The claw shielded them from the patrol boat, and the last burst of tracer passed harmlessly yards behind them.

They hit the shelving sand of the beach, running aground and juddered to a stop almost as violently as if they had hit a brick wall. Kenyon was braced for the impact, but Coleman and Sarah were thrown forward against the bulkhead. Blood streamed down Coleman's face. In the sudden silence, Kenyon could hear the deep rumble of the patrol boat's engines, somewhere out of sight behind that claw of land. He picked up Sarah, who seemed to be badly shaken but otherwise unhurt. 'Ashore,' he said. 'Get ashore.'

Coleman was dazedly feeling his head. He took his hand away, and stared vacantly at the blood on it. Sarah tried to lift him.

'Leave him,' Kenyon ordered. 'Hurry up, for Christ's sake, before they start shooting again.'

Sarah obeyed. She climbed forward, and levered herself over the bow. Kenyon heaved Coleman to his feet, threw him over the side without ceremony, and fell in after him into four feet of water. It was like being suddenly encased in a block of ice. Kenyon gasped with shock, spluttered, found his feet, grabbed Coleman round the waist, and hauled him ashore.

Sarah was there waiting. She was wet through as well, and shivering violently.

'Keep going,' Kenyon panted. 'Up to those trees.'

On this unbroken spread of snow, they stood out as conspicuously as three flies on a white tablecloth. Coleman was regaining his senses; the blood came from a cut on his head which was not serious. They hurried and stumbled, ploughing through the clinging, deep snow towards the handful of dark tree trunks.

They were lying in the shelter of the trees, shaking uncontrollably with cold, gasping for breath, when the patrol boat found the position it was looking for and put a long burst of tracer into the cabin cruiser. The cruiser accepted the thudding bullets for ten long seconds, and then the fuel tanks exploded. Bits of the cruiser sailed through the air in all directions, plopping into the sea, falling on to the snowy beach. The remainder burned merrily, like an enormous bonfire.

Kenyon cursed obscenely. In the brilliant light of the flames, the tracks they had left as they stumbled through the snow could be seen with crystal clarity, leading inexorably towards the clump of trees under which they now crouched.

'We've got to keep going,' Kenyon said, between teeth clamped tight to keep them from chattering. 'These people don't seem to have much respect for neutrality and the three mile limit.'

As fast as they could, which was not very fast in the clinging snow, they crossed the rest of the claw-like promontory so that they were out of sight of the patrol boat, and turned left, heading inland.

After what seemed a long way, Sarah fell to her knees and supported herself on her hands, gasping and straining for breath. 'I'm sorry,' she managed to get out.

Kenyon glanced back. Dark shapes were moving. They had put a small boat ashore.

'Not yet,' Kenyon said. He pulled Sarah up. Coleman had recovered. He took Sarah's weight on the other side, and between them they supported her as they forced their way through the snow.

They came to some woods, where the snow had not penetrated so deeply, and they were able to make better speed. Spaced out in the trees were small wooden huts, shuttered and empty. In summer the area would be alive with holidaymakers, wearing shorts and light dresses, swim suits and bikinis.

They stopped. Kenyon could see no one behind them in the trees. He listened. Coleman supported Sarah who was out on her feet.

'She's exhausted,' Coleman said. 'We could break into one of these huts. She'll freeze to death if we don't get her into shelter.'

'We're still leaving a trail,' Kenyon said. 'Even through these woods. They'd find us in five minutes flat. Listen.'

They strained their ears. At first there was nothing but the ghostly silence of a snow-bound land, as if the earth had been sound-proofed. Then Kenyon thought he heard someone call, in a language he did not understand.

'The further inland we can get,' Kenyon said, 'the less they'll like it. Unless they propose to invade the bloody island, and occupy the capital. This is a holiday site. People drive here in summer. There must be a road.'

Coleman nodded. Half carrying Sarah, they came to a clearing in which was a much larger wooden building – a restaurant and shop during the summer. In front of the building was a large, flat, empty space, which, if it was a car park, should have a road going somewhere.

It did. They hurried along it as fast as they could. But it was clearly only an approach road, narrow and badly surfaced. They slipped in pot holes, and once Kenyon fell, bringing the other two down with him. His body cried out to stay there, just to lie where it was, and let them come, anything, it did not matter, so long as this awful cold, this fearful weariness was brought to an end. Coleman was in no better shape. They dragged themselves to their feet, and helped Sarah along. Behind them in the camp site a shutter was rattled and tested.

'We've got to get off this road,' Kenyon said. 'It's too bloody straight.'

Shelter lay to one side where a thick hedge bounded a field. They struggled through the hedge. Twigs snapped. Lumps of frozen snow fell to the ground. Beyond the field was a wood, and they headed for that. Kenyon had never craved the shelter of dark trees so much in his life.

'I can manage now,' Sarah said.

The two men released her, and they all tried to run, forcing their weary legs towards that wood. As they approached it, the headlights of a car passed somewhere the other side of the wood, and disappeared round a bend.

Once among the trees, they stopped and rested, drawing deep, painful gulps of breath. Kenyon looked back. The trail they had left in the snow wandered unpredictably from side to side, as though left by three drunks.

A small group of men appeared beside the hedge and came to a stop. A conference seemed to be going on. 'They're getting worried,' Kenyon whispered.

Perhaps they were, but they came on, eventually, just the same. Kenyon took Sarah's arm and made her run again. Coleman was just behind them. Kenyon knew they could not keep this up. The men behind had gained on them a lot. It was only a question of time, and very little time at that. The road, he thought. Where one car had passed, at this time of night, there could be another.

They ran through the wood, dodging tree trunks, stumbling over roots hidden in the snow. They ran and ran and ran, until they came to the road. It was empty. There were no headlights coming from either direction, and no sound of any engine. A signpost told them that there was a village one kilometre to their left. They would never get to that village, Kenyon knew. Not all three of them.

'Listen,' he said to Coleman, in a soft, clear whisper. 'Take Sarah across this road. Then turn left, but walk in the ditch until you get round that bend. Then go like hell, and get her to the village. You'll be all right there. They won't risk going anywhere inhabited.'

'What about you?' Coleman whispered back.

'I'm going to lay a false trail, and draw them off. I'll meet you in the village later. Get going,' Kenyon whispered urgently.

Sarah looked back at Kenyon once, and then they were across the road, and walking left in the ditch. Kenyon frenziedly scuffed out the tracks leading into the ditch, and then went back a few paces, rendering their footprints on the road a confusing mass. He looked round. Coleman and Sarah were moving round the bend, in the ditch, and then they were gone. Kenyon loped along the road, in the opposite direction, as fast as he could, dragging his feet in the snow as he went. He hoped they would not notice that the trail was somewhat different.

He could hear them faintly, now, but he kept going along the road, hoping to get to the point where the road meandered round an outcrop of the wood to his right before they broke cover and saw him. He thought he had made it. He left the road, and crouched behind a tree just inside the wood. He took out the automatic. He had only fired one shot from this gun, but it had been immersed in the sea. He hoped it was as finely engineered as it looked, and was water proof.

No more than a minute passed, but it seemed like forever. No men were coming up that road, and Kenyon thought that he must have failed, and they had turned left after all, and headed for the village. But then he heard slight sounds, first from one side of him and then from the other, and he realized that he had not made that corner unseen after all. They knew where he was.

He lay there, listening to himself being outflanked. He wondered what they were armed with. If they had machine pistols, he would probably be unable to get in even one shot. He thought about Michael Meacher, obsessed with dreams of girls. About the blackened wreckage of his car, in which Meacher had died. About Sarah Brooks, who had offered him her body, as if in love, and flown to Harry Coleman when she thought he was ill, without so much as leaving a note behind her.

He listened to the faint sounds in the wood, and realized

he had been mistaken about one thing. They did not know exactly where he was. They knew he was there somewhere, but not precisely where to find him. From their cautious behaviour it was conceivable that they shared some of his apprehension and fear. The thought gave him a little comfort. Just the same, caution or not, they were working methodically towards him, he could tell that from the faint, tiny sounds in the wood. In a minute, or less, one of them would see him. Perhaps he could see that one first. Perhaps he would be able to get off at least one shot.

Kenyon was concentrating so hard on the wood that he almost missed it. His ear was tuned so intently to the whisper of a leaf, the protest of a frozen twig, the compression of snow taking a man's weight, that he almost missed the quiet hiss of tyres on a snow bound road.

He swung his head round. Blazing headlights illuminated the road, from a car which would have passed him in another few seconds.

Kenyon dived out of the wood like a rabbit, and stood in the middle of the road. The headlights blinded him momentarily. The car swerved, skidded, nearly went into the ditch. Kenyon leapt aside. The wing brushed him. The car came to a stop. It was a Mercedes. The driver, white faced with shock and fury was shouting what Kenyon presumed was 'What the bloody hell do you think you're doing, you stupid bastard!' in Swedish.

Kenyon ran round the car so that its body was between him and the men in the wood – with some disregard for the Swede's safety if they started shooting – and snatched the passenger door open.

'Do you speak English?'

'Yes.' The Swede's expression softened. 'Is something wrong?'

'My car skidded off the road,' Kenyon said, getting into the Mercedes unasked. 'Two friends of mine are in the village. Can you take me there?'

'Sure,' the Swede said, driving on. 'Where's your car?'

'Some way off,' Kenyon said. 'We were lost. We had to walk.'

'Far?' the Swede enquired sympathetically.

'Quite a way,' Kenyon said. He hoped that would account

for his clothes, which had been wet, and were now half frozen. It was mercifully warm inside the Mercedes.

He glanced back at the wood as it receded behind them. The trees and bushes wore a mantle of white snow. The wood itself was dark and silent and peaceful. Nothing moved. There was not a human being in sight.

14

A chauffeur-driven Ford Lincoln met them at London Airport. The chauffeur saluted Coleman respectfully.

'Drop me off somewhere, if you're going to the Embassy,' Kenyon said.

'I'll see Sarah home first,' Coleman said.

'Fine,' Kenyon said. 'I live that way.' He subsided into a brooding silence. He had not had a minute alone with Sarah, not in Visby where the obliging Swede had taken them, nor in Stockholm, nor on the plane back to London, when Coleman had sat with Sarah and Kenyon had been three rows behind.

Coleman was himself again, and was showing an attentive charm which Kenyon supposed was normal for him, but which he had not seen before, in their short acquaintance. But then Coleman had been under a lot of stress in Gotland. Now, he was relaxed, smiling and confident.

Kenyon glanced across Coleman at Sarah, as the car emerged from the Airport Tunnel and moved smoothly on to the motorway. She was smoking, and listening to Coleman. She did not look at Kenyon.

The car whispered to a stop outside Cleeve Court. The chauffeur opened the rear passenger door. Coleman and Sarah got out. Kenyon followed.

'Take the car on to your place,' Coleman offered. 'I shan't need it for a while.'

'I'll walk from here,' Kenyon said. 'It's not far.'

'I've said thank you already Mr Kenyon,' Coleman said. 'But thanks once more.'

His handshake was firm and warm and friendly. Kenyon thought that he would like Coleman, if he did not hate the man so much.

'I don't suppose we'll meet again,' Kenyon said. 'So I'll say goodbye. Goodbye, Miss Brooks.'

'You must come round for a drink some time,' Coleman called after him.

'Thanks very much,' Kenyon said.

Coleman gave him a smiling wave and took Sarah's arm. They went into Cleeve Court. The Ford Lincoln drove off. Coleman would send for it tomorrow morning, no doubt, Kenyon supposed. The thought hurt; an almost physical stab of pain.

There were a handful of letters in Kenyon's box. He took them downstairs, opened his front door, and dumped them on the breakfast bar without looking at them. The flat was cold, dark, dank and dreary. Kenyon switched the electric fire and lights on, and gave himself a whisky which was on the large side, even by his standards.

The phone rang. It was Tom Bradley.

'I shudder to think what you've been up to, Sidney,' Bradley said, 'and kindly don't ruin your career by telling me.'

'I took a short holiday,' Kenyon said. 'That's all.'

'An Englishman who, strangely enough, seemed to be using three different passports, has been fished out of the Baltic Sea by a Swedish Customs boat,' Bradley said. 'He'd been shot, once, through the heart. The bullet came from a type of automatic manufactured in East Germany. You know nothing about that, of course.'

'Not a thing,' Kenyon said down the phone, lighting a cigarette at the same time.

'Fine,' Bradley said. 'Exactly what I thought. Just the same, a fair bit of shit has hit the fan. I'm going to be quite busy trying to turn the stink into the sweet smell of roses. I'd rather you were safely out of the way for a couple of weeks. Do you fancy a trip to somewhere remote, like the Kalahari desert?'

'It's time I saw my father,' Kenyon said. 'He lives in Saffron Walden.'

'Even better,' Bradley said. 'Take a well-earned rest with your father, leaving today if you don't mind. And Sidney,' he went on, 'I know you were only interested in getting your favourite female company back, but some of us are well pleased.'

Bradley hung up. Kenyon went into his bedroom and packed a suitcase for a two week stay. He brought the case back into the living room, put it down, and gave himself another over-sized whisky.

The phone rang. This time it was Detective Superintendent Pinder. 'I gather you're touring for a fortnight, and can't be reached,' Pinder said. 'I wanted to catch you before you went. That transfer to Potters Bar. There was a cock up. Someone got the paper work wrong. Up to you, Sid, but if you'd rather come back to Bayswater, when you've finished your leave . . . ?'

'Any time,' Kenyon said. 'Thanks very much.'

Kenyon supposed he ought to open his mail before he went. The first three were bills, which he put in his briefcase. He would pay those from Saffron Walden. The next was a thick, manilla envelope, almost entirely encased in cellotape, with no stamp on it, addressed to 'MR S. KENYON' in block capitals, and marked 'BY HAND'. The sender had been so lavish and enthusiastic with his cellotape, that in the end Kenyon had to cut the corner of the envelope off with a pair of scissors, and then rip it open by hand. He also seemed to have cut off the corner of a dog-eared ten-pound note. There were twenty-nine more used ten-pound notes in the envelope. Three hundred pounds in all. There was no note inside.

For a few blank moments, Kenyon stared at the money as though it had appeared by magic, deposited on his breakfast bar by some unknown genie. He could not account for it at all. Then it came to him. Of course. Jackie must have learned that he was definitely going to get the reward money, and had scrupulously delivered Kenyon's rake-off in advance. He stared at the notes for a period which spun into minutes. That Long Firm Fraud. It seemed an age ago, but it was not. Kenyon had forgotten all about it. Jackie had not.

Finally, Kenyon carefully repaired the ten pound note he had damaged, put all the money in a clean envelope, went out, and found a taxi which took him to Green Park, where he caught the Tube train to Hounslow.

Kenyon had not even known Michael Meacher's home address, until he had taken half an hour, after his death, to compose a stilted, unreal letter of condolence to his parents. The house was a workman's cottage, two up, two down, now modernized. Mrs Meacher was about fifty. She might have been a good-looking woman once, but not now. Her face was heavy and strained. Her eyes were a pale blue, and sad. Her manner was composed, but remote.

Mr Meacher was a guard on British Railways, and would not be home until late that night.

Kenyon gave her the money. 'This is Mike's,' he said. 'We run a savings group. That's his share.'

'Are you sure?' Mrs Meacher was puzzled. 'We were sent his Post Office Savings Book, and I thought that was all he had.'

'It was kind of unofficial,' Kenyon said. 'Just a few of us, saving up for holidays, that sort of thing. Sorry for the delay, but we had to work out how much interest there was.'

'Well, thank you,' Mrs Meacher said. Although a few hundred unexpected quid was obviously not going to change her life very much. 'It's very kind of you to take the trouble to come all out here. Mike told us a lot about you. He admired you very much, Mr Kenyon, but I expect you know that . . .'

She went on some more about how marvellous Mike had thought Kenyon was. Kenyon wondered if she knew that her son had met his death in his car, that by pure random chance he had taken Kenyon's place in the furnace where he was cremated. If she did know, she did not mention it.

Kenyon declined the offer of a cup of tea, and escaped as soon as he could. The emptiness that Mike Meacher had left behind in that tiny house, and in the mind and thoughts and heart of his mother was only too obvious, and Kenyon found it too painful to endure. On the way to Hounslow Station he saw a taxi and hailed it. The fare back to Paddington would be expensive, but today Kenyon did not feel that money was worth worrying about very much.

In Gloucester Terrace, Kenyon paid off the taxi. Sarah Brooks was waiting, literally, on his doorstep.

'I phoned twice, but you weren't in,' she said.

'What do you want?' Kenyon enquired, ungraciously.

'I'd like to talk to you,' Sarah said. 'May I come in?'

Kenyon took her downstairs. She saw his suitcase at once. 'Are you going away?'

'Yes,' Kenyon said. He looked at his watch. There was a train from Liverpool Street Station in one hour's time. He should telephone his father to say he was coming, and then order a taxi.

Sarah glanced round the flat. 'It's quite nice,' she said. 'But I don't think I could stand being underground like this.'

There were questions Kenyon could ask, but Sarah had said she wanted to talk to him. He waited for her to do so, but she said nothing, merely continuing to examine the living room in an interested sort of way. Kenyon thought that the questions could wait. She was, after all, here in his flat, of her own volition, and not in her own.

'The bedroom's quite small,' he said, 'but there's a part of it you might like to study for a while.'

'Really? What?'

'The ceiling,' Kenyon said.

Sarah lay on her back. She was breathing deeply and slowly. Her clothes mingled with Kenyon's on the floor. Kenyon lay beside her, staring upwards.

'White emulsion,' Sarah said. 'Nothing unusual about it at all.'

'Give it a while,' Kenyon said. 'It may grow on you.'

'I thought you were going somewhere,' Sarah said.

'I'm supposed to stay out of the way for a while,' Kenyon said. 'I thought I'd drive up to the Lake District. Do you want to come with me?' he asked, ditching his father without a qualm. He remembered that his self-drive car was still at London Airport. He would have to get it back.

Sarah hesitated, but then she said, 'Yes, all right. But I'll have to get to Winchester by the twenty-fourth. I always spend Christmas with my parents.'

Kenyon was astonished to realize that it was that near. The festive season had not figured much in his thoughts, of late. 'OK,' he said. 'I ought to go and see my father anyway. I'll deliver his Christmas whisky in person.'

'I'd better stay for New Year,' Sarah said, 'but you could come and stay for a day or two, if you're free.'

'Fine,' said Kenyon.

'There's one thing, though,' Sarah said, seriously, 'which I'd better explain.'

'Your parents don't like coppers,' Kenyon suggested.

'No.' Sarah seemed embarrassed. 'You won't be able to sleep with me while we're there, I'm afraid. I think they'd be shocked if I brought someone home and went to bed with him.'

Kenyon tried to suppress it, but it was no use. He began to laugh.

'It's not funny,' Sarah said, flushing.

'All right,' Kenyon said. He ran his hands down her slender, familiar body. Sarah squirmed. 'Where's Harry?' he asked.

'He phoned the Embassy,' Sarah said. 'He had to fly to America at once.' Her eyes had grown intent, and her mind seemed not to be on her reply.

'Is he coming back?' Kenyon enquired.

Sarah kissed him, and took hold of him. Kenyon lost interest in Harry Coleman's movements, and concentrated on his own.

Postscript

No organization, whatever its political hue, is as monolithic and efficient as those who fear it often imagine. Lines of communication are never perfect, and enthusiasts are prone to feel that the men at the top are hidebound and over cautious.

Early in the new year simultaneous but sporadic outbreaks of violence took place in West Germany. An attempt on the Chancellor's life failed. A junior minister responsible for the police was seriously wounded. Strikes in Hamburg and Bremen did not spread. An army unit near Bonn continued with its manoeuvres, and no tanks entered the city, as some had expected. Leaders of industry, who were meeting in Stuttgart, publicly supported the government and security forces in stern measures to restore order. Another statement of a different kind, which might have been issued in other circumstances, had been destroyed, and none of the industrialists present at the meeting cared to remember it.

A Communist leader in Bavaria, who had not got the message, staged a mass rally and demanded a government comprising all freedom-loving, democratic parties of the Left, to deal with the neo-Nazi outrages. He himself would be duty bound to accept some portfolio, such as Minister of Internal Affairs. No one took any notice.

The American and Soviet ambassadors both expressed their governments' sympathy with, and confidence in, the duly elected West German leaders. Both added their confidence that the West German government was clearly in control of the situation. The East Germans said nothing.

The Communist leader in Bavaria received a telephone call suggesting that he take a holiday. He departed for a ski resort in Rumania.

The world press treated the whole affair as an abortive attempt by the extreme Right to seize power and reflected with satisfaction on their failure. In different parts of the world powerful organizations studied the events, drew what lessons they could, changed existing contingency plans, and began work on fresh ones. Other organizations strove to anticipate those plans, or better still, find out what they might be, and made contingency plans of their own.

For most people, in most parts of the world, the events engineered by what the press called 'The January Nazis' were soon forgotten. Most people worried about their loved ones, their jobs, their homes, their bills, their health, and their taxes, as they always had done.

As the New Year wore on into spring, Detective Inspector Sidney Kenyon wondered sometimes why he did not move his things out of his flat in Gloucester Terrace, w2 and move in with Sarah. But he did not. There were still times when he wanted to be on his own. Also, Sarah seemed to have become restless and occasionally moody. Bed sometimes allayed the mood, but sometimes it did not. When it did not, Kenyon went back to his flat for a few days, until she called him, or he decided to call her. He had the feeling that something was expected of him, that certain words should be spoken, but he could not bring himself to use them.

In the end, Sarah said, 'Harry called. He's getting a divorce. I didn't ask him to. It's his decision.'

'Really,' Kenyon said, distantly. 'I hope he enjoys his lifetime of guilt.'

'He loves me,' Sarah said. 'He wants me to marry him.'

'What do you expect me to say?' Kenyon enquired, bleakly.

'Nothing,' Sarah said. 'If you'd had anything to say, you'd have said it before now.'

When Sarah flew to America, Kenyon did not offer to see her off. For some time after that, he worked seven days a week. He could not quite decide if a very pleasant affair had ended, as affairs did, or if he had gratuitously and casually abandoned the best thing which had ever happened to him.

He thought about that a lot, and very little about the events in Gotland.

THE SWEENEY

Ian Kennedy Martin

Jack Regan is one of the Heavy Mob.
He's also a loner, intolerant of red tape and
insubordinate to his superiors.
And he just happens to be the best detective in
Scotland Yard's crack Flying Squad.

When Regan receives orders to co-operate with
Lieutenant Ewing, over from America to trace a cop
killer, Regan is pursuing his own case and ignores
them. But he soon discovers that Ewing is as tough as
he is – and a dangerous clash of personalities
develops. As the two cases begin to merge into a
sinister and violent network of IRA provos and
murderers, the two men close in for the kill . . .

Ian Kennedy Martin is the creator of Thames
Television's enormously popular TV series, starring
John Thaw.

THE ULTRA SECRET

F. W. Winterbotham

'The greatest British Intelligence coup of the Second World War has never been told till now'
Daily Mail

For thirty-five years the expert team of cryptanalysts who worked at Bletchley Park have kept the secret of how, with the help of a Polish defector, British Intelligence obtained a precise copy of the highly secret and complex German coding machine known as Enigma, and then broke the coding system to intercept all top-grade German military signals. Group-Captain Winterbotham was the man in charge of security and communication of this information. Now he is free to tell the story of that amazing coup and what it uncovered.

'A story as bizarre as anything in spy fiction . . . the book adds a new dimension to the history of World War II'
New York Times

'Military historians, like the general reader, will be astonished by this book . . . Group-Captain Winterbotham cannot be too highly commended'
The Listener

'Superbly told'
Daily Express

THE SEVENTEENTH STAIR

Barbara Paul

The velvet silence of the tower hung like a pall around her . . . she lay, drenched in a chill sweat of terror, straining to hear the sound that had woken her . . . then it came again . . . a low sobbing cry echoing through the lonely chateau.

Rosella Eastwood was summoned to Paris by her guardian, but when she arrived she found no one to greet her, only a will bequeathing her the Chateau de Louismont in the Loire Valley: a place of hated childhood memories, where she had to face the hatred of the Louismont family, the agony of loving a man who could never be free, and the evil secret of the west tower.

BEN HALL

Frank Clune

Australia in 1860. A time of exploration, gold rushes, gun fights and the cruel tyranny of the cat over transportees. A time when gangs of outlawed robbers and escaped convicts roamed the outback, bushrangers achieved immortalisation in song and legend. Men like Donahoo, Frank the Darkie and bold Ben Hall – men who'd rather die in a bloody battle with the traps than perish in irons.

This is the true story of those pioneer days, of the men and women who took the challenge of their new, wild, unmapped continent and tamed it.

'Ben Hall' is now a major television series from BBC/ABC, created and produced by Neil McCallum.